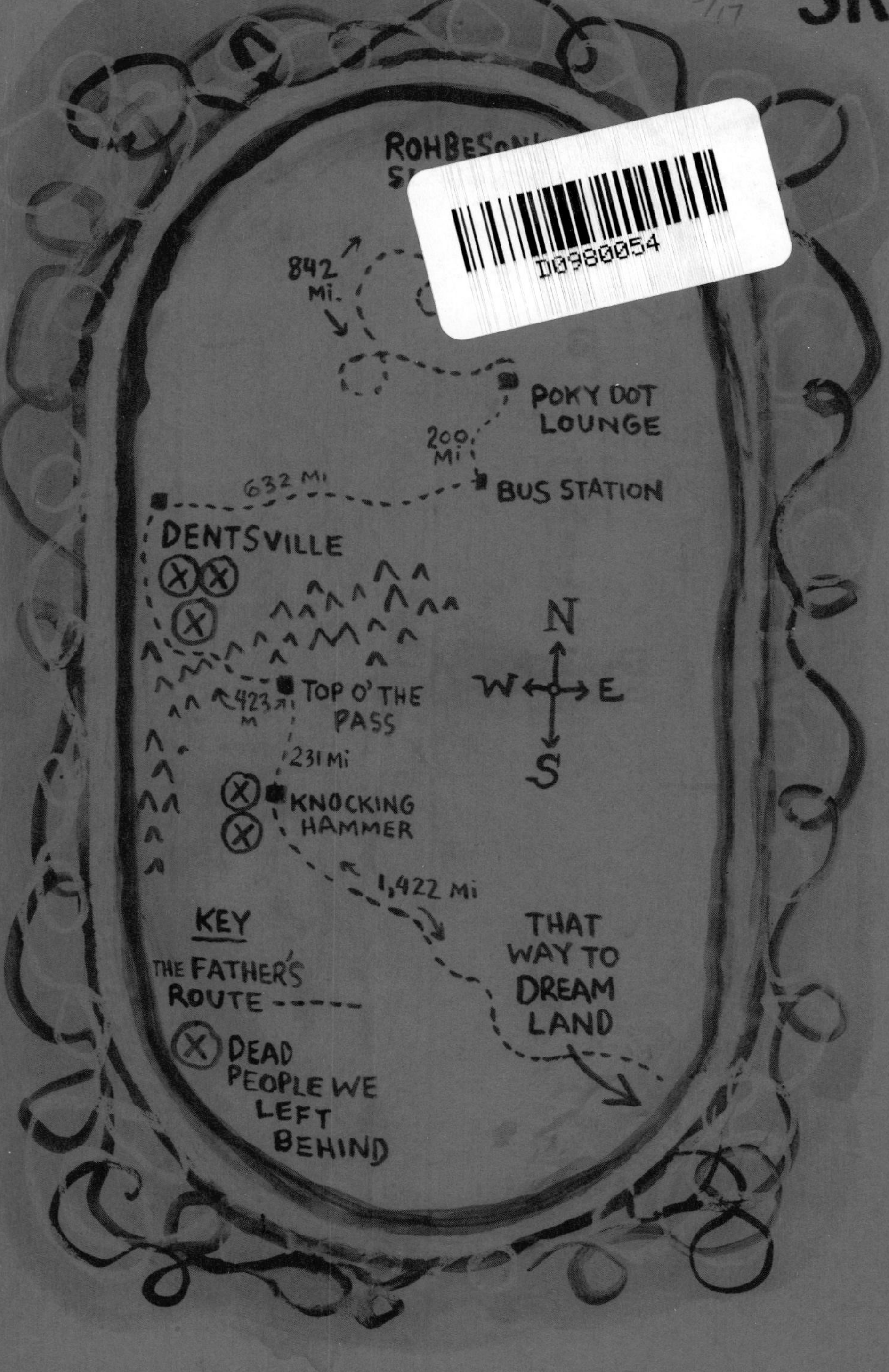
842 Mi.
POKY DOT LOUNGE
200 Mi
BUS STATION
632 Mi
DENTSVILLE
N
W
E
S
TOP O' THE PASS
423 M
231 Mi
KNOCKING HAMMER
1,422 Mi
THAT WAY TO DREAM LAND
KEY
THE FATHER'S ROUTE
DEAD PEOPLE WE LEFT BEHIND

CRUDDY

an illustrated novel by
LYNDA BARRY

SIMON & SCHUSTER

SIMON & SCHUSTER
Rockefeller Center
1230 Avenue of the Americas
New York, NY 10020

SIMON & SCHUSTER and colophon
are registered trademarks of Simon & Schuster Inc.

Designed by Tom Greensfelder & Kevin Dean

Manufactured in the United States of America

10 9 8 7 6 5 4 3

Library of Congress Cataloging-in-Publication Data

Barry, Lynda
    Cruddy / Lynda Barry.
        p.   cm.
    I.   Title.
    PS3552.A7423C78   1999
    813'.54—dc21   99-26418
                                        CIP
ISBN 0-684-82974-6

*The author wishes to thank: Liz Darhansoff, Robert Mecoy,
Tom Greensfelder, Susan Grode, Ben Sandmel, Caroline and
Barry Ancelet, and The Ragdale Foundation*

For L.C. and K.K.

Such bright blood is a ray enkindled
Of that sun, in heaven that shines
And has been left behind entangled
And caught in the net of the many vines.

— Francesco Redi

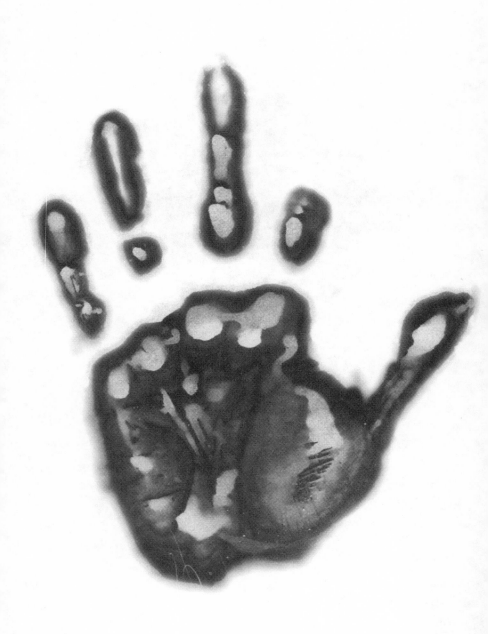

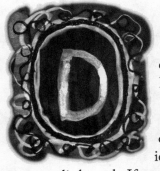

ear Anyone Who Finds This,
Do not blame the drugs. It was not the
fault of the drugs. I planned this way before the drugs were ever in my life. And
do not blame Vicky Talluso. It was my
idea to kill myself. All she did was give
me a little push. If you are holding this book right now it
means that everything came out just the way I wanted it to. I
got my happily ever after.

Signed, Sincerely Yours,
The Author,

Roberta Rohbeson
1955 – 1971

HEN WE first moved here, the mother took the blue-mirror cross that hung over her bed in our old house and nailed a nail for it in the new bedroom of me and my sister. Truthfully it is a cross I have never liked. The Jesus of it seems haunted. He's the light-absorber kind. In the pitch-black middle of the night he will start to glow green at you with his arms up like he is doing a tragic ballet. Some nights looking at him scares me so bad I can hardly move and I start doing a prayer for protection. But when the thing that is scaring you is already Jesus, who are you supposed to pray to?

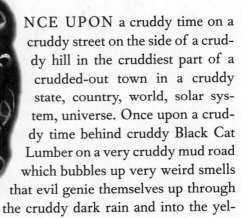

Chapter 2

NCE UPON a cruddy time on a cruddy street on the side of a cruddy hill in the cruddiest part of a crudded-out town in a cruddy state, country, world, solar system, universe. Once upon a cruddy time behind cruddy Black Cat Lumber on a very cruddy mud road which bubbles up very weird smells that evil genie themselves up through the cruddy dark rain and into the yellow lit-up window of the cruddy top bedroom of a cruddy rental house where a cruddy girl is sitting on a cruddy bed across from her cruddy sister who I WILL KILL IF YOU TOUCH THIS, JULIE, AND IF YOU DO I SWEAR TO GOD I WILL KILL YOU, NO MERCY, NO TAKE-BACKS PRIVATE PROPERTY, THIS MEANS YOU, JULIE, YOU! The cruddy girl named Roberta was writing the cruddy book of her cruddy life and the name of the book was called Cruddy.

Cruddy by the author Roberta Rohbeson, who is grounded until September 8, 1972. Only eleven months and five more days to go.

Cruddy. The famous book by the famous author Roberta Rohbeson who can't even CONCENTRATE TO WRITE this because her little sister will NOT shut up she will NOT shut up SHE WILL NOT SHUT UP and Roberta is about to BASH her little sister's HEAD IN IF SHE DOES NOT SHUT UP AND—

Now it is later.

Now Roberta is back from just getting in huge trouble for throwing the Cutex Nail Polish Remover bottle at her sister. Roberta was aiming at her sister's ARM but it wailed on the sister's HEAD by accident. Roberta was trying to explain to the mother it was an ACCIDENT! AN ACCIDENT! But the mother never believes anything Roberta says anymore since the night the mother got called to the emergency room where the author was tripping out on drugs very badly and the mother started screaming, "DRUGS?!! DRUGS?!! DRUGS?!!" and the cords on her neck were sticking out extremely and she had to be restrained by others to keep from killing the author, and the police kept sticking their freaky heads in close to the author's face and their breath was quite squidly and they kept saying, "Where did you get the substance, Roberta, who gave you the substance, Roberta, where did you get it, the substance, Roberta?"

And in the next cubicle the restrained and tripping Vicky Talluso was screaming, "DON'T YOU NARC ME OUT, ROBERTA! IF YOU NARC ME OUT I SWEAR TO GOD I WILL KILL YOU!"

But the author didn't want to narc anyone out. All she wanted to do was deliver the fantastic message of Truth plus Magical Love equals Freedom, but this was obviously a message the police and the mother could not comprehend.

And rushed to the operating room was the Love Interest, also tripping violently and hemorrhaging internally, and it was not looking good for the Love Interest, and the police were asking me if I had any information, did I know how he fell, how long he was laying there, about the slashes, the knife wounds, about his hereditary medical condition, did I know where his parents were, did I have any information at all besides the fact that he was the love of my life?

Meanwhile, back at the ranch where the author was getting screamed at by the mother for ACCIDENTALLY bashing ID-

IOT SISTER JULIE on the head with the nail polish remover, AN ACCIDENT, the author was sitting very still on a ripped kitchen chair and staring at the chunks of crud on the floor. The mother is what they call a main character. The mother is a very main character who says I live to torment her, that I only wailed the Cutex Nail Polish Remover bottle at the head of Julie because I want to torment her, who says the reason I do anything is just to torment her.

Now you need to know the scenery. First the house. The address. 1619 East Crawford. A rental in a row of rentals all the same, all very hideous on a dead-end road between Black Cat Lumber and the illegal dumping ravine. People have been heaving off old mattresses and old stoves and dead dogs ever since I can remember even though there is a huge nailed-up sign that says NO DUMPING! VIOLATORS WILL BE PROSECUTED! But in all the time of our living here I have never seen anyone get prosecuted once. I don't think a prosecutor even exists.

In the garbage ravine there is a nude man who crouches among the trash piles and his name is Old Red and he has very yellow skin like freezer-burned chicken and his thing in life is to suddenly run out and do a two-second display of his dinger and then run back in. People say he is actually a businessman, an executive at Boeing, very high up. I have never seen Old Red, but I believe in him. There have been nights when I have heard the drifting sound of his lonely yodels.

Our house slants. Like if you lay a jar on the floor of the kitchen area it will start rolling very rapidly. The back of the house is shoved right into the dirt of the hill and the front is on sinking wooden legs and there are scabby gray streaks all over the beige paint and wet chunks of mold growing all over the roof and there is a broken TV antenna that turns in the wind and makes noises that will freak the bravest person out.

There are a lot of trees behind the house, mostly scrub maple and pine and a lot of nasty smells that come from the garbage ravine and more nasty smells that come from the mud in front of the house and all day there is the sound of the loudspeaker calling in the lumberyard for Mike. Mike to the front desk. Mike, you got a call on line three. Mike to the loading dock. And I have watched out of my window to see which one is Mike, which one of the men on the forklifts inserting the smashed-flat Dracula teeth under stacked loads of wood is Mike, but every time they call for Mike a different guy goes inside. Maybe they are all Mike.

In our backyard is a rusted-out oil barrel hooked to the house and a T-pole clothesline with a hole in the metal of the T-pole called a weep-hole. It is there for drainage and ventilation but it also sometimes catches the wind and makes a sad "hoooooo-hoooooooo," sound, very lonely. And there is also the "hooooooooo-hooooooooo" of the trains passing on the other side of the hill, and once when I was just standing in the backyard I heard the T-pole and the train hooooooo-hooooooooo at the same time and my eyes went instantly wet, for what reason I do not know.

There is no sidewalk on our road. Just mud and mud and mud. The mother says there is something wrong with the ground. It bubbles. Julie says a shrunken man inhabits the mud and she has seen his face rise to the surface and she has seen the whites of his eyeballs opening at her, she has seen his muddy lips and freaky teeth and he tries to speak to her but she always runs inside before he can deliver his message. Julie is not the kind of person who makes things up and she swears it is true about the shrunken man.

I said, "Julie, you are lying."

She said, "Roberta, I am not."

I said, "If you are telling the truth then poke this pin into your hand."

Julie shoved it in all the way to its head. That is her style. And so I have been freaking on the possibility of the existence of the rising shrunken man because the way Julie did that pin thing was so sincere.

East Crawford is a road of trash people. Teeth missing and

greasy two-color hair on the women and regular greasy hair on the men and all of the people come in two sizes only, very fat or very skinny. And all of them are hacking and all of them are huffing on cigs constantly. I smoke too at times. So does Julie. It is very hard not to smoke here.

There's a lot of dead cars parked sideways and some are filled with junk to where it is pressing against the window glass and there is green mold growing on the junk. There are rotten porches and slamming doors and constant yelling inside the houses and constant yelling outside the houses and two doors down there are two little fish-faced girls who just stand in the mud and do contests of who can scream the loudest.

And the people are constantly falling. Falling down all the time. In the yard, in the mud of the road, out of cars, down the steps of the houses, and two nights ago the saggy underwear man next door was on his porch screaming "I AM what I AM and that is ALL I AM and I AM *IT*!" and then he fell over the side rail and into a bush.

The owner, the landlord of all the houses is Harmong. Mr. Harmong is the cheapest chintziest most pig-lipped tightwad skanked-out lardo king landlord of all time. He weighs sixty million pounds and has to walk with a metal cane with four legs on it just to keep from falling over from his personal fat, which also makes him wheeze and choke and who has face skin that looks like it was rubbed with greasy pink Brillo and who wants the actual cash rent laid in his actual hand on the first day of every month, which is the job the mother makes me do while she locks herself in the bathroom until Mr. Harmong goes away.

The last time he was here he clamped his fingers on my hand tight and stuck his pig lips out and asked me if I was old enough to have a boyfriend. I said no. He said he better not see no coonasses sniffing up after me because he has people watching us. He says he has people watching every last one of us. The saggy underwear man is his chief spy. Always walking the porch in droopy drawers and looking our way.

For the inside of the house there is not much to say. The bottom floor is just one room. There is a kitchen area and a living room area. There is the mother's TV and the mother's chair and the mother's lamp. All new. All fancy. Presents to her from the grateful people at her hospital. The mother is a nurse at Veterans.

There is a very skanky rug in the living room area that Mr. Harmong actually had nailed to the floor to keep anyone from stealing it and some of the nail heads have worked themselves up and Julie and I have snagged our toes on them many times. I have a certain rock I brought in just to use on the nail heads but they won't stay down. Even the nails are trying to get out of this place.

The only other mentionable thing is a gas furnace, big and brown with dented and taped-over ducts and bubbled-up scorch marks up the side, caused by a thing called roll-out. When the furnace comes on sometimes flames shoot out orange into the room. Supposedly it's not dangerous. Mr. Harmong says it's nothing to worry about. He says if it gets out of hand, throw some baking soda at it.

Where the mother was screaming at me was in the kitchen area. The walls look like gray velour from the layers of grease and dust. There are swaying cobwebs hanging. The refrigerator is very loud and it leaks and it shakes. The final thing to mention is the kitchen table with fake wood patterns which can look very lively when you are tripping on certain substances; you can see moving heads in the patterns, nodding at you, giving you advice. And even though the author was not on any substances while she was just getting screamed at, out of the corner of her eye she could still see the lively heads moving under the plastic surface of the tabletop. It turns out that once your mind gets expanded it is very hard to shrink it back down again.

Out of the other corner of her eye the author could see Julie sitting at the top of the stairs and smiling because she was happy the mother was screaming at the author. Julie was almost laughing at the scene because JULIE IS EVIL, SHE IS AN EVIL PERSON.

The author was sitting very still in a blue-flowered Sears nightgown with one rip under the arm caused by the author insisting on sitting with her knees up and the nightgown pulled tight over her knees which she knows causes rips but she does it anyway because she has NO RESPECT no GRATITUDE because she thinks THE WORLD REVOLVES AROUND HER plus she is a stupid, stupid idiot because she is barefooted, what if she stepped on a needle, one of the mother's dropped embroidery needles? What if she stepped on a needle and it went right into her foot and Roberta would not feel it and the needle would rise and rise and rise through the veins leading up to the heart and then the needle would STAB HER IN THE HEART and Roberta would DIE and it would be VERY PAINFUL, this according to the nurse mother, a medical expert on Freaky Ways to Croak. It was the mother who stole the *Stedman's Medical Dictionary* Golden Jubilee Edition even though it had HOSPITAL PROPERTY DO NOT REMOVE stamped all over it in red. A book the author has fallen in love with and reads at night during the lonely hours.

The mother shouted that she knew several people who died from the Rising Stab of the Unfelt Needle, or RSUN, she has seen cases of it many times and not ONE PERSON HAS SURVIVED IT.

And the author sat very still but she was thinking AS IF!!! As if I wouldn't feel a needle go into my own foot. As if I don't have enough vein biology information to know a needle would never make it to my heart. AS IF! AS IF! AS IF!

But Roberta kept her mouth shut and her eyes on the floor where she continued her study of the chunks of crud. She did not make a peep while the mother blorked out her fake medical information in horrible breath explosions.

The author has a very sensitive nose.

Once in the olden days of Roberta's life there was a dog named Cookie. And the mother was also always screaming at Cookie for everything, smoking and screaming because Cookie had incurable skin problems caused by the mange creature Demodex and Cookie was always itching and scratching and all her hair was rotting off and wet scary dog scalp was showing and the sound of the chewing got on the nerves of the mother who threw things at the dog and shouted, "YOU AGGRAVATE ME!" And then the mother said Cookie had to go and Roberta begged and begged her no but all the mother did was wait until Roberta went to school and when she came home there was no Cookie. Instead there was a bag of white-chocolate stars from the famous candy place beside the Aurora Bridge. The famous dumping and jumping bridge. And the mother had bite marks on her hand and she said to Roberta, "Have a candy star."

I said, "Where's Cookie?"

She said, "I have no idea."

And Roberta stood on the porch and called and called until the mother yanked her inside and shouted, "You want to call that dog? Here! You call her!" And she grabbed the telephone and bashed the receiver into Roberta's face. A broken nose. A boxer's nose. One of my many distinctive features. My sense of smell has been very sensitive ever since.

I have not mentioned yet the real mystery of this story. The gruesome and bloody scene in a parking lot on the edge of the restricted area of the Nevada desert known as Dreamland. A real place. The Lucky Chief Motel Massacre. Only two known survivors. One was Cookie and the other one was me. Maybe you saw pictures in your newspaper. It was very famous. But I am jumping ahead. Because I have not even mentioned the father yet.

Julie got a major lump on her head from the nail polish remover bottle and the mother made her come downstairs so I could feel it and know the full terribleness of my personality and maybe it was cold-blooded of me to press down on it as hard as I could but there is such a thing as hatred in this world. The hippies are trying to cure it but I do not think they will be able to. No hippie could make me say peace to my sister right now, who is laying on the bed faking being asleep. She is doing her imitation sleep formations like hanging her mouth part open and breathing long breaths and slightly rolling her eyeballs under her eyelids and I will say she looks very convincing. Julie is an idiot and I hate her but she is very talented at certain things. Faking things.

I do feel slightly bad about bashing her head so hard. I feel slightly bad about so many things I have done. But I do not feel bad about killing him. Because it was me who killed him. And I'm not asking any forgiveness for that at all. It was a good idea and I'm glad I had it.

Truth plus Magical Love equals Freedom. The author knows this is a lot of details to remember for your reading comprehension but the author badly wants to give you the who, what, when, where, and how of this story right away because the author very badly wants to get to the question of why. The burning question of why she turned out the way she did and why she ended the way she ended.

Ask a burning question, get a burning answer.

chapter 3

ND NOW the story can be told, and must be told, the truth can finally be revealed about that mysterious day long ago when the authorities found a child calmly walking in the boiling desert, covered with blood.

The authorities said, "Who are you? Where have you come from? What tragedy has occurred?" But the child could not answer. The child's bloody face could only stare without blinking for the child was in the medical condition known as shock, the same condition as the freaked-out little girl in the movie *Them!* Called *Them!* because that was all she could scream when they found her walking in the desert because her mind was blown out by what she had witnessed. All she could say was "Them! Them! Them!" So she could not give the authorities any information about why she was the only survivor and everyone else was laying around in hacked-up pieces. What gruesome attack by unknown forces had taken place? *Them!* is a great movie. They show it sometimes on *Nightmare Theater,* Channel 7. If you see it in the *TV Guide* you should really watch it because it has ideas in it that could come in handy someday if you are ever facing the authorities in the desert and you are covered with blood that is not actually yours.

And now the story can be told. And must be told. In this book the truth will finally be revealed about the horrible murders and then the author must die. And people may be sad about that and wishing there were more books by the author, Roberta Rohbeson, but sadly, it will be too late. There will be only one Dewey decimal system number for her. Sadly only one. And if they ever find her body, and if she could have a final request, that number is what she would like engraved on her gravestone.

After the authorities found us, found me and Cookie wandering, and after they spread newspapers out on the backseat of the patrol car and told us to get in, our picture was in the next morning's Las Vegas newspaper. Me and Cookie's picture was. We looked bad and crusty. The caption called me the Mystery Child and the story underneath told of my shocking condition and amnesia and asked did anyone recognize me, anyone in this world? The picture was of the very olden me, my hair very very short, shaved like a boy's and my arms and legs so skinny and my expression very paralyzed, me holding Cookie in my breadstick arms. And even though most of the blood was washed off of us we were still very convincing because the newspaper photographer told the Christian Homes lady to please leave some of the blood, he did not want all of the blood showing, but please leave a little because blood was the drama and the interest but too much of it was an appetite wrecker and it was a morning paper.

So the Christian Homes lady took me and Cookie into her cement backyard, all cement but painted green, and she made nauseated faces at our condition and also at the swirling fly families that had become our devoted followers and she unrolled the garden hose and said, "Stand right there," and then, "Take off your clothes and put them there," and when the reality of the nude version of me was revealed, she freaked totally. Because up until then, everybody thought I was a boy. When it turned out I was a girl, that was a surprise no one was expecting.

The father taught me. Against the odds, he taught me his wisdom: No matter what, expect the unexpected. And whenever possible BE the unexpected.

Chapter 4

ND NOW a word from our sponsor. You should know about Vicky Talluso. In fact, if you are tired of your life, if you want your life to turn instantly amazing, you should KNOW Vicky Talluso. Things happen around Vicky Talluso. Incredible things. Meeting incredible people. Having revelations. Running from the cops.

I met her at school on the day of my fifth-year anniversary of the Lucky Chief Motel Massacre. Public interest had finally laid down with its arms crossed like a vampire in a coffin. No one cared anymore who did it. No one cared if I ever told the story or not. It was what I had been waiting for, but when it finally came it was slightly a disappointment. On every other anniversary someone had always called us, someone from the Las Vegas paper, some reporter asking the mother, "Has she remembered yet? Has she talked yet?" And the mother got her chance at publicity, which is something she dearly loves. But this year the phone did not ring and the mother started looking at me with a little more squint to her eyes, like she was deciding something.

I was expecting to feel relieved when the story died. I was expecting to feel proud. The father always talked about the value of being able to really keep your mouth shut when it mattered. I kept mine shut for five years. It took five years for the parade of interest to finally pass. I thought I was going to feel happy when it did. I didn't expect the empty street it left behind. I didn't expect the old faded trash swirling in devil-cones around me.

They didn't find him. They didn't find his body, but I was thinking it was still there. I was thinking that if I really wanted to, I could take the money I have hidden and I could buy myself a Trailways ticket and I could go check on him. See if he is petrified like the shiny beef jerky man called Sylvester at Ye Olde Curiosity Shoppe who is on display beside actual shrunken heads with sewn-up eyes and lips. Or maybe he is all skeleton now, picked clean and bleached out like the displayed bone with WHALE PENIS written underneath it. Ye Olde Curiosity Shoppe is a good place to go when you are left wondering what finally became of the person you stabbed and then left in the sun.

On the anniversary of the fifth year I was thinking, What was the point? If it could all end with such a nothing feeling. If it could end with a nothing but the mother's squint, what was the point of getting away with it? The father would have called me an idiot for asking that question. He would have said, "Clyde, sometimes I'm not entirely sure you are my son."

Clyde is what he called me. He wanted a son to pass his wisdom to. Me being born a girl was just a technicality. The world spun a lot smoother once you understood what you were bound to live by and what you weren't. "Clyde," he said. "Your average man thinks he needs to grab the world by the balls. That's why your average man will never get ahead. He grabs at what only wants a tickle and a kiss. Hell. Try it on a bull sometime. See for yourself."

The father came from meat people. Generations of them that could be traced all the way back to the time of the monkey. "The monkey with the most meat wins," said the father.

I said, "I thought they just ate fruit."

He said, "Oh no, hell no. Look at their teeth. Fangs like that? If one bit you, you'd know it. Meat people run things, Clyde. Always have and always will."

It's in my blood. I know it is. Meat person. I am hell with a knife and there is nothing I can really do about it but try and keep my mouth shut and try not to let it show.

Vicky Talluso came toward me across the empty track field and she was walking too fast. I didn't really know her but she was in one of my classes and I had seen her around in the halls. It was hard not to notice Vicky. She had extravagant ways, too much makeup and very bright clothes and sort of a burnt-rubber smell she tried to cover-up with Chantilly. People automatically turned away from her. No one could really stand to look. In the Navy they call it dazzle camouflage. It was the Navy that figured out you could paint something with confusions so horror-bright that the eyeballs would get upset to where they refused to see. Battleships were painted this way and the bomber planes just passed them by. Dazzle camouflage is Navy. The father was Navy too. "Navy all the way, Clyde. Every goddamned inch right down to the end of my pecker."

It was lunch, and I was sitting in my usual place up in the weeds on the embankment near the track field. Passing time there. Some people would call it hiding there. My school is a violent place. People need people to knock over or sock in the gut. I stand out to them for some reason.

During my first days in the weeds I was not disturbed or even noticed by anyone. And then Vicky Talluso came walking right toward me, staring straight at me, wearing shocking-yellow crinkle-vinyl knee boots with super-stacked heels and twisted purple stockings and a pink and orange psychedelic shirtdress with a lime green collar. Her long hair was swinging and she was wearing a kind of hat called a tam, a tam made out of hypnotizing red velvet and she was moving so confidently and so fast and she was flipping me out completely, freaking me extremely. I could not think of one reason why a person like her would be walking so rapidly toward a person like me. Because I am her opposite in every single way. I am about as detailed as a shadow.

I nervously started yanking up grass and weeds and made a

pile out of them and when she was very close I started staring at the pile very seriously like it was a science project I was working on, but her face had already been flash-burned into my vision. She had slightly bulged-out eyes with a lot of violet eye shadow and globbed-on mascara and she had a long nose that humped up in the middle and white frosted lipstick coated thick on very chapped lips and her lips protruded forward because her twisted eyeteeth bucked-out, a defect that was weirdly alluring. One of her many weirdly alluring defects.

I smelled the Chantilly and then burning rubber and I wondered about it. What could make a person smell like that. I later found out it was from the hair-removing cream she constantly used because she is a very hairy person. Quite naturally hairy all over, her eyelashes were incredibly long but so were her arm hairs. And the eyebrow hairs of her right eyebrow. The other one was completely missing. I noticed it right away. She was very bald above her left eye. The skin there was crusted.

"Hey," she said. I didn't say anything back. "Hey, deaf," she said. "You. I got your message." She sat down too close to me and started yanking up grass and throwing it on my pile. "I received your message this morning and the answer is yes."

I said, "Message?"

"You're Roberta, right?"

"Yes."

"Yessssssssss," she said, imitating my habit way of saying the word. The mother went insane if me or Julie said "yeah," because only idiots said "yeah." She wanted us to say "yes" very clearly. Make the "s" very clear. She did not want to be known as the mother of two idiots.

"Yessssssssss," said Vicky Talluso. "That's so sick. Yessssss."

She was yanking up the grass vigorously, yanking up roots and dirt clods and I noticed her hands were very small and wide and her fingernails were also small and wide with silver nail polish caked up in chipped layers.

She said, "You have ESP, right?"

I squinted.

"You have ESP and you have contact with an Unfortunate Being, right? You were doing the Ouija board this morning."

I shook my head. She saw me staring at her missing eyebrow. It was inflamed looking. Slightly scabby. I was thinking of the mange creature Demodex. I said, "Do you got a dog?"

"It's 'have,'" she said. "Not that it matters. But it's 'have.' You called me this morning on the Ouija board and said to meet you here because you have something you need to give me.

Only you don't know what it is. You said you needed for me to come to you and tell you what it is you are supposed to give me."

I shook my head no.

She said, "Yessssss." She said, "Do you have any cigs?"

I shook my head again and she yanked up a clump of grass with a huge root clod attached and threw it. She said, "I hate this place. I hate this school. I hate this world. I hate this universe. Do you have any cigs or not?"

"No."

"And you weren't trying to contact me this morning?"

"No."

"Liar. Not that it matters, but liar."

From her purse she pulled out a flat chipped metal case that made a spronging sound when she opened it. Inside behind a filigree bar were three cigarettes.

"My last ones. Do you smoke?"

"Yes."

"Yessssssssss. That is so sick. Do you care if I steal it? Yessssssssss. That is how I'm going to say it from now on. Yessssss. Yessssss." She offered me a cig. I took it. I took it because the father said that when anyone offers you something, including a new identity, you should always take it and see what it leads you to. Once he found a nudist camp that way.

She pulled out a lighter with USN engraved on it. Big and silver-colored. Special issue. Made for people in windy conditions. You could not blow it out. I said, "Your father Navy?"

She snorted. "My father? Not hardly."

We sat in the weeds awhile blowing stale Newport smoke into the air. I felt a weird electrification from being beside her. Partly it made me want to leave and partly it was what made me stay when the first bell rang and neither of us acted like we noticed it. Lunch was over. We had five minutes to get to fifth period.

"You don't need to lie to me," she said. Blue smoke came out of her nostrils.

"OK," I said. It was the Navy thing to say. The thing the father told me to do. Agree and agree. See what the person has in mind.

"So you did contact me."

"Yes."

"Yesssssss."

Five years is a long time to go around obeying and not talking and having a boring life. Maybe I did contact her. Or maybe my Unfortunate Being did, whatever that was. Maybe it was time to finally tell the story and maybe Vicky Talluso was the perfect person to tell it to.

The second bell rang. Vicky was chewing on grass, grinding down with her front teeth and then actually chewing the grass into a wad. She said, "Roberta. Roberta. Hey." I looked up and her mouth opened and her tongue shelfed out and there was a two-inch wet black ball of grass on it.

I said, "Dag, Vicky!"

She said, "What?"

She saw me looking freaked. Possibly she was more Navy than I was. She said, "Know what is so amazing about that? About chewed-up grass?"

I shook my head.

"Milk is made of only that. Of chewed grass and nothing else. Grass is the milk's Unfortunate Being. Get it? We're skipping fifth, right? You're skipping with me." She picked up her purse and stood up. Some clouds behind her were doing that thing of suddenly looking all shadowed with white glowing edges. She said, "Roberta."

"What?"

She showed me the grass wad again.

Was it me or Clyde who jumped up and followed her when she took off running?

Was Clyde the Unfortunate Being she was talking about? Or was it actually me?

Chapter 5

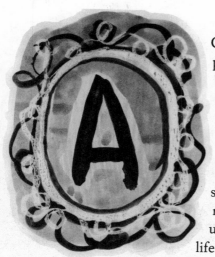

CCORDING TO the newspaper version of the story, the father stole me, kidnapped me, snatched me up in the middle of the night and left the mother a note saying if she contacted the police or tried to find either one of us he would not hesitate to slit my throat. According to the newspaper article he was a man unhinged by recent events in his life. The hanging suicide of his own father in the meat-packing room, the failure of the family business, and the breakup of his marriage for reasons too personal to mention like finding out Julie was the child of a man the mother worked with, Dr. Cush, ancient and ugly as an unwrapped mummy, but loaded with money and looking for love. Unhinged by the events that unfolded in the space of forty-eight hours, he did what desperate men do in desperate situations. He packed up his knives and his kid and screeched out of town in a dented green DeSoto, never to be seen again.

According to the newspaper version of the story, it was a miracle I survived. The father is the main suspect in the Lucky Chief Motel Massacre. His face is still pictured in some post offices, thumbtack holes all over it from other more important notices stuck on the bulletin boards over the years. I have collected a couple of them. They are the only pictures of him I have. The mother took a lit cigarette and pushed it into every other photograph of his face that existed.

She has told me many times that she thought long and hard about what to do when she opened the newspaper and saw my picture above the caption that said, *Mystery child still unidentified.* A lot of papers picked up the story. The picture she saw was a later one of me sitting on the front counter of the police station in Las Vegas. Looking a little fatter. Happier. Holding Cookie but still not talking. They guessed my age to be six or seven. I was eleven and a half. The mother never could stand seeing an error in a newspaper. Maybe she called because of that.

She thought long and hard about what to do. Dr. Cush gave the mother a little something to help her get started elsewhere. Not much. Not nearly enough. But she took it, bought a sky blue Rambler American, packed up Julie and didn't look back. Do they remember us there anymore? The family that became unhinged and blew away?

I have wondered too why the mother decided to make the identifying call. Maybe she was afraid of what I would say if I finally started talking. How I might tell the truth, that it was her who shoved me into the backseat of his car in the middle of the night. Her who piled the clothes on top of me and said if I said one single word, if I made a peep to let him know I was back there, she would pull my eyes out.

Or maybe she called because she could not stand to see me getting all of the publicity. She had always wanted her picture in the newspaper. Maybe she just could not stand the thought of me hogging all the action.

In the little teeny grease spot on the map where I was born the name Rohbeson meant quality meat. Rohbeson's Slaughter and Custom House was famous for five counties. Rohbeson's methods were strictly Old World. Everything done by hand. The rounding, knocking, bleeding, gutting, skinning, splitting, dressing, aging, curing, pickling, packing, bone and hoof boiling, all of it done right on-site.

The father slammed his hand down on the kitchen table and made the forks and knives jump. He said, "I'll challenge anyone to come up with better tasting meat. That shit what's coming out of Chicago now? Out of those big houses? That ain't meat. I don't even know what to call it. It's what you get when you pack half-dead cattle nose to asshole, scare the living hell out of them with shock prods, blow their brains out with a bolt gun louder than a cannon and then hoist them up to bleed 'em on a chain line."

"Uh-huh," said the mother, yawning and stirring a tiny spoon into a jar of Julie's baby food. Julie was sick. Something was very wrong with her. She was giving off smells.

The father was taking straight pulls out of a bottle of Old Skull Popper. "With line crews, it's output, output, output. They don't cull. A carcass comes down the belt with tumors as big as your head and worms wiggling from hell to breakfast and you know what they do? Send it down the line. Let the next bastard worry about it. They got the inspectors in their back pockets, they'd stamp USDA on a dead rat. You know what USDA stands for? *You Stupid Dumb Ass.* That's what a customer is who buys that shit. Them line men piss right into the pickle vats. I know for a fact they do."

"Except it's a 'Y'," said the mother.

"What?"

"'You' begins with a 'Y'." said the mother. "Not a 'U'."

The father stood to inherit Rohbeson's Slaughter when Old Dad died. He was next in line. He was the only man in line. The last standing Rohbeson. "And he just sold it out from under me. Never said word one. I was out there running things, up to my nuts in blood and sawdust every day, telling him we were going to turn it around. 'Those big packing houses got nothing on us, Old Dad. The stores are going to come back begging, Old Dad.' And all that time he was nodding, blowing smoke up my ass.

"We could have goddamned turned it around! You know that half the cuts we do you can't even find anymore? A whole world has just died out and no one gives a damn about it. Pretty soon you won't see an independent butcher anywhere. Gone. Shit. Gone."

"Uh-huh," said the mother.

"I'm glad the bastard hung himself. If it was up to me I would have left him swinging with the carcasses right where he was. I would never have cut him down. I would have bled him and dried him and made him a goddamned mascot. A goddamned tourist attraction. Come on down over to Rohbeson's Slaughter and meet Old Dad. Get your picture taken with him and have a free hot dog.

"Bastard sold it all out from under me. Paid off the mortgages. Packed what was left over in three Samsonite suitcases, cash money delivered to settle the last of what he owed. Note said, 'Sorry, son. But at least I'm not leaving you in the hole.'"

"Well, that *is* something," said the mother. Julie's head was hanging forward. She was asleep and her face was sweating.

"SOMETHING?" screamed the father. "It's SQUAT! Not even a goddamned life insurance policy! SQUAT!" His hands bounced some additional slams onto the table and then he stood up.

This was our last dinner together. We were eating chipped beef on toast.

"You better start looking for a job," said the mother. "We're supposed to be out of here by the first."

"JOB?!" shouted the father. The night went on like that. And the next day the wife of Ardus Cardall was rushed into St. Martha's, the tiny hospital where the mother worked. Someone had blasted her arm off point-blank with a hunting rifle. When the mother came home from work she was squinting hard at the father who squinted right back.

He said, "Marie Cardall. She going to make it?"

The mother said, "What do you think?"

The newspaper version of the story said witnesses saw a man in Elkwood-issue coveralls near the house the night an escapee bulletin went out on the wires. Marie's car was stolen and no one knew what else. She was shot with her husband's rifle. The newspaper version said her husband Ardus was being questioned about it.

"His alibi is tight," said the father. "Can't get much tighter than being in jail yourself when the crime occurs. She going to pull through?"

The mother said, "What makes you so interested?"

"Hey," said the father, "I don't give a damn about Marie Cardall. I'm just making conversation."

Suspicion was cast on Ardus Cardall because he was bitter about his wife turning him in and testifying against him. Bitter wasn't the word. And he was a string-puller.

It was Marie Cardall who contacted the police when Ardus came home from work and told her he might have buried the little boy that was lost, the boy the town was turning itself inside out about. He told Marie there was a pretty good chance he buried the Leonards boy alive in concrete while he was pouring the foundation for the new church. He said that by the time he noticed there was nothing he could do. The boy was gone. So he just kept pouring. He told Marie he was just hoping the whole thing would somehow blow over.

"And she turned him in," said the father.

"She was right to report him," said the mother.

"Well, Ardus saw it differently."

"For god's sake."

"If you think that she went to court because she gave a damn about that Leonards boy you are ignorant as living hell."

"Why, then?" snapped the mother.

"Figure it out. It ain't long division."

The mother snorted. "No. I guess it *ain't*." Saying "ain't" with special emphasis.

"Well?" said the father. "Did she make it or not? Is Mrs. Cardall still among us?"

"You tell me."

"My guess is she pulled through."

"Ha," said the mother. "Ha-ha. You're funny."

It was that night she shoved me into the backseat of his car and told me not to show my face. It was that night he told her he was leaving on a business trip and would probably be gone for a while.

Chapter 6

ICKY CUT along the top of the embankment, ducking and keeping close to the Cyclone fence that ran through the half-dead pine trees. Different P.E. classes were coming out onto the field. Different gym teachers were blowing black plastic whistles and shouting. Fifth period. First time I ever skipped.

We kept going. The Cyclone fence ran out. We came to the far, far end of the school and then crossed over into where everything was growing wild. The area people called no-man's-land, because it was between the school and the reservoir. There wasn't anything there but a decrepit old outbuilding, in a place everybody called the Dip. It was at the bottom of two embankments and the sticker bushes grew high all around. There was no direct path down, but little juvenile delinquent trails zigzagged through the Scotch broom and the disturbing trash you always find in abandoned places along with the drifting smell of human pee.

Vicky went very fast through the paths, not pausing at all when the fly families lifted around her and then settled and then lifted again. It was the beginning of September, still very warm for Cruddy City, but at the bottom of the embankment it was bright and actually hot. There were piles of rabbit evidence, and a pile of someone's old stiff clothes giving off a close smell, like in a hot secondhand store, and there was the smell of the out-building itself. "I have to go bad," Vicky Talluso said. "Guard me." She squatted down.

The building was wooden and rotting with a half-falling-in roof. A curved, military-style roof, the kind you see on the buildings at Fort Stilacoomb. There were old NO TRESPASSING signs nailed on it and the paint was peeling off in long green scabs. Along the top near the corroded roof edge were three rows of shiny small-paned windows painted black from the inside and mostly broken. Pigeons flew in and out constantly. On the door someone had carved the words BIG DICK MEL.

Everything was seeming very quiet and the sun was sending down rays that made everything look washed out. Vicky stood back up and looked at me. "You paranoid?"

"No."

"Because I hate paranoid people. If you are paranoid you better tell me right now."

"I'm not."

The door was big, like the door on a barn. It had some rusted link chains across it, but Vicky knew where to pull so that a gap opened up wide enough to push through. "You," she said. "You first. I'll hold it for you."

I hesitated and she saw it. I hesitated even though the father told me a thousand times, DO NOT HESITATE. NEVER, EVER HESITATE. The father said hesitation is for your average man and your average man always loses. Vicky made a tiny move of impatience and it freaked me forward. I squeezed myself into the blackness. It felt like all the light in the world got sucked away.

The smell of the building was thick and rank. It was moist. The smell of rodents and pigeons and rotting straw. I felt the ache of my eyes dilating too fast. In the ancient days of our school, the building was where the maintenance men kept things. It was where the archery bales were stored when people still took archery in gym. The famous story was that the targets got hauled across the field and set in rows and sophomores stood holding

bows and sharp arrows waiting for the gym teacher to signal the moment to shoot. And one time a dog wandered onto the field and before the teacher could call it away one of the kids just shot it. And then everyone was running to help the dog and the kid shot another kid and he just kept on shooting until he got tackled. He said he wasn't a disturbed person. He said he was just a plain normal person that sometimes had to kill people with arrows.

I didn't know if the story was true or not. There are a million stories that float around a school. But as my eyes adjusted I saw putrid stacks of gray hay with torn bull's-eye targets still hanging on them.

Vicky found a place to sit. Shafts of light fell down around her from holes in the roof. I saw the familiar glue-sniffer brown paper bags laying around. There were the magazines showing nudeness. Pink flobs of skin and black wiry hair. A leak of sunlight slid across Vicky's back as she leaned down to look at one closer. Tilting her head at the page like she was trying to read a message in bad handwriting. "Look," she said. A picture of a man having an interaction with a slime flower fold. "Do you know that Jesus loves him just as much as he loves you and me? Isn't that cracked? Sit down. I want to give you a transformation. I am so good at transformations."

In the old days of the father I was in many situations where everything around me was screaming DANGER! DANGER! FREAK OUT AND RUN! but he taught me to go forward. He taught me to remember I was Navy all the way and to go forward without fear. Compared to what I have seen in my life, Vicky Talluso's world was nothing. But I was out of practice. It had been a long time. I was rusty and all I needed was a little oil. That is what the father would have said before he passed me the flat bottle of Old Skull Popper. "Clyde, you have nothing to fear 'til you run out of beer."

Mostly he was right. Mostly what looked like a horrifying scene at first turned out to be nothing at all. Like the transformation Vicky wanted to give me. All she meant by it was she wanted to put makeup on me. She said there was no reason for me to go around looking like a skag when I didn't have to.

She pulled out a pink rattail comb and moved me into a pool

of light. "No offense but your hair is horrible. You need to grow it, OK? You will look a lot better with long hair. I am going to do beauty for a living. I just have it in me. I can just look at a person and tell exactly what to do." The feeling of her combing my hair made a nice sensation in the back of my throat.

She said, "Do you have a boyfriend?"

"No."

"Did you ever have one?"

"Nuh-uh. No."

"Well, when I finish this, I know the perfect guy for you. Do you get high? You ever drop before?"

"No."

"Because you're against it?"

"I'm not against it."

"Then because no one ever got you high before, right?"

"Right," I said.

"God. You are going to be soooooo thankful that you met me. You are going to love me so much after today. You haven't ever done anything exciting, have you?"

"Partly I have."

"What?"

"Well, I killed somebody once. A couple people, actually."

She was snort-laughing. I felt her breath on the back of my neck. It had a scent that surprised me. Under the cig smell there was a cherry cough drop smell I hadn't noticed before. Part medicine, part pretty candy.

She said, "You killed people?"

"Yes."

"Yessssss. God, you are sick. How. How did you kill them?"

"With Little Debbie."

She was laughing again. Pushing my head forward and ratting my hair high. She said, "Roberta, this guy I was telling you about? He is going to *love* you."

chapter 7

HE FATHER drove through the darkness. He drove and he drove. I curled up in the well of the backseat floor and felt the vibrations of the road beneath us. The father sang with the radio. He had a decent voice. He thought he could have been a famous singer and maybe it's true.

He talked to Old Dad. Old Dad, you bastard. Old Dad, you lying sack of shit. He glugged Old Skull Popper and every once in a while he talked to Marie Cardall, another sack of shit, just like her husband. He threw cig after cig out the open window and a couple of them got sucked back in and landed in the backseat. I smelled the smoke before he did. And then he shouted, "SON OF A BITCH!" and slammed on the brakes. I was thinking we were on fire, but it was a roadblock.

Troopers came to the car from four directions with strong flashlights and the flying night bugs were going wild. The father hated troopers. He hated all cops, but troopers most of all.

"Hands on the steering wheel where I can see them." A blinding flashlight beam shot around the inside of the car and hit me in the eyes. When the trooper saw me he lowered it. He said, "Sorry there, sweetheart. Don't be scared." The father whipped his head and when he saw me his eyes went wide.

"Daddy," I said. Reaching up my hands to him just like he

taught me. If we were ever stopped by cops it was what I was supposed to do. Call him Daddy. Act scared. Start to cry. And if I could manage to throw up, that would be handy.

"Aw, honey, I'm sorry," said the trooper. "Didn't mean to scare you. Did I wake you up?"

"It's OK, 'Berta," said the father, and he reached back for me and pulled me over into the front seat. There were times when it was handy for me to be a girl. It was one of those times. I pushed my face into the father's shoulder and wondered if I should barf or not. It would have been no problem. I'd been feeling carsick for miles.

"I'm sorry to bother you, sir. Can I see some ID?" The trooper leaned his head in the window.

"I'm looking," said the father. He was digging in his pockets for his wallet and trying to keep his face down so the Old Skull Popper fumes wouldn't rise up the trooper's nose. I could see how nervous he was. I said, "Daddy?" I pointed to the torqued-out rectangle of leather on the dashboard. "You looking for that?"

"Oh thank Jesus. Yes. Yes, baby doll. Thank-you." The father handed his license the trooper and said, "She's the brains of this operation."

The trooper smiled and shined his flashlight into the backseat again.

"Something burning in there?" Wispy smoke was curling up from the clothes.

The father yanked the clothes out of the backseat while the trooper took his license and registration back to call it in and the other men shut their flashlights off and went back to talking with one another. The father threw a few looks my way and shook his head a couple of times and laughed under his breath. "Missed your old man, huh, Clyde? Couldn't stand to see me go, is that right? Don't worry. I'm not going to whip you. You just saved my ass, son. When we get out of this, I'm going to buy you a hamburger."

The father found the smoldering clothes and stamped them

out. The trooper came back with his ID and handed it back through the window. He had a warm bottle of RC. "This is for your little girl. Wish it was cold for her."

"It don't matter," said the father, passing it my way. "She's a garbage gut. She'll eat and drink anything you put in front of her." I hated pop but I took a drink anyway.

The father said, "You hunting that escapee from Elkwood? Is that what this is about?"

The trooper lifted his eyebrows. "You know something about it?"

"Heard he blew her arm off point-blank. Heard she was bled out terrible by the time they brought her in. My wife worked on her. She's a nurse at St. Martha's."

The trooper bounced a look off of me and then back at the father like he should know better than to talk about something like that in front of a little girl.

He said, "Your license said Rohbeson."

"That's right."

"Rohbeson's Slaughterhouse?"

The father nodded.

"My daddy drove across two counties to get to your place. Said you couldn't beat Rohbeson's. Took his deer there every year. Your outfit turned out the best venison sausage I ever tasted. I'm real sorry about your old man."

"Yeah, well." The father looked down. "Chicago and all. We couldn't compete. That's progress."

"Your whole operation's shutting down then?" said the trooper.

"It's shut down. My old man had it mortgaged to the gizzards."

"It's a shame."

The father nodded. "It is."

"All right then," said the trooper. "I don't need to tell you not to pick up any hitchhikers."

"Hell no," said the father, feathering the gas pedal. "I wouldn't dream." He waved out a half salute and eased up the clutch. When we curved the next corner he snatched the pop out of my hand and whipped it out the window. His forehead was sweating. He was trying to get a fresh pack of cigs unwrapped but he couldn't do it. "Help me out here, Clyde." He tossed the pack to me. "Have one yourself if you want. You earned it. We just about got caught by our short and curlies. Reach under the seat and pull out my medicine. Take a pull. It will put you righter than RC any day. Whoooooo! Son-of-a-BITCH! I about crapped my pants when I saw you back there. Take a pull off that bottle. Go on. Hold your nose when you do it and you won't taste it so bad. It burns like hell but what comes after is a true reward. I am sure goddamned glad to see you, son."

And I will admit I was glad to see him too. And I was feeling pretty good with the radio on loud, lighting his cigarettes for him and watching the bugs splat against the windshield while the father raced down the black back roads, singing.

And then in the middle of nowhere on that nowhere road, a woman stepped out of the darkness holding a suitcase. A large woman wearing a head scarf and a bathrobe, setting a suitcase down and waving both of her big hands in the air. The father slammed on the brakes and the car fishtailed her way and slowed to stop and then at the last second the father floored it. He floored it right into her. There was a sick crunching and a thumping and a moment of flesh pressing against the windshield in front of me. A smashed face hitting the glass with horrible features flattened, and then thumps sounding over my head and then nothing. Just silence and a weird weightless feeling all around. A feeling like when you stand up too fast and the spots of light swim around your eyes. The father checked the rearview mirror. He looked at me. "Think I hit her?" He was smiling. He threw the car into reverse and ran over her again. He drove back and forth several times and then jumped out, grabbed the suitcase, and held it up.

"Not a scratch on it, Clyde! It's a Samsonite! We could do a goddamned commercial!"

chapter 8

OOOOOOOOO!" THE sound made Vicky jump and mess up my mascara.

"Hooooooooo!"

"What's that?" she whispered. She grabbed my arm.

"Hoooooooo!" A chill went straight up my back. It was a person for sure and for a second I thought it was someone it could not possibly be unless the dead do truly walk.

"Hooooo did you killlll?" said the voice.

Vicky's eyes locked on mine.

"Hoooooooooo!" It was coming from behind a stack of targets. Vicky shoved me. "Go see," she whispered. "Go look."

I crawled forward a little and poked my head around for a second and then whipped it back. "It's a guy," I whispered.

"What kind of guy?"

"I think it's a hippie."

Vicky stood up and took a few creeping steps around the stacked bales. I saw her yellow boot swing back and deliver a hard kick.

"OWwwwww!" said the hippie.

"I hate spies," said Vicky Talluso. "Roberta," she said. "Get over here."

He looked very relaxed laying on his back in the straw. He seemed to be somewhere around our age, a little older maybe, and he was looking very much like a typical glue-sniffer dropout. The extreme relaxation of the guy was interesting to me. A very fat fly lifted itself and made a worn-out buzzing sound and flew a lop-sided circle around his face. He followed it with his eyes and said, "Not now."

Vicky said, "He's wasted."

She nudged his leg with her boot and it was quite rubberized. Except for the slightest movement of his open hands he was still and I saw he was extremely pale. Dark circles ringed his eyes. His hair was white-blond and longish, looking greasy and clumped to-gether. All of him was looking very white except his eyes, which were black, weirdly black and crowded with fringes of too many white eyelashes. His fingers wiggled a little, and I started thinking of a white moth on its back moving paper-colored legs so slowly.

He was wearing a red-and-white-striped surfer shirt, very large and ugly high-water bell bottoms, tight to just below the knees and then flaring out the wrong way. He didn't have socks on and his shoes were the most insane pimped-out beige patent leather with scuffed gold buckles and high stacked heels that were worn down to almost sideways. They looked big on him. He saw me staring and said, "These are the Lord's shoes, Hillbilly Woman. We traded. Now I walk in his shoes and he walks in mine. And guess whose fit better?"

"He's completely wasted," said Vicky. "Look at him." She clawed at her forehead, digging her short fingernails into the bald eyebrow skin above her left eye. It was the reason she was bald there. She clawed at it whenever she was trying to figure out what to do next. And she had such an active life that the hair never had a chance to grow back. The father taught me to watch the hands. Always watch the hands. The hands will tell you everything you need to know.

"Hey. Spy," said Vicky. "You tripping?" Her voice was too loud for the situation. "You drop? Hey. You. Talk. Answer."

He didn't look at her. He kept his black eyes on me. Vicky no-ticed it. She said, "He's in love with you, Roberta."

She meant it as an insult. The guy did not give off normal vibrations and nothing about him was cute, but it made her mad that he was noticing me instead of her. When she said it, he smiled and the sudden alive pinkness of his gums and his wet teeth sent a shock through me and caused an involuntary jerking. Sometimes the autonomic nervous system is called that, the involuntary. And sometimes the passageways are frayed or badly wired. I have certain bare spots and he found one.

Vicky was kneeling beside him, bending over his face while her hands were quick going through his pockets. "Yeah, you're tripping aren't you, little hippie man? His pupils are totally blown. Is it acid? Hey. Answer. Is it mesc? What's your name?" She pointed at me. "You like her? She doesn't have a boyfriend. Right, Roberta?"

She gave me the olden look. Maybe the oldest of the olden looks. The go-along-with-it point of the eyes. The father would have laughed at her. She was so obvious. She had no style at all. I felt a little disappointed. The father would have bent over laughing.

"Roberta doesn't have a boyfriend and she loves getting high. Right, Roberta? Are you going to get her high? What's your name?" Vicky's fingers worked her way into his bagged-out shirt pocket without trying to hide what she was doing.

"I am the Turtle," he said. "You know me as the Turtle."

"Yeah? What's this?" Vicky pulled out a round flat container with a metal lid. "This your stash?" She shook it and there was a damp scratchy sound.

"Since 1822," said the Turtle.

"Yeah?" said Vicky.

"It satisfies."

"What is it, hippie man? Hash?"

The Turtle said, "It's a new day so let a man come in and do the popcorn," and then snatched the container out of her hand before she could pry off the lid.

I thought of a trap-door spider. He moved as quick as that.

"Don't be so tight," said Vicky. "I wasn't doing nothing."

The Turtle tossed it back to her. He said, "Why don't ya check it ouuuut and lock it dowwwwn!" Every time he talked he changed his accent. I was getting interested in him.

Vicky sat down and pried off the lid. Inside was a dark flaky substance that looked like hairy mud. She sniffed it and pulled her face back. "Smells like horse piss. What is it, Turtle?"

I sat down next to her. I said, "It's Copenhagen, Vicky. Chew."

"What, like hash?" she said. "A kind of hash?"

"No," I said. "Chew. Tobacco."

She said, "But it does have, like, hash oil in it, right? Because I have a very sensitive nose. I can tell hash."

The Turtle propped himself up and did a French accent. "Like, I want shit, man, hey. Will you stone? I want to smoke shit for example. Is it?"

I was getting more and more impressed with him. He reached into the same shirt pocket and pulled out a bent white paper twist. Club-shaped and very fat, which he held out to Vicky.

"Trade ya," he said. "It'll talk to ya." He wiggled the twist and I watched Vicky try to figure out if she was being tricked or not. Vicky looked at me for my opinion. The father would have fallen on the floor laughing.

All three of us held in and exhaled our clouds. The Turtle called it the Ancient Substance, something I'd been hearing about in Health, something featured in the film our 1,000-year-old teacher Mrs. Fields showed us called *What Are Drugs?* When I started laughing, Vicky said, "What? What?"

I said, "What Are Drugs?" I said, "Getting a trip is groovy, man. I am groovy. I can flyyyyy." I told them about the movie. About how it started with warped music and a close-up of water that someone was dropping food coloring into and what looked like some little balls of aluminum foil. I told them about the whispering voice. "*I am groovy. Getting a trip is groovy.*"

"Getting a trip *is* groovy," said the Turtle.

"Oh yeah!" said Vicky. "I saw that movie in second period! And it was so fake! And people kept cracking up! And Mrs. Fields turns on the lights and says, 'Shut up or you have to go to the office!' And me and these two black guys could not stop laughing and we got sent to the office." She inhaled another cloud and passed me the twist. I was staring at her. In a pinched back-of-the-throat voice she said, "What?"

I took my inhale. I wondered was she just being a very bold liar or did she really not know I had that class with her. I was sitting two rows behind her. And I knew what she said never happened. Mrs. Fields turned on the lights and told us to shut up but she didn't send Vicky Talluso to the office. She didn't send anyone to the office.

"Hillbilly Woman," The Turtle timed it so that Vicky was on an inhale when he spoke to me. "You must continue your story."

Vicky blew her cloud out. "What story?"

"The murder," said the Turtle. "Little Debbie."

Vicky pulled her head back and looked at me. She said, "What Little Debbie?"

"The Hillbilly Woman killed the people with Little Debbie. I heard her say so."

"Oh," said Vicky. "That. She was just bullshitting."

"Were you?" The Turtle was looking at me and his black eyes were like sucking holes.

"No," I said.

From the back of her throat Vicky said, "Lie," and some little wisps of smoke curled around her teeth. She was hogging on the roach and it was burning her fingers. The Turtle tossed her a beat-up cough drops tin with a flip-top lid.

"What's this?" she said. "Another fake-out?" Vicky shook the box and there was a dry rattle.

"Careful," said the Turtle. "Don't bruise them."

Vicky opened the lid. She sniffed and said, "Chocolate mesc! Is it? Is it? Is it chocolate mesc?"

"Is it?" said the Turtle.

She took out a clear cap filled with what looked like powdered cocoa and held it between her fingers. "It is," she said. And before the Turtle answered she closed the tin and slipped it into her purse. "I'm keeping it for you, OK, Turtle? You are very wasted, OK? It's easy to lose things when you are wasted, so I'll keep it for you."

He was fast. He was holding the stash box before Vicky could even finish shutting her purse. She moved her hand quickly to her mouth and swallowed the cap. She said, "It's mesc, right?"

"Is it?"

"TELL ME!"

The Turtle shook his head. "No, Violent One. It is not."

"What is it then? Will it get me high?"

"It has a name but it will be unfamiliar to you."

"I know a lot of names," said Vicky. "You would be amazed."

The Turtle stood up and brushed off bits of straw from his clothes. "We need to stroll," he said. "We need to be with the people."

We pushed ourselves outside and my eyes cramped down hard from the light. The name of the drug was Creeper. The Turtle was right. Vicky Talluso had never heard of it. As we followed him up the embankment she said, "Is it like microdot?"

"It's not like anything," said the Turtle.

Vicky hunched her shoulders up and down. "Does it give you rushes?"

The Turtle pulled out the box and offered it to me. "Do you wish to partake, Hillbilly Woman?"

"Why do you call me that?"

"Because you are a hillbilly girl lost in a hillbilly world."

Vicky Talluso said, "She is! She is!" and started laughing uncontrollably. Then she said, "I'm not feeling it or anything. I just get so excited when I drop. Roberta, you have to drop. She's never dropped before, Turtle. Come on, Roberta. Didn't I tell you I was going to get you high?" I held my hand out to the Turtle.

"Yesssssssss," said Vicky Talluso. "Yesssssssss."

chapter 9

HE FATHER drove with his headlights off for a while. I had no idea how he was staying on the road, it was so black out. A train came up alongside us out of nowhere, barreling hard out of the blackness on the parallel, blasting and screeching and over the noise the father shouted, "Freight cars are empty, that's why she bounces." And that sentence got stuck in my head and played awhile. And then the train curved away from us, rattling away into the darkness and it was quiet, just the car sounds and the father sighing now and then and saying "shit" because the radio station was going out of range.

We came to a set of grain silos, giant and white beside the tracks and I was thinking how train tracks were everywhere. Train tracks were where nothing else was. The father circled around the huge silos until he found his way around back to where there was a little wooden office up on stilts. Truck-window height. Behind it was a service area with a water hose attached to a spigot and neatly coiled. "That's a good hose," said the father, "and they leave it like that where anybody could take it." He shook his head. "Farmers. Bless their hearts."

He got out of the car and the minute his face was turned away I jumped into the backseat. He had the hose going and was getting good pressure by holding his thumb over the end, giving the bumper and the hood a good wash down. It seemed to me the sky was getting lighter. That the night was finally ending. But when I looked again it was just as dark as ever. When the water exploded onto the window next to me I screamed and saw him laugh. Through the cascading water on the window his face looked rubber, looked like it was melting away. He threw down the hose without winding it back up and got in the car.

"What you sitting back there for, Clyde? Don't be like that. Come on back up here. We just did the world a favor. You know who it was that we hit, don't you?"

I didn't say anything. He started the engine and said, "Oh, damn," and hopped back out to get the Samsonite suitcase. It needed a spray-down too. And I was thinking I should run. Right that second. Just open the door and take off running into the black scrub on the other side of the tracks. Would he come after me? I didn't know. And then what? What would happen after that? If he caught me or if he didn't.

Some people cannot forget the location of the jugular and the carotid any more than they could forget the alphabet. After a certain amount of time it's just burned into your mind like a song on the radio, the vascular system, the skeletal system, all the different cuts; standing rib, Porterhouse, round, eye of round, Delmonico, fillet, strip, skirt, sirloin. The knives you want for each. Obviously I am talking the language of meat. Of course I mean cattle. I do not think there is anything that could be called a specific cut on a human being. We have organs in common with cattle, we share many systems of the body, but I am not sure there is such a thing as the Delmonico area in a person.

I didn't run. We drove on. From the backseat I watched the back of his neck as the sky began to lighten around it. He was half in the bag. It took more and more glugs of Old Skull Popper to get him there, but the sounds of his words were smudged and he was getting philosophical.

"Used to be a father would never turn on his son. Would never sell the business right from under his own son. Used to be you could count on your old man not to cut your balls off and feed them to the squirrels. You understand what I'm trying to tell you here?" His eyes searched me out in the rearview mirror.

I didn't think a squirrel would eat a man's balls. Rats might. I offered him that comment.

"Son. I'm trying to say here that you have to be prepared for the unexpected, because, son, it's out there." He tapped on the windshield in front of him and the car swerved slightly. The empty land around us was pale and still in the shadows. "It's everywhere you look, it's waiting for you like the goddamned Apaches."

When he saw me close my eyes he shouted, "You can't go to sleep on me, Clyde. Talk to me. Ask me anything. You figured out who it was yet?" He meant the lady we ran over. I didn't answer.

"You got all the pieces. Now put them together. Didn't that lady strike you as strange? Ugly as a hog and big as sin? Walking in the middle of the night like that? Standing in the middle of nowhere. Think, Clyde. And tell me, whose fat head put that dent in my hood?"

His eyes found mine in the rearview for just a second before I looked away.

"What if I told you it wasn't a woman? That help you any? It's not someone you know to remember, exactly. But you heard about him."

I closed my eyes and the father swerved the car hard on purpose to wake me. "You're the only thing keeping us on the road, son. You better not fall asleep or we'll both be crow meat."

The first fingers of sunlight fell across the horizon. Colors came back. "You forfeit?" asked the father.

I nodded.

"You remember Doolie Bug?"

I shook my head no.

"One of my cousins used to baby-sit you? That crazy son-of-

49

a-bitch? You know that round scar on the top of your hand? Doolie Bug did that with a Tiparillo. I told your mother, I said, 'DB's out of his frigging mind, honey, don't leave our little baby with him.' But she's contrary. If I told her DB was a cannibal from the planet Mars she'd throw a birthday party for him just to piss me off.

"Well." The father laughed and coughed. "It took a while, but I got him for you, Clyde. Better late than never, they say."

The scar on the back of my hand is real. It is round and has pale marks radiating from the middle because it had to stretch with my growing. A nickel lays in it perfectly. I have laid a cool nickel upon it many times. It is real, but I was not so sure about the story of the father. I know we hit someone and hit them again and I know we left them laying there but it was the cousin part I wasn't sure about. He told a lot of dead cousin stories. Cousins who got what they deserved. Stingy ones who fell through the ice going after a dropped penny. Snoopy ones who blew their own heads off with a came-upon gun. Stuck-up ones who died on the toilet. He said that one got written up in the newspaper. *Stuck-up Cousin Dies on Toilet.* Front page. According to the father who could have been a famous singer. Who could have been a movie star. Who could have bought out Armour and Hormel both on what he would have made if Old Dad hadn't shafted him.

The father was tired of playing by the rules. The father was calling himself Billy Badass, the outlaw that always got in. And I was his partner, his sidekick, Clyde. The Old Skull Popper was really talking to him and we swerved all over the long empty road.

The scar on my hand is real but the mother always told me it was him, the father himself who gave it to me.

Chapter 10

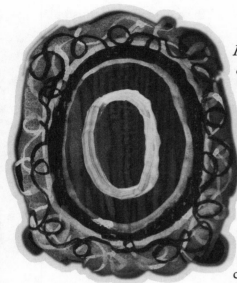

H 'BERTA, oh little 'Berta, can't you hear me calling you?" The Turtle was singing and his voice was decent. Sometimes high and sometimes hoarse.

The Turtle said, "Would you ladies like to join me in New Orleans? Would you like to experience the malodor of the sad drunk's urine in Pirate's Alley? Would you care to gaze upon the House of the Rising Sun? The Great Wesley and I are planning a trip and you would be most welcome. We have nearly everything we need. We have a car and it is quite a car. But we lack a driver."

Vicky scratched at her eyebrow. "Who's the Great Wesley?"

I said, "I can drive."

"Stick?" asked the Turtle.

"Yes."

"Yessssssss," said Vicky Talluso. "Roberta tells another lie."

"I've been driving since I was eleven," I said.

"Leprosy of the face comes from lying," said Vicky. "You get leprosy and then your nose falls off."

We were on the embankment beside the reservoir, leaning and pushing our faces into a high Cyclone fence with our fingers on the chain link. We were there to watch the high jets of water shoot out of the Jefferson Park Reservoir. Water must be kept in motion or the result is stagnation. For creatures it's blood that

51

must be kept in motion or there is putrefaction. I mentioned this. Vicky stared at me. The Turtle nodded. "Yes," he said. "Absolutely. Even in the achievement of ataraxy there must be motion." Vicky stared at him. She was squinting.

The Turtle said, "Leprosy of the face is totally misunderstood. It is not nearly as bad as people think. Leprosy of the mind, however, is a disaster."

In the distance I heard the three o'clock bell. School was over. It was time to return to East Crawford. To the mother and my life there. To Julie, the evil half-daughter of the crumbling mummy called Dr. Cush, who made no provision for her when he croaked. Who left her nothing, not a Band-Aid, not even a hair ball.

It was different for me. The father left me a fortune. Getting to it was my problem. I knew the way, but I needed transportation. I was tired of the current version of my life. The mother and I, we had serious mental problems with each other but it was her who had the knives. Who screamed that she could cut my throat and Julie's throat and her own throat and who could stop her from doing it? Who? Who in this world?

I do believe that if she got in the right mood she could slit my throat with no problem. And I think she could do Julie. But I'm pretty sure that when it came to doing herself she'd run out of gas. I mentioned all of this to Vicky and the Turtle and Vicky's eyes went round.

"A fortune?" she said.

"Yes."

"Yessssss," she said. "What kind of fortune? Are you lying? Because if you are lying I am going to get very violent. I get extremely violent when people lie to me. Is it money?"

"Cash money," I said. "Three suitcases full."

Vicky snorted but kept her eyes on me. The Turtle didn't say anything. His thick white eyelashes didn't even flutter.

I watched the motion of the shooting water, shooting high and white, then gone, then rising again. It's called pulsing. It happens because of the differences in pressure. Blood shoots for the

same reason. You would be surprised by how it can spray. Blood can hit the ceiling and drip back down on you. But usually blood on the ceiling and the walls is secondary. It is from the knife or the ax in fast repeated motion. Back-splattering. Meat people know how to keep it to a minimum but it is still an unavoidable part of the job. I mentioned this too. Vicky said, "You're sick, Roberta. Is the money real?"

The fountain jets shot up and behind them in the blue sky the clouds were moving fast. The visual combination made me dizzy, and I saw the little bright spots come swimming from the sides of my eyes.

I said, "I need to sit down."

The Turtle sat down next to me. "Tell me about the dangerous adventures of Little Debbie."

Vicky said, "You two are perfect for each other. I can't wait for both of you to get really high and have a conversation because I want to be really high and listen to it because I can't tell what the fuck either one of you is talking about."

She had one cigarette left. She lit it with the USN lighter. The flame blew sideways in the wind and I smelled the fluid and my fingers itched to take it apart. Slip it out of its metal case and take a dime to the screw at the bottom and open it. I wanted to tilt up the flicker wheel and pull out the red flint. I said, "Can I see your lighter, Vicky?"

She said, "People who lie can't touch anything of mine."

The Turtle suggested we move down to a little hollow beside the fence where we would be completely hidden. Vicky got mad. "Once I light a cig I hate to move, OK? I'll do it this time but next time you'll know so there will not be an excuse."

We followed the Turtle a few yards to a hollow in the embankment. Someone had dug a hole under the fence.

"That's where he went in," said the Turtle.

"Who?" I said.

"The fellow. The dead fellow."

Vicky was blowing smoke out of her nostrils and staring up at the tilted razor-wire top that was added to the Cyclone fence after the day the dead man was found in reservoir waters. A man who had been floating in the water supply for some time.

The Turtle said, "I knew him."

Vicky said, "No one knew him."

"I did," said the Turtle. "The Great Wesley did."

The Turtle said, "The fellow was a homo and this was difficult. His parents were never in the mood for this information. They sent him to the Barbara V. Hermann Home for Adolescent Rest. The Great Wesley and I were so fond of him. We were saddened by the news of his self-inflicted homicide."

"Suicide," said Vicky.

"Not at all," said the Turtle. "It was murder."

Vicky snorted. "You can't murder yourself."

The Turtle shook his head. "If only he had known."

Vicky said, "I'm not feeling anything. If this Creeper is a burn, Turtle, I'm serious. You do not want to know what I do to people who burn me."

I leaned my head forward because I felt like I was going to throw up.

Vicky said, "You feeling it, Roberta? You getting the rushes? Look at me. Let me check your eyes."

But my eyes were normal. Chills came clawing up my back. Was it the rushes? Something was happening. My jaws felt tight. I said, "I heard he was in there for at least five days before they found him. You guys ever wonder how much of the dead guy's water you drank?"

Vicky made a little heaving sound. She shivered. Was because of the Creeper? I looked over at the Turtle. His face was very calm. His eyes were on the pulsing jets. Who was he? What was his deal?

"I'm having a nic fit," said Vicky. Her hands were shaking bad.

The Turtle pulled out his Copenhagen and told her how to do it, how to pinch up the tobacco and how wedge it inside her lip. Vicky tried it. Her eyes watered and she started spitting violently. Little black flecks were in all the crevices of her teeth. She was clenching and unclenching her fingers. "I think I'm feeling it. You guys have to guard me, OK? Because I can get insane when I drop. Very insane."

"Will you come to New Orleans?" said the Turtle. "We have an appointment at Dorothy's Medallion that the Great Wesley really would like to keep. Have you heard of the place called Dorothy's Medallion where large women wear small golden bathing suits and squat for the audience? Can either of you dance?"

Chapter 11

LIES ARE messengers. One was on a blade of dead grass right below where I was trying to barf. It was scrutinizing me and I did not like it. I said, "Sometimes I am in the mood for fly scrutinization and sometimes I am not."

"So be it," said the Turtle. "Absolutely."

"New Orleans," said Vicky Talluso. "Is that serious? Because seriously I could go. Because my philosophy is just, like, screw it, I'm going. Now I don't feel it. Roberta. You feel it? Were you lying about the cash money?"

I shook my head no.

"No, which?" she said. "No you don't feel it? No you're not lying? Which?"

"Both," I said. My stomach was in ripples and I could smell tripe, fresh and unrinsed and very strong. Memory smells are a problem for me. Actual smells can be difficult, sometimes almost impossible for me to stand. But actual smells are things a person can get away from. The memory smells are impossible to fight. The tripe smells steamed. I started heaving. The fly continued to scrutinize.

Flies have always been part of my life. In the days of Rohbeson's Slaughterhouse, flies were everywhere, crawling up the walls like living designs. I used to fall asleep looking at them.

Thinking about their world. Their society. Did they have kings? Did they steal from each other? My light fixture was black-full with bodies of them. I used to think they had feelings about certain people. People who noticed them. Certain people. Me.

There was a fly in the car with the father and I. I wasn't sure if he was a slaughterhouse fly or just a middle-of-nowhere fly. One that got in when no one was noticing. And I wondered what it was going to be like for him when he got out again. What would he think when he flew out of the car and didn't recognize anything or anybody?

Only in a fairy tale could he ever get home again. In fairy tales it happened all the time. It was possible. I was thinking it was really very possible. And while I was thinking this, the father snatched the fly out of the air and mashed him with a gesture so quick I barely saw it. Meat men can do that. They can snatch flies right out of the air.

The father checked on me in the mirror and asked if I was hungry. He said, "I still owe you that hamburger."

I started throwing up but nothing came.

"Roberta, Roberta," said Vicky Talluso. "Are you OK? Is that going to happen to me, Turtle? Because really, I cannot throw up. I mean actually physically I cannot throw up."

The long fingers of the Turtle touched the back of my neck as he gathered my hair away from my face. "It will pass," he said.

Vicky said, "What if it doesn't?"

"I'm OK," I said. "I'm OK."

"Lay back." said the Turtle. "Just be cool and feel the peace and be free and feel the love raining down on you and it will pass."

Vicky said, "If that Creeper-whatever makes me do that? If I start talking about flies and dry barfing? I'm going to seriously kick your face in, Turtle."

The Turtle was right. It did pass. Like a snake it slithered away out of me, dividing the grass as it went. My head was on the Turtle's lap and he was looking down at me through his eerie fringes of white eyelashes. He said, "Hillbilly Woman."

I said, "Turtle."

Vicky said, "Unless I get a cigarette, I'm going to claw someone's face off."

Vicky wanted to go the Washeteria to get cigs. She said the lady there was a troll with a million warts on her face and incredibly sagged-out boobs and she would not give you change but if you had your own change you could buy cigs from her machine without her caring. Vicky was talking very fast and some of her words were warping but I followed her meaning. I walked next to her and the Turtle walked next to me and I noticed he was shorter than I thought.

I was walking in the wrong direction if I ever thought about going home again. I knew the mother was home and she was waiting. She was waiting right by the door. Her shift was night. She was in her white uniform and stockings and shoes. Her hair was in a French twist. She was smoking. She was muttering. Where in the hell was I?

I have lived a restricted life since the mother saw my picture in the newspaper and met the surrounding reporters and felt the flash of the photographers' bulbs. Our reunion created quite a stir. The reporters wanted to be there when she came to get me. And they were. And the city of Las Vegas was glad to host us. We were given free rooms at the Golden Nugget and all-you-can-eats everywhere we went. At night from the window the lights glittered and glittered and glittered. Julie watched television and sucked her thumb. I watched out the window. What the mother watched I do not know. She left just as it got dark and didn't come back until just before morning. We passed a week this way and then it was over.

I never told what happened at the Lucky Chief and she never once asked me about it. She told her made-up story on how the father kidnapped me, how he snatched me away from her. And how she was frightened he may return. He was the main suspect in the murders. When she was asked if he seemed capable of such a horrible crime, little glittering tears dropped from her big eyes and she nodded. "Yes. Oh yes. He's capable. I am so afraid."

But in the newspaper pictures she doesn't look afraid at all. She looks happy. And beautiful. Did I mention the mother is beautiful? She is what they call a knockout. A stunner. Drop-dead beautiful.

The pictures are on the wall in the living room area. Just her. No caption. No story. Just her very beautiful face smiling on famously. She was so happy when her picture was in the paper. But now no one was calling, and the mother was squinting at me.

I'm what a person might call a dog. Very much a dog. Guys have actually barked at me and offered me Milk-Bones. My face cells divided into the shape of the father, who even for a man was on the homely side. Jug ears and no chin and a wide nose and hooded eyes. Bad skin. Thin hair. All of it revisited in me by means of somatic mitosis, *Stedman's Medical Dictionary*, page 954.

I have looked like a boy since the beginning of forever, a pug-ugly one was how the father said it. Unusually ugly. A face strangely shaped. It hit him early in our journey together that I could pass for a mongolian idiot with no problem. That was his name for it. Mongolian Idiot. Also in *Stedman's*, page 957. The name of the mental condition suggested by my face is real. It's my epicanthic folds. I have what some people call slant-eye.

He told me how to do it. Be this type of idiot. And he was proud when I first pulled it off. In Moorehead, North Dakota, he took me into a Salvation Army. The clothes the mother threw into the car for me were mostly dresses and he didn't want me in dresses. The lady at the counter felt so sorry for us she didn't even charge us.

"Clyde," said the father as we rolled out of that town, "You are a treasure."

This story was tumbling out of my mouth as we walked to the Washeteria. It tumbled out in broken chunks and pieces. The Turtle was listening. Vicky wasn't. She was talking at the same time and her words sounded like scribbles.

I said, "Turtle, I want to go to New Orleans. I can't go home, I am too late. The mother is waiting and she will kill me, I mean actually kill, and she will blame it on aimless men, she will tell the newspapers it was the aimless men."

"The aimless men?" said the Turtle. Vicky was buzzing loud in my other ear. Her words were repeating but I could not make the meaning of them come together until she was shouting and what she was shouting was, "DO YOU HAVE A NICKEL? I NEED ONE MORE NICKEL. DO YOU HAVE A NICKEL? HEY, ROBERTA, HEY."

My saliva was squirting down the insides of my mouth and tasting sweet. The Turtle gave Vicky a nickel and said, "The aimless men?"

And I explained the aimless men, how they are always hiding and waiting for the girl who moves with no purpose. Killer men who would drag me deep into the woods and stab me forty-nine times and cut off my hands and cut off my head and throw my hands into the bushes at Golden Gardens and throw my head off Pier 99 and they would roll the rest of my body down any sewer hole. The mother knows about these men, these killer men because she gets the details from sinister magazines, all of them with TRUE! in the title.

"*True Crime*," said Vicky Talluso. "*True Confessions. True Detective*. Those stories are bogus. Very fake. Anything with 'True' in the title is a lie."

I told how the mother says if I do not come directly home after school the aimless men will capture me and strangle me and shoot me in the forehead and tie me to a tree and cover me with gasoline and light me on fire and then have an ax attack to my face.

"See?" said Vicky, and she was indignant. "That's not even logical! The guy would do the ax part *before* he lit you on fire. Bogus. Clearly. Obviously. Wait out here, because, Roberta, you are very sensitive to drugs and you are freaking out and you don't even know it and I hate that. Come on, Turtle." She held the screen door open for him, but the Turtle stayed with me. He stayed right beside me and listened to my spilling story while we leaned on the telephone pole. Through the window the lady watched us. And she was everything Vicky said, the million warts and the saggy boobs. The shadow of the window-painted word WASHETERIA was falling on her face, the "W" was. She was exactly like Vicky described except on her face it wasn't warts. It was moles. Beige moles, a million of them growing one upon the other.

The Turtle listened to my speeding words and then held up a long finger. "Wait. Tell me one thing," he said. "Are you wanted?"

Chapter 12

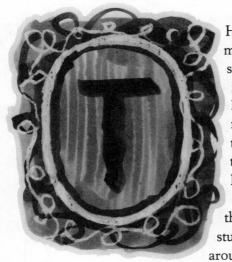

HE FATHER never treated me like a kid unless there was someone around. When the father looked at me, I do not know what he saw. Maybe a midget. Maybe an elf. I don't think it ever entered his mind that I was a kid. He knew it, but he never thought it, and it was what a person thought that mattered. That was the stuff you could twist a dream around.

During our journey he gave me cigarettes, glugs off of Old Skull Popper, bought me coffee and talked to me about the Navy, about things he saw when he was stationed here and there. He mentioned vultures and hornets and some things naked people did under red lightbulbs. He told me he had seen it all and he wasn't even near forty. "There isn't a thing left on this earth that can bug my eyes out anymore, and Clyde, for a man my age that's a tragedy."

We drove the back roads, sometimes it seemed like we were going in circles, but the father never used a map because the roads he needed to take, the gravel roads shooting pinging rocks and choking dust, were never on them. Where were we going? I wanted to know but I couldn't ask him. My mouth just wouldn't move around the words. I was in the front seat again. After the bright daylight came, what happened the night before faded out of me a little. We were miles away from it. I didn't think about it. Behind

63

us in a cloud of dust a truck was coming fast. The father looked in the rearview mirror and I saw him freak a little. I saw his hands get tight on the steering wheel. The truck swerved around us without slowing down. It pulled a bouncing empty cattle trailer with LITTLE BITTY DREAM written on it in custom letters.

"Shit on that," said the father, and shoved a cig between his lips.

"You know that Marie Cardall, Clyde? That got her arm shot off by them men?"

I told him I thought it was one man.

"See there? Just like the police. They think the same thing. That that one escapee did it. Just because someone thought they saw him in the vicinity with his Elkwood's on. Hell, any man can run in a prisoner's coveralls. That don't take no talent. That escapee was probably halfway to Texas before anybody touched Marie Cardall's doorknob. Do you know she still don't lock her doors? Lock your doors, Clyde. Always lock your doors."

The dash lighter popped out and he held it tilted while he sucked up some fire onto the end of his cig.

"So you figure out who did it yet? Because you know the parties involved. God, Clyde, I'm about laying it at your feet here."

"Doolie Bug."

"Yes, the squashed sack of shit had a role in it, that's sure. But the second man. You know what the second man is doing right now?"

I shook my head.

"Driving this car."

I sat very still while he unspooled the story. He wanted to tell it so bad. It was just wriggling inside of him.

"Marie Cardall was just begging for it. First time I talked to her about Old Dad delivering a suitcase to her, she told me she never got any kind of suitcase from anyone. I said, 'His tally book says you got one.' But she says no. She never saw or heard of any suitcase from Old Dad. I hate it when people lie to me. Don't you ever lie to me, Clyde."

He was pointing a square-topped finger at me. It was missing the tip, from the only slip of the knife in his whole career and it only happened because Mrs. Hannis came asking him to grind up some kidneys for her cat, and he hated cats, and he hated Mrs. Hannis, and most of all he hated running kidneys through his grinder because they make a hell of a mess. It was because of Mrs. Hannis he picked up the wrong knife. An unexpected extra inch of blade can make a big difference. A finger's worth. He was proud that he kept moving like nothing happened. Ground up the kidneys and smiled. Thought about putting a can of ant powder in with them but couldn't chance tarnishing the reputation his people had built over centuries. Whenever he saw Mrs. Hannis on the street the father always said, "That old goat owes me a finger."

The father told me how he rode up to Marie Cardall's place on a bicycle and Doolie Bug was waiting for him in the shadows.

"We get through the door, I throw on the lights and she pops up out of bed looking like Edward G. Robinson in a nightie, she grabs Ardus's rifle, points at me and says, 'I don't got your goddamn money.'

"Now, get logical. If she didn't have it, why'd she bring it up like that? It's ugliness, Clyde, to point a rifle at a person and tell them lies at the same time. If you got a rifle you don't need to lie. I said, 'Marie, you've known me since I was little. Don't you blow a hole through me.'

"She said, 'Get out of my house or by god, I will.'

"But she hesitated. Don't ever, ever hesitate, Clyde. Don't lie, and don't ever hesitate. Marie Cardall did both and look what it got her. And the damn suitcase was right under her bed the whole time. I about laughed out loud. I told Doolie Bug, get her car keys. I threw some of her clothes at him and told him to put them on, it came to me right then to do it. Doolie Bug's so little and ugly, he was shaking like a girl. In the dark he could have been her easy."

The father told Doolie what road to take, what culvert to

dump the car into, how far to walk and exactly where to wait with the suitcase. "I told him, the bend on R1114, right in the exact middle of the bend. I said, 'DB, I'm relying on you. If you screw this up? I'll hunt you down and make a vest out of your skin. But if you pull it off, there's two more suitcases just as full as this one. You help me and it's straight fifty-fifty between us. Clean. Are we partners? Prove it to me.'

"Stupid bastard. He knew I hated his ass. What in the hell would make him believe I would ever be partners with him? But he wasn't stopping to think, see. Clyde, you have to stop and think. Doolie Bug believed that just because I handed him the suitcase, I trusted him. And if I trusted him, he could trust me too. Well, shit on that. It wasn't like he just met me."

And this is when I first heard it explained, the concept of dazzle camouflage, invented by the Navy and modified by the father, who explained all the variations while booze fumes filled the car and the tires ground dry ruts on back roads getting smaller and smaller. Shooting a woman's arm off with a hunting rifle was a form of dazzle camouflage if what you were camouflaging were the slits in the jugular and the carotid. With the right knife you could do such great damage. The father said he knew they would concentrate on the arm. It would take them a while to notice the tiny punctures all up and down her.

"What about Doolie Bug?" I asked.

"What *about* Doolie Bug? He's a smashed sack of shit now, isn't he? With Marie Cardall's clothes on and his prints in her car. Case closed. And I did it for you."

I looked at him squinting into the slanting sunlight.

"I killed him for you, Clyde. No hesitation. When you look down at that Tiparillo scar on your hand, I want you to remember that your old man came through for you. I killed him five times over for you, Clyde. And I'd do it again in a minute. Because that's the way I feel about you. And I would like to think you feel the same way about me, that you'd do the same thing for me if it ever came down to it. That's what it means to be partners. Are we partners, Clyde? That is what I need to know before we go a mile farther." He pushed his foot hard down on the brakes and the tires spat gravel. When you have been rolling for so many hours, stopping the car is always shocking. I have always felt nervous in a suddenly stopped car.

"Look at me, Clyde. Can I count on you?"

I nodded yes.

"You promise to Jesus?"

"Yes."

"Because he'll know if you're lying and that is just as bad as stabbing him in his heart."

I said, "I'm not lying," but my voice wasn't so convincing.

The father said, "I'm going to have to work on you."

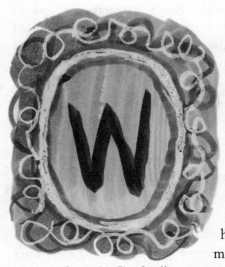

Chapter 13

HEN VICKY came out of the Washeteria, the Turtle had his arm around me. I was feeling a slight electrocution from it. Normally I do not like for people to touch me, I have a weird problem with it, a doggish problem. When people touch me I want to bite them. I have had this problem since I can remember, and I had been wondering if maybe I'd finally grown out of it, but my jaws rippled when he put his arm around me. It was all I could do to keep my teeth together tight.

Normally I do not like being touched, but I have wanted a boyfriend in my life. I used to think about the ways it would be possible. I read a story where a freaky-looking girl met a blind guy and told him all kinds of lies about what she looked like, like how her eyes were blue instead of brown, which I thought was idiotic of her since the guy wouldn't know color anyway. I thought of him, the guy in the story, and how I could take him from her with my truthfulness. I thought it could work out between us.

I have liked certain guys at school. Guys that never even look at me. One has a silver front tooth. One is tall and has a face like a deer. One spoke to me once. He said, "Don't you know it's rude to clip your nails in public?" And there is Billy the Kid, the DJ on KHR, who I sometimes sneak calls to in the middle of the night. He asks me how old I am. I tell him seventeen. He asks me if I ball. He tells me to call him when I'm eighteen. I request different songs. "House of the Rising Sun" is one of them. I never thought it was a real place but the Turtle said it was and he would take me there and I had to wonder if there would be a red lightbulb.

In my restricted life, the mother has tried to make me afraid of the aimless man, but truthfully I have never been afraid because I never thought I was the aimless man's type. I did not think he would keep his eyes on me long enough to hunt me. That I would be as noticeable to him as a gray clothespin on a sagging line. In my restricted life it was the mother who I was afraid of. The Turtle had his arm around me, and if she saw that, my life would be over.

Vicky said, "What, are you two together now?"

She was having a hard time unwrapping the cellophane from her cig pack. She was doing it so slowly, concentrating on the red pull-strip and the glinty shine. And then I noticed we all were concentrating on it, leaning our heads over it and watching it intently. It seemed like a miracle item to me. Vicky held the end of the pull-strip and let the top piece of cellophane hang and flutter and we stood there very amazed by it. And I was thinking how we are always surrounded by incredibly beautiful things but we don't know it, and that from then on I was going to know it, and then I looked up and the Washeteria woman's freaky head was right next to the window and she was darting little pig eyes at us and moving her lips at us and her beige moles were wiggling and I was screaming very loud and the Turtle and Vicky were pulling me down the street and Vicky told me to shut up because she hates people who scream. This is one thing I can say about Creeper. It makes everything you look at very loud.

We went to a scrudded-out little park that was mostly weed grass and one set of swings and some warped splintered seesaws and the Turtle said he wanted to seesaw with me so I sat down and then watched him walk over to the swings. Vicky laughed. She said, "Suc-kah! Rober-tah!"

The Turtle started swinging. One of his shoes came off. There was aluminum foil inside his shoe and it caught the light and sent a ray into my eye that knocked me over. Then Vicky was laughing very hard and contorting on the grass also. The Turtle said, "Hillbilly Woman. Tell her the story of the Poky Dot lounge, the Violent One missed that part. Tell her what was written on the door."

"No," said Vicky. "Tell the part about the money, Roberta. What about the money?"

The Turtle fished his shoe back on. His toes were also very long, unusually long, you could even say disturbingly. He said, "Fuck ALL people of Indiana!" He said, "Indiana people SUCKS SHIT!"

"I don't get it," said Vicky. "What? What's funny?" Because me and the Turtle were laughing very hard. Were we together? It was possible.

The Poky Dot Lounge was what appeared on the horizon an hour or so after the father hung another cig from his lips and said, "Last one." He balled the cig pack and flung it out the window. In my side mirror I watched it bounce away behind us. Bounce and roll and vanish. We crossed a wide river and then everything changed. There were no more fields, no houses, no trees, not even telephone poles. Even the colors were gone, all of them except brown and gray and the blue of the late-afternoon sky. The world got emptier and emptier until it looked like a brown ocean of dead velvet, just emptiness covered with short dry grasses and low scrub.

We were on a one-lane road and behind us the stirred-up dust hung in the air. Some creatures bolted in the distance, looking like deer, but not deer. The father said, "Give you fifty bucks if you can tell me what them are."

My head was hurting and I was hungry. I ate what the father ate. Coffee and cigs and aspirin and Old Skull Popper and an ancient vending machine candy bar and the rancid taste was still in my mouth. I was hungry but I felt like if I ate I would heave instantly. My eyes were burning and I had a sensation in my throat like I'd swallowed gulps of sand.

71

"Give up?" asked the father. "You owe me fifty bucks. Them are pronghorns. Some people are wild about them, but I never could stand the flavor. You know what they mean by gamey? I've dressed a few. They say the sausage ain't bad. Never tried it."

We rolled on through the plucked world. He huffed his last cig down to the filter and his lips made a little popping sound when he threw it out the window.

He yawned and then I yawned, and he said, "It's catching."

He said, "Talk to me, Clyde, ask me some questions. Ask me anything. I'll always give you a straight answer."

I said, "Where are we going?"

He said, "Oh, that's a surprise."

He said, "Clyde, we are knife people and have always been knife people and people who use guns are pismires. But I want you to know there is a rifle in the car with us. We're knife people but there's always exceptions. There could come a situation where we are glad we have it, understand me?"

I nodded even though I didn't and he smiled and showed his curved yellow-gray teeth. Did I mention I loved the father? At the beginning of the journey I loved him a lot. They say love for a father is natural and nothing can change it. I don't know about that.

"Shit," he said. "Out of gas and out of smokes. Better start saying your prayers, Clyde."

The time ticktocked undisturbed for a few miles and then across the horizon I saw the silhouette of telephone poles and a square shack up on cinder-block legs. The father said, "We're saved."

It was painted a faded-out pink. Shaky circles were drawn on in tan and brown. On the door it said,

POKY DOT LOUNGE
NO MINOR
NO LOITER
NO INDIAN

Someone had added an "A" to the end of INDIAN and then

wrote "Fuck ALL people of INDIANA. INDIANA people sucks SHIT!!!"

The Turtle was laughing again. He was curling and uncurling himself like a shrimp and laughing hard.

"That's IT?" said Vicky. "I'm starting to hate you guys."

"Tell it again," said the Turtle.

"No," said Vicky. "The money. Tell me it's real."

"It's real," I said. "And I want you all to keep acting very normal. Turtle, you need to pick up your stash because it fell out of your pocket and then we should get up very normally and walk very normally away from here because there is a cop watching us."

The Turtle took off running. He tore across the street and cut down an alley. He was amazingly fast considering his shoes. The cop was in an unmarked car and he wasn't wearing a uniform but I knew he was a cop, I'm a trained cop spotter, I know their ways. He pulled out rolling slow, keeping his eyes on the Turtle and turning down the same alley.

"Where?" said Vicky. "Where's a cop?" She was looking in every direction.

I said, "He just left. He just went down the alley after the Turtle. The car that just left. That was a cop."

"What car?" said Vicky. "I can't believe how you lie." She picked up the Turtle's stash box and wiggled it. "We got it." She dropped it into her purse and then pulled out a mirror to check her face.

"Roberta, I have a question I really want to ask you but it's personal to me, OK? But you have to tell me the truth, because I really want a truthful answer. Swear to god, OK? Swear to Jesus?"

"OK," I said.

She pointed to her missing eyebrow. She said, "Roberta, is this noticeable?"

The first lie I ever told her was right then.

Chapter 14

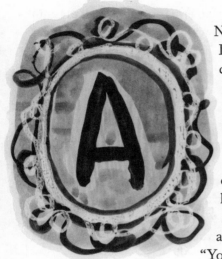

ND BEHIND the Poky Dot Lounge a train came roaring, coal cars filled and packed down into rooftop shapes that can survive the wind. A Northern Pacific, at least a mile long. And I was standing by the car watching it and the father was around the other side taking a pee and then he came up very quiet behind me and he put his arms around me and squeezed me to him and said, "You like trains, little girl?"

And then he screamed, "SON OF A BITCH!" and tried to grab me but I was two steps out of his reach. He clutched at his forearm and shook it, looking at it and then coming at me so fast I couldn't think to run. He delivered such a slam I saw blue light streaking. I was on the ground and he kicked me.

You remember I mentioned my biting problem.

"GODDAMNED CLEAR TO THE BONE!" He kicked me again. The blood from his arm splattered across the dirt and I was thinking it was adding its molecules, the father's blood was adding its molecules to the composition of the dirt, I was concentrating on the molecules because I have learned that concentrating on the smallest things can proved a distraction, an escape hole to disappear down. I was concentrating on the molecules and particles and atoms while he kicked me, the spaces between the molecules can be demonstrated by taking a gallon of water and a gallon of rubbing alcohol and pouring them into a two-gallon container and you will see that it will not make two gallons, it will not reach the two-gallon line because—"YOU BIT ME! YOU FUCKING BIT ME!"

Human bites are ferocious with bacteria. They can give you kinds of infections that are hideous, very dangerous, every meat man knows about the danger of bacteria introduced deeply into open wounds and there was only one bottle of Old Skull Popper left and the father was very angry about having to waste the precious drops on sanitizing. I heard him making ow, ow noises as he poured it on.

"What the hell got into you, Clyde?" His voice was calmer. I rolled myself up and felt the stabbing pains in my side. "I could have killed you right then. Don't put a man in that state, ever. He can't be held responsible."

He dripped the clear harsh liquid on the shell-shaped wound. "If it was just one inch over that way I'd be ripping your guts out for a tourniquet. What in the hell got into you?"

I was not able to reveal the true answer. The train wound away into the distance.

"Was it that little squeeze I gave you? You think I want something from you? What the hell do you have that could interest me? You ain't even female to me."

But he had said "little girl." The train was a pinpoint on the horizon that vanished away. I thought that's what he said but I didn't feel sure. Ears played tricks. Eyes played tricks. Fingers and hands played all kinds of tricks.

It was true I like trains. I have had a certain problem around trains since I was very little. I have been very attracted to them stopped or moving but especially moving. I have never been able to get close enough to them and while trying I have done things that would make an average person scream. I have laid on my stomach flat and close to the tracks to let the roaring pass over and shake my molecules hard. The exhilaration. The exhilaration. Everything is always easier after the exhilaration.

In my restricted life there has not been much opportunity for the exhilaration. The mother has given me a type of exhilaration by throwing sharp things at me, screaming about the various ways she is going to kill me, but it's not the same thing at all. I never feel better afterwards. There is never any relief that comes from it except maybe to her.

I can hear the trains from my bedroom window at night, but I have never walked to find them. In my restricted life I have not been allowed to actually go anywhere except school.

I have had nightmares about the coal-car train. The truth of what happened roars back to mind, the father's flesh gives way between my teeth, his fist knocks me down, his blood splatters across the dirt. Back-splatter. It's one thing the evidence people look for at the crime scene.

The father broke the door to the Poky Dot Lounge. He needed a cigarette bad. He needed Old Skull Popper, and a tank of gas, but most of all cigarettes, and there could be other things he needed depending on what he found inside.

I was stationed at the door to watch for trouble. The sun went down and the world stood empty. No dust stirred anywhere.

The father said, "Clyde, give me a hand. You see a goddamned light switch anywhere?"

There was a pull string that brought a bare bulb to life. The place smelled hard of pee and the walls were filthy. Someone had gone insane with a spray can, blasting out dripping dots of paint on the rough walls and sagging ceiling. There was a short bar, a couple of stools with cracked vinyl tops, a pool table with a grease spot in the middle the size of a man, and a nasty-looking blanket. And there was a record player. A kid's record player, the kind that plays 45s. There was one record. Hugo Winterhalter and his orchestra doing "Canadian Sunset." I switched the record player on and it spun. When I put the needle down the sound of sudden music made the father jump. He said, "Jesus! Give a man some warning!"

It was strange to stand in such a decrepit place listening to the sounds of pianos and violins. The father was getting frustrated.

"This place is such a shit hole. Goddamn train bums. I don't know why I wasted my time beating that front door open because the back door ain't even attached. Always walk around a place before you bust into it, Clyde. Remember that."

The father gave up hope of finding anything he could use. He said bums were better scroungers than the civilized man. He said he was surprised the record was still there. He handed it to me. "Want it? Keep it. It's yours. Shows I don't got no hard feelings against you, but you try another trick like that and I'll flay you in six pieces and drag you behind the car."

He took a last look around the room. "Firetrap. Nobody would miss this place." The father made a high pile of burnables and threw on a match.

Don't ever disappoint the father when he needs something. Ever. You see what happened to the Poky Dot Lounge.

chapter 15

O," SAID Vicky Talluso. "You ready to meet him?" We were cutting through different back ways, different alleyways, heading to her house. I said, "Who?"

"*Him.* The future love of your life."

"Oh." I shrugged. I was feeling tired. Still floaty from the Creeper but it was a downward float. What I really wanted to do was sit down somewhere and just stare. I didn't care at what. My legs were feeling rubbery and Vicky Talluso was starting to get on my nerves. I hadn't known her very long but I already noticed she never asked a question without expecting a specific answer. She never asked, for example, a free-form question, like what was your opinion on something, or for more details about something you mentioned about yourself, like how you killed someone. And then I realized I hadn't asked her any questions either. I tried to think of one but nothing came.

We turned onto another alley. I had no idea where I was, the alley was dirt and the tire ruts were deep. A smell of garbage circled us. Vicky said, "You better not screw this up, Roberta."

"Screw up what?"

And the story came out that the guy who was so perfect for me was the brother of Dane, the guy she was wanting for her boyfriend. Dane said for her to bring someone for his brother.

"What's his name?" I asked. Vicky didn't know. It turns out she had never actually seen him. But she figured he would be amazing because Dane was so amazing. I got a sick feeling in my stomach at the thought of an amazing guy meeting me.

"I don't know, Vicky."

"You don't know what?" She shoved my shoulder. "You don't know now that I've gotten you high and I'm taking you to my house to get you some decent clothes so you don't look like such a skag and I'm taking you to meet an amazing guy who lives on the View in an amazing house with a heated swimming pool, and no parents home for two weeks, you don't know about THAT?"

She was shouting at me and it made a huge dog start barking behind a tall wooden fence and the dog started leaping and saliva wads were flying off its lips and then Vicky ran over to the fence and started kicking it with her yellow boots and the dog went insane and a window flew open on the second story of the ratty house behind the fence and a bald man stuck his head out and said, "Get the HELL away from my dog!"

"GO FUCK YOURSELF!" Vicky shouted so hard the veins on her neck were out.

"WHAT DID YOU JUST SAY?" The man's face started contorting. Vicky shouted it again and he left the window.

I said, "We should go, Vicky."

She screamed, "I'LL *KILL* YOUR FUCKING DOG IF I WANT TO!"

I will admit that it was me that tripped her. The father taught me how to do it. A simple flip with your foot, you catch them right under the heel when they are walking. The father said, "If you do it right, they don't even feel it. They're on their butts before they know what happened. All you have to do is look concerned and help them up and you have made a friend."

I reached my hand to Vicky and she slapped it away. She took her purse and threw it into the sticker bushes. The gate flew open and the dog lunged. Vicky jumped and rolled and was on her feet running. You never run from a dog. Ever. What you do with a dog is step toward them and then keep your hands by your sides and stay very still. You can glance at their eyes but don't hold a stare. They may jump up and tear your face off anyway but at least you will have a chance. If you run you are dead. Especially with a big dog like Brother. And if you run you won't see that Brother is on a choke chain held by the bald man.

Brother was a beautiful dog. Even while he was making vicious leaps at me I noticed it. Have you ever seen a chocolate Doberman with his real tail and ears? Beautiful is the word and I guess I kept saying it because the bald man finally stopped shouting and Brother stopped barking. That was what I wanted to stare at. A dog like Brother with golden eyes and the dog smell that has always calmed me.

I said, "Sir? I'm really sorry about my friend acting like that. Her father just died, sir." I don't know why I said the thing about Vicky's dad. It just followed the first sentence right out of my mouth.

The man turned very understanding. Brother let me pet and fuss over him. The man got a rake and held the sticker bushes away so I could get Vicky's purse, and then told me to keep an eye on my friend. If she kept acting like that she could end up in the hospital.

On his arm I saw a faded USN tattoo.

I said, "You Navy?"

He smiled at me big.

But where was Vicky? Where was Vicky Talluso? I had her purse, I found her hat, her red velvet tam laying in the next alley but where was she? The light was fading fast and I realized I had nowhere to go.

The father said when you are lost you can follow the telephone wires. If you are stuck in the middle of nowhere having fits because you have no cigs and no booze and your car ran out of gas on you so you lit it on fire and it's flaming behind you in the dark and you have that lonely craving for the opportunities other people can provide you with, by all means, follow the wires.

"This damn thing is heavy as shit," said the father. He had the suitcase in one hand and his USN duffel over his shoulder. My bag was also USN, less wide but longer with a drawstring top. In it were a few of my clothes and the rifle, broken down and carefully wrapped along with some boxes of shells. "Why do you keep turning back to look at the damn car, Clyde?"

I told him I was waiting for it to blow up. In the movies when cars started on fire they always blew up.

"Not when they don't got no gas in them they don't," said the father. "That's just common wisdom." And he was about to lay more common wisdom on me when the explosion happened.

"What the hell," said the father. "I'm still right."

He said he burned the car because they might be looking for us. The authorities might. And we needed to start covering our tracks. And then he said where I bit him was throbbing like a son-of-a-bitch and he reminded me that he almost twisted my neck, he could have snapped it easy, he knew how to do it. He was a hand-to-hand man. The Navy was sad to lose him. He said he could snap my neck and who would ever know? There wasn't anybody looking for me. He asked me if I could think of a single person who would report me missing.

I couldn't.

We slept that night in the weeds alongside the road. We were both so tired it didn't matter. When I heard the father's sleep breathing, I pulled my duffel farther away.

In the morning we were walking again. The father was wearing fresh slacks and a fresh short-sleeve shirt. I could see his sleeveless undershirt through it. He told me to change my clothes too, and at first I wouldn't because there was no place to change. Not a thing to stand behind.

The father said, "What are you worried about? Hell, I've only seen you bare-assed all your life. I won't look. There ain't nothing to look at."

But of course he did. He waited a few moments before he turned around and watched everything.

We were saved by a man in a truck who jerked his dirty thumb back toward the direction we'd been walking and said, "Your car blowed up," and then shot a jet of tobacco spit through the air. "Hop in." The father got in first.

"Bub-bub-brother?" The father had his shoulders slumped and he was stuttering. Dazzle camouflage. "H-have you g-got a ci-ci-cigarette on you?"

"Naw," said the man. "Take dip?"

"If yyy-you can sp-sp-are it."

The man passed the Copenhagen to the father who took out a huge wad, stuck it in his lower lip and held the can out to me.

The man's name was Syd. He was very tan and his clothes were very faded but he looked like a very together sort of person. His hair was oiled and combed in the Robert Mitchum style. I was admiring the comb-tooth pattern when the father nudged me with the can. I took a pinch.

Syd said, "Your boy chew? He don't even look eight years old." Syd's eyes looked friendly. Bloodshot but sincere. He didn't look old but his face had a million creases. Later the father said you could have poured a gallon of water into that face and not a drop would spill out. The sun did it. It dried the strongest men out like jerky.

"Hhh-he don't ttt-talk. Eh-eh-eh-pilepsy."

Syd said, "Epilepsy? I got a sister has epilepsy and she talks fine."

The father started tapping his hand on the dash. Watch the hands. He taught me that. Watch the hands. They will tell you everything you need to know.

"Bbb-brain damage fff-from fff-falling."

In the wing mirror I caught a glimpse of my face. It was swollen bad and the color around my left eye was deep and purple-red.

"That what happened to you, son?" Syd leaned forward to adjust his straw seat cushion and took a longer look at me. The father caught it. After that, whenever Syd leaned, the father blocked his view.

"Muh-muh-muh-mongoloid."

"No shit," said Syd. "Epileptic mongoloid with brain damage to boot. Somebody dealt you a real bad hand, son. I'd fold if I were you." Syd leaned forward fast and winked at me and I got a sudden bolt of fear in my stomach. I'd never met someone who could see through the father before. I didn't know it was possible. And I had no idea how the father would handle it if Syd pushed him. But Syd didn't. He reached under the seat and pulled up an old pop bottle for the father to spit in and that was about all that happened until Syd dropped us at the Trailways.

The father told Syd to come see us anytime. He peeled off the Copenhagen label, wrote a fake name and address on the back of it and said, "My www-wife's real p-p-pretty and she'd g-get a kuh-kick out of you." He told Syd he could look forward to a free haircut because the father had his own barbershop.

Syd gave me a wave from his window. He said, "Keep your old man out of trouble." A piece of paper fluttered into the air behind him as he drove off.

"Look there," said the father. "Stupid shit already lost my address."

chapter 16

N THE bus station the father handed me five dollars and pointed me to the lunch counter. "Get yourself something to eat." He went into the men's room and when he came out his hair was combed and aftershave clouds were drifting off of him. He shoved our bags into a metal locker and put the key in his pocket. At the ticket counter he asked for two tickets to Dentsville. The ticket lady was looking at him in an interested sort of way and he was looking back at her like a mirror. "Two?" she said.

"Yeah. One adult and one pain-in-the-ass nephew."

She looked over at me and laughed. I lifted my upper lip a little and showed my teeth. Sometimes I did this. I picked it up from dogs.

There were some hours to kill before our bus left. I watched the ticket lady's eyes follow the father as he walked out the glass door to find the liquor store she gave him directions to. She liked that he had turned to look at her. She put a sign out that said PURCHASE TICKETS AT NEWSSTAND AND SUNDRIES, grabbed her purse and told the waitress she was taking lunch.

The waitress shook her head and wiped the counter in front of me. She was old but not ancient and she had a hair net on. I saw her flick her eyes at the round-headed man sitting behind the sundries counter and I saw him flick his back. He was smoking a cigarette that had gotten very wet around the lips. He picked up a

bent fly swatter and went back to staring out the window.

I asked for pancakes but it was too late for pancakes. The waitress seemed very insulted that I would even mention the word "pancakes." She pointed to a big clock with a yellowed face and a wig of greasy dust. She pointed to the menu. She said, "Read? Tell time?"

I ordered french fries and a large milk. It was a down time between buses. There weren't any other customers. The station was small but with very high ceilings that made sounds echo. The hanging lights had the longest pull strings I'd ever seen and there were flies hanging on them, swaying in the weak little breeze made by a dying fan.

The milk was ice-cold and I drank it so fast I got a stabbing headache. I was pushing on my forehead hard with both hands and the waitress's face got a little bit softer. "Thirsty, huh?" I nodded. "Where you headed?" I shrugged.

"Your uncle said Dentsville. Did I hear him say he was your uncle? You have people out that way?"

I said, "Can I have another milk?"

She put it in front of me and I went for it. I couldn't put it down. She started laughing when I asked for a third one. She said, "Good lord. I hope you don't drink your liquor like that!"

I said, "No."

The man at the sundries counter laughed and then started coughing.

The waitress put the third glass down. She said, "Dentsville. Dentsville. Your uncle military?"

"Navy," I said.

"Fort Madley then, maybe." She called over to the fly-swatter man. "Fort Madley, isn't it? Outside of Dentsville?"

He said, "I believe so."

The waitress said, "Is it Navy, Fort Madley?"

He said, "Army, I think."

She looked at me. "You said your uncle's Navy?"

I nodded. "Down to the last inch of his pecker."

She covered her mouth and said "Lord!" with the word drawn out. The fly-swatter man was laughing. He said, "Sounds like a Navy man to me."

"Well," said the waitress. "My."

In a lower voice she said, "What happened to your face?" I looked down at my hands. She said, "Where's your folks at? Where's your mother?"

I looked up at her, just barely. I said, "Passed away."

She leaned into the little window to the kitchen and convinced the purple-nosed cook that it wasn't too late for pancakes.

I had noticed in many stories that it was usually an advantage to have a dead mother. Opportunities came your way that wouldn't have otherwise. I was starting to think of what it would be like to stick around the bus station. I liked what I saw of the little town. The sun was bright on everything and there was a little park across from the Trailways station where a couple of old guys stared at things from benches. I started thinking about Syd. What life would be like if I were his kid. What it would be like to sit up on the bus station's silver and red spinning counter chairs and eat a plate of pancakes he bought me because I did so good on my report card. Eat a banana split. Listen to him brag on me to the waitress.

The fly-swatter man let out a snort and popped a fly in mid-flight. It went sailing through the air and skidded on the floor. He said, "You see the size of that bastard!"

"Language," said the waitress. "Children here."

"Oh the hell," said the man.

The fly lay there for a while, and when no one was watching, it left. Where it went to I do not know. It outsmarted all of us.

The waitress was setting paper cones for water into a row of metal holders. She was moving fast. There was a bus due. She tore off my check and told me I had to leave the counter and to pay the fly-swatter man. She didn't charge me for the pancakes or the extra milks. I had a lot of money left over. I stood looking over the candy and picked out some sour-grape gum, some fireballs, a bag of barbecue potato chips. The fly-swatter man said, "Quite a shiner. How'd you manage that?" And then the people started pouring in. "Fifteen minutes!" shouted the driver. "Fifteen and fifteen only!" He had his own coffee cup and he pushed past the people and slid it onto the counter.

I watched the people shovel food down and listened to their voices bouncing off the ceiling. And then the bus driver shouted the time and they were gone.

The waitress cleared the counter. She looked mad again. She kept looking over at the empty ticket window and pushing her lips together. She flipped a rag over her shoulder and clattered a stack of dirty plates and kicked the swinging door open with her shoe, calling to the fly-swatter man, "Must be nice not to give a damn about anybody but yourself." The door swung shut behind her. The fly-swatter man grunted.

I went back to looking at the things he had for sale. There was a row of push-button pens hanging on a display string. I kept staring at them.

The fly-swatter man peeled some tobacco crumbs off his lip. He was a sad-looking man. His lower eyelids hung so you could see the insides. There are certain dogs this happens to. They are not born that way but somehow it happens. I noticed too that he had large earlobes with creases in them and strange dentures that looked like wax.

I said, "Can I buy a pen, please?"

He said, "What color?"

He took down the blue pen I asked for. "Also," I said, "do you got paper?"

"Stationery?"

"Is that your paper?"

He nodded and looked on a shelf behind him. "All I have left is airmail. You want airmail?"

He pushed a flat pale blue box across the glass counter. It was dusty and it had a red loop of ribbon taped around it. On the front of the box was an indented silver drawing of a plane and the trail it left spelled out "Airmail" in the most beautiful longhand.

"Oh," I said. "It's so nice."

He said, "Stamps?"

I nodded.

"How many?"

I said, "I just turned eleven. It was just my birthday."

"How many stamps?"

"Eleven," I said. "Because I just turned eleven." I don't know why this information made him so gruff. I was thinking maybe he would give me the comment of "Happy Birthday" or, "Congratulations," or whatever it is people say to kids who just turned eleven.

He laid down my stamps and pushed my change at me and picked up his wet cig and his fly swatter and started staring out the window again.

I said, "Know that fly you hit before?"

He made a short little noise.

I said, "Well, it got away."

His sad eyes looked me over.

When the father came back through the glass door our bus was just ready to start boarding. He was walking fast and his hair was wet-combed back and he had his usual tall liquor store sacks and he smelled very strong of cigarettes and perfume and a kind of booze I didn't know. "C'mon, Clyde." He got our bags and hurried me along, jerking his head toward the bus door and saying, "Go, Clyde."

The ticket lady came in a few minutes later. She didn't look at anyone but the father, who never looked back at her once.

The father hunched and stammered and asked the people in line if it would be all right with everyone if I got on first, being as I was an epileptic.

There was a whoosh of the silver door and the high steps were revealed. It was my first time on a bus and it seemed incredibly royal. I paused at the top of the steps and felt the father's instant shove. "All the way to the back. Move it. Go."

He let me have the window seat and he slouched low, hit the recliner button, and shut his eyes. I watched the ticket lady searching the passenger windows as the bus pulled out of the station.

Dentsville. On the front of the bus it said DENTSVILLE.

The father poked his head up when we were out of the bus station. I said, "Are we going to Fort Madley?"

He said, "What the hell's Fort Madley?"

I took out my stationery box and slipped the ribbon off. Inside was pale blue paper, thin enough to see through. The envelopes had the same airplane on them with the same perfect writing behind it. Airmail.

When the father spoke, I jumped.

He said, "What's that there?"

"Airmail."

"Airmail? You spent the money I gave you on that? Damn it, Clyde, who in the hell are you planning on writing? Santa Claus?"

I put it away and waited for him to fall asleep.

It was coming toward evening and we were in the open land again and it was good to see it. The colors had done their last flares and were draining away. I was having a hard time looking out the window because the wires and poles were making me dizzy. The constant up and down. When I tried to ignore them they seemed to get even more obvious. Even when I stared straight ahead they were getting into the corner of my eye.

Who was I planning on writing? Who was I planning on writing? The father's question was bothering me. I looked over at him. He was snoring so slack-jawed and his breath was squidding out horror fumes in my direction. I saw his Navy bridgework that always gave him trouble. His head was tilted away from me. And I will admit I looked at his neck to find it. The light pulsing of the carotid. The involuntary pulsing. As involuntary as my eyes studying it.

There are two kinds of dying for every single person. There is the moment when your personality dies, when the you of you drains away into the air, and then there is the part where your body dies, organ by organ. And then three days later there are the flies.

Dear Jesus,

Hi, how are you? Please excuse my bumpy handwriting but right now I am on a bus.

I kept trying to find a way to turn myself so that I couldn't see the telephone poles or be in the path of the father's breath. I was feeling dizzy and then very sick and the father was shouting, "WHAT THE—GO TO THE HEAD, DO IT IN THE HEAD! DON'T PUKE ON ME, CLYDE! CLYDE!"

I never did finish my letter to Jesus. I tried for a while but I couldn't think of anything else to say besides, *Have a Good Summer and Stay Crazy.*

chapter 17

WANDERED AROUND after the streetlights came on, wearing Vicky Talluso's hat and carrying her purse and sending her ESP vibrations even though I was doubtful either of us had ESP. Vicky said she did, but I think she just needed a girl to bring for the brother of Dane, and maybe I looked hard up enough to believe it was a spirit who sent her to me. Was I that hard up? It was possible.

I was walking down hills I'd never walked before and around me the windows of the people's houses were all jumping with the berserk light of the TV. I doubted that I had ESP because if I had ESP I do not think my life would have turned out the way it did. If I could have seen the unexpected before it got to me first.

I was thinking of the Turtle. His arm around me. What did it mean? Was it meaningful? Vicky never said his name after she got his stash. What mattered was the stash and not the Turtle. I felt in Vicky's purse. The stash was there. It was there. I could call the cops and say "I have drugs," and get arrested if I wanted to.

I was wondering was it meaningful, the Turtle's arm around me, was it? And what was the deal on him? He was such a weird combination of skorkish clothes and vocabulary I didn't know and then his teeth, which were small but very straight and white and had the little ridge across them that braces leave. He wasn't from my side of Dunbar Avenue, that was for sure. Did it mean anything, his arm around me? He was interested in my story. He asked me questions. That one question. "Are you wanted?"

I was thinking it would be not so bad to run into him and I did some ESP vibrations to him too but it felt fake. I came to Twenty-third Avenue. I knew where I was again. Now what. Now what.

In Ye Olde Curiosity Shoppe down at the piers along with the bone of the whale penis and the dried-out beef jerky man called Sylvester there were the shrunken heads. It was from the eyebrows and eyelashes you knew they were real. And little downy hairs on the faces. Their mouths and eyelids and nose holes were sewn shut. Someone stitched them like the mother said she was going to stitch me. She was going to sew me shut. It was during one of her furious screaming nights when anything goes. When Julie and I are just supposed to sit on the floor and take it. She wanted us on the floor. I don't know why. Julie was the one who got her mad. She told the mother we were watching TV and the movie was the *Curse of the Mummy's Tomb* and when the mummy walked out I said, "Look, Julie, it's your dad."

You should never bring up Julie's dad to the mother for any reason. She gets the most furious when she remembers all of the ways she's been ripped off in life. The mother told me she was going to sew me shut for saying that and she got the needle, the right needle that came from the hospital, stainless steel and curved into a half circle with a blade point. It was already threaded. She crouched down and held it up to my face. She said, "This is what I'm going to use."

I suddenly felt so tired of trying to keep her off of me. I was thinking, I don't care anymore. Get it over. Get it over with. I crossed Twenty-third and headed home.

East Crawford doesn't have streetlights. There's some light that leaks onto the mud road from the lumberyard, and there are people's porch lights but most are burned out. Ours is. The square front room window had the blue TV light behind the curtains and from a side gap, a shard of light from the mother's lamp fell jagged on the wooden steps. She was home. The lamp was never on except when she was home. She was home.

My hand was shaking when I put my key in the lock. I kept thinking, Get it over with, who cares, get it over, but the scream-whistle was starting in my ears anyway. I put my key in the lock and twisted it. I knew the mother heard it. I knew right then she was looking up, her posture getting instantly straight, she was waiting for my head to enter her world. But the door would not open.

I pushed and twisted the lock and tried the doorknob and twisted the key again and freaked. She did something to the door. She did something to make sure there was no way I could just walk in. I was going to have to knock. She wanted to make sure she was ready for me. It took a long time to get my hand up. Knock-Knock.

Her lamp switched off. There was a tiny sway to the curtains. And then the door flew open and two claws went into my face.

It was just Julie. The mother wasn't even home. She wasn't home when Julie came home from school. "WHERE WERE YOU?" Julie was screaming, we were on the floor tearing at each other. She's smaller than me but not by much and she is strong and fearless when she's mad. She was gouging my skin and trying to bite me. She spit and I spit back and I shoved her against the furnace, which made a loud blamming that traveled the duct-work.

She lay on her side making noises like she couldn't breathe and I was thinking she was faking, what a faker, and then I saw her eyes go wide and I turned to see what she was looking at. The mother was standing in the doorway.

A man stepped into the room behind her. A skinny man with a black suit on. He had a long yellowish face with a lot of folds, old dry hanging folds and a long nose with emerging puffs of nostril hair and spotted sagging lips looking like two bad internal organs with curved rodent teeth bucking out between them. His hair was very blond and obviously a wig. And his eyes were blue. That terrifying pale blue you see on dolls that have eyes that open and shut. His looked like they would shut forever once you knocked him over. His smell was very clean, slight antiseptic mixed with lavender. A rich person's smell. He was perfect. He was the kind of man the mother had been dreaming of.

"This is Dr. Canning," said the mother. She was smiling. Her hair was fixed. Her hand gestures were very graceful. She had a new gold bracelet on. She didn't tell him our names. What she did was flick her fingernails at us and say, "Get upstairs."

Julie instantly started putting on her pajamas. "You're dead," she whispered. "You are killed." It wasn't any use to ask Julie not to tell the mother. Begging didn't work with Julie. Neither did beating her up. She might bust me to the mother and she might not. There was no way to tell.

Her elbow got bent-jammed in her nightgown sleeve hole and she hopped in a circle trying to get it loose. She said, "What's wrong with your eyes?" She said, "Help me." And then the nightgown ripped and she started crying. She just fell onto the floor and cried.

The mother's feet came up the stairs. I said, "Julie, get up, get up. She's coming." But the mother was going to her own room. We heard the padlocks on her door unlocking, we heard some bumping on the other side of the closet. Her suitcase. She was getting her suitcase down. Drawers opened and closed, and then the door padlocks were snapped shut.

Then it was quiet. Perfectly quiet. She was standing outside our door. The mother did this. She made you wait. She made all the freaking gather hard within you and then she made her move. Our door opened about a foot and the mother's head came in and the mouth of it opened and some words were said and then the head retracted and the door shut. For a million dollars I could not tell you what she said because of the scream-whistle flooding my head. I saw her but all I heard were the scream-whistles blowing my mind out.

The mother and the suitcase went downstairs. The voice of the pancreas-lipped doctor came up the stairs. Then came the sound of the mother's fizz-laughing, sounding very fake, and her voice calling to us in a merry way, saying Aunt Caroline would be over any minute and for us to be good and mind Aunt Caroline, and the mother would see us next week. The front door closed and then there was just the TV sounds of a very excited person singing about their toothpaste.

"Who's Aunt Caroline?" said Julie.

We both minorly started to laugh. It was a weird giddiness that sometimes hit us both at the same time when the mother left the house.

"What's wrong with your eyes, Roberta?"

I got up to look out of the bedroom window, making sure it was real, that she was really gone. I saw the red taillights moving away, leaving cherry red trails suspended in the dark.

In the corroded dresser mirror I saw my pupils were blown. No iris at all. I said, "Let's go downstairs."

chapter 18

E CAME rolling into Dentsville in the middle of the afternoon. I was starving. The father was afraid I'd get sick again so he wouldn't let me eat anything. All I got to drink were the half-melted ice cubes from the bottom of his spiked pop. It had been a long ride. I slept through a lot of it but the rest of the time I couldn't really tell you what I did. Stared out the window, mostly. The father didn't want me to talk to anyone and he said he wasn't going to talk to anyone either. "L.L.S.S., Clyde. Loose Lips Sink Ships." Would that have been so bad?

I kept my part of the deal. I didn't say a word. The father had some long pulls off of a new bottle of Old Skull Popper and then got a fat lady to stand in the aisle and try to dance with him. The back of the bus was the party section. A lot of smoking and booze fumes. The father was the star like he was always the star in a group of drinking people. The star, the mayor, the president. Even I could not help admiring him in my own mongolian idiot way.

People in the front of the bus turned irritated heads toward us but the driver was on our side. He had a face like a leather-covered skull and while he and the father were sneaking fortifying glugs during rest stops the driver said this run was his last. After that, he just did not give a damn. Dentsville was on one end of the map and his wife was on the other. And he wanted to keep it that way. He told the father he was chucking it all. Retirement, pension, free bus rides for life, all of it down the hole.

"We must be married to the same woman," said the father.

"Cheers," said the driver. "Hell."

In the Dentsville bus station it smelled nose-burningly strong of disinfectant and people, too many people. The waiting chairs were the dip-plastic kind, orange and blue alternating and there was someone in every seat except one that had creeping gunk on it. The lights were fluorescent and flickering and made the people look greenish. The cafe was separate, in a different room altogether, and through the glass I could see that it was packed too.

"OK, Clyde, listen up here." The father stowed our bags. He looked bad and so did I. The swelling on my face was down but the bruises were turning greenish-black. It was dramatic. The father said, "Don't clean up. The worse you look the better for where we're going."

I said, "Where?"

He said, "I ever mention your uncle Lemuel to you?"

I shook my head.

He said, "That's because he's a worthless piece of shit. And he's not your uncle either."

We were standing on the sidewalk. The father was tucking a fresh pack of cigs into his pocket and looking up and down the street, trying to get a fix on where he was. The sky was gray and the air was cool and had an edge to it that I couldn't identify. It wasn't unpleasant but it was distinctive and it got me curious.

Across the street was a bar called The Golden Egg. The father's eyes lit up when he saw it. "This ain't like back home, Clyde. I can't bring you with me. I need a couple of hours." He slipped his watch off. Its face was scuffed and it had a pinching silver band. There was old blood dried in the cracks and crevices. "Here. You come back at five. Five on the dot, got it? Say it back to me in Navy. What time are you going to be back here?"

"Seventeen hundred hours," I said.

He pulled ten dollars out of his wallet. "Don't go wasting this on that shit you bought last time. Now go. L.L.S.S. Navy all the way."

I headed down the street and then turned to see him slip through the black-glass door of the Golden Egg.

I decided my direction by that cool-air smell, fresh and weirdish and coming strong from down the street. I headed into the downtown of Dentsville.

It wasn't such a happy city. People were mainly hunched and staring downward and the buildings were tall but empty looking, like whatever was happening had already passed and wasn't coming back.

A guy with teeny eyes and huge eyebrows was blasting aggressive music on a crooked trumpet and kicking a coffee can at his feet that had rocks and change in it. He got pissed when no one dropped money in and blow-gunned notes at the back of their heads. I watched for a while and then I crossed the street. There were some ladies in pastel chiffon scarves who peered at me with too much curiosity at a corner where I waited for the light, so I bolted and jumped in the way of a bus. It wasn't anywhere near hitting me, but the driver blasted his horn and mouthed furious words anyway. Dodging a bus is nothing. Not after you get good at dodging trains. And I was very good at that.

The air smell was more powerful, it wasn't a good smell, not like flowers or food, and it wasn't a rotting smell either. It was complicated, it had many parts, and one of the parts was a core of coldness, if coldness has a smell. To me it does.

At the next corner the smell was knocked to the side by a different smell, doughnuts, slightly rancid but plentiful. The doughnut shop was on a corner of a street that turned very bummy and skruddy with trash and there were little movie houses with faded pictures that displayed ladies bending and squatting with black tape across their eyes and naked boobs. The pictures were warped and greenish and of course there were the dried-out dead flies laying below them. Flies die in so many lonely places. Across the street from the doughnut shop was a two-story neon clown holding a sign that said AMUSEMENTS! but the windows on that building had the boob ladies also.

There were sailors everywhere. Tons of them dressed in white with little caps and black hanging ties, going in and out of the shops and walking close together and laughing. And I was a little bit dazzled by their actualness, their pure Navyness, their handsomeness, and I was thinking it would be a Navy man I married. Only a Navy man. Navy all the way.

And then two of them came up to me. One said, "You got a friend? Will you do two-sies?" The other said, "Shit, Quiver, he ain't even ten!" Horrible waves of nasty booze smells came off of them and one had blood on his teeth. I turned and went into the doughnut shop.

If in your mind a doughnut shop is a clean place with a clean paper-hatted man behind the counter and displays of innocent doughnuts and pots of coffee and good cold milk, well, this place was not like that. Not anything like it. There were people on gummy stools slumping and freaking in slow motion over the sticky counters. No-teeth people smoking, and scary teenagers also smoking, some girls with too much makeup and some boys with scars on their faces and hanging hair. And behind the counter the man was little and harassed looking and his apron was filthy with something that could not come from doughnuts and when he saw me he said "What?" and his voice was harsh. It was hot in the doughnut shop. Super-heated rancid grease air blasting out of vents with dust tentacles waving. "What?" he said again, and rapped on the counter when I looked away.

Behind the swinging half-door to the back there was a loud commotion going on. Someone was yelling "Fuck you, motherfucker, no, uh-uh, it ain't going to be like that, I ain't playing no games, motherfucker, no."

There were flies on the doughnuts walking free. The counterman turned his head toward the shouting and then said, "Blooma!" and a big man who had been staring out the window looked up. The counterman tilted his head toward the shouting and the swinging door flew open and a little matchstick person with a greasy ski jacket came stumbling out backwards yanking on a fur coat that someone else I couldn't see was trying to yank back.

The counterman lifted his eyes and said, "Blooma!" again, and the big guy whose sagging belly was hanging exposed under his shirt, sighed, and got up and walked toward the matchstick man. He had a bulging fat roll on the back of his neck and he looked bored even when he pulled out his sticking knife. When the matchstick guy saw it, he let go of the coat and put his hands up. He said, "Hey! Ain't no need for Bo-bo! It's cool! We cool! Shit. Get Bo-bo off my back, motherfucker, and we cool."

The big man followed him back through the swinging door.

Hardly anyone in the doughnut shop was even looking up. The counterman's eyes came back to me and landed on the father's watch. He reached his hand out for it and said, "Two dollars. What else you got?"

A few blocks farther down the streets were still ratty, but empty. The odd smell was very strong, and all of its parts had increased. The alluring part and the repulsing part and the cold core that seemed to make the colors around me sharpen. There was a buzzing inside of me, nerves buzzing, and I was thinking it would be good to have something to eat, it didn't matter what it was, and I saw a laundromat and I was thinking that would be a good place to sit, get a candy bar out of the vending machine and listen to the sounds of clothes washing and drying. It would be good for the buzzing, which was making me grind my teeth.

The Laundromat door opened an inch and then stuck and I had to push very hard to get it to go wide enough to let me in. It was empty. There were gumballs in the gumball machine that were bleached two-toned from facing the sun, and a rubber tree plant next to the window that had been dead for a few years. There was the buzzing of tube lights and a higher-pitched sound coming from a clock that was broken but still trying to move, the red secondhand stuck but jerking anyway. Cigarette burns were melted into the chairs and tabletops.

I was looking at the candy bar machine and thinking how rank all of it probably was, how it was weird to see a Sir Goober candy bar next to Salvo laundry soap because the soap was mixed in with the candy. I put my money in and counted the red pull knobs carefully so I would get the Sir Goober and I pulled that knob. The Salvo package landed in the tray.

"Shit," I said. "Fuck." I didn't normally swear, but I was in the mood to try it out. "Fucking piece of shit," I said. A sharp voice said, "HEY!"

There was a person in the room. A woman who was very large sitting in a chair I swear she wasn't sitting in before. She had a greasy pageboy haircut and smeared glasses and she was wearing a change apron. When our eyes met she pointed at the hand-lettered sign above her.

THE TEN COMMANDMENTS OF THIS ESTABLISHMENT

1. NO sitting or STANDing or LOITERING on Laundry Tables

2. NO eating of Food on Laundry TABLEs NO Wet Drinks

3. If Attendant is Absent DO NOT ask The TAstee Chicken King For Change as the Tastee Chicken King wants it known there will be NO CHANGE for LAUNDRY

4. We are NOT responsible for ANY Injury Loss or Damage

5. Pay Phone for Patrons ONLY do NOT tie up PHONE

6. NO arguments just Take It Outside

7. NO Toilet available for any Reason

8. Do NOT ask the TAstee Chicken King to use its Toilet As the Toilet of the Tastee Chicken King is Reserved For The Tastee Chicken King Only

9. NO Dying is Permitted in ANY Machine

10. No FOUL language this IS A CHRISTIAN Establishment WE CALL POLICE!!!!!

The lady watched me read all the rules. She tapped number ten significantly.

I said, "You spelled 'dyeing' wrong. On number nine. Unless you mean actually die in your washing machine."

She said, "What the hell are you talking about?"

"Dead people in your washing machines."

"Get the hell out of here."

I held up the Salvo. "I wanted a Sir Goober."

She said, "Cram it up your ass."

I figured out where the cool smell was coming from. It was coming from a thing called The Sound. The Dentsville Sound. Along one side of Dentsville was a body of water, an inlet of salt water coming in from the ocean. There was land on both sides, so it wasn't the ocean, but I was thinking that must be what the ocean would smell like. It had a tide like the ocean and the tide was low and I saw exposed barnacles and clusters of pinched-looking shells, deep blue-black in color. And varieties of seaweed hanging off of things and floating in the water with cigarette butts and pieces of Styrofoam and striped drinking straws. There were dark shapes moving especially deep, I couldn't tell what they were. Possibly fish. But I was thinking of the movie *The Creature*, and I was thinking how now that I saw the kind of water he hung around in, I understood him better. And then I saw a jellyfish. Whitish, nearly transparent, the first one of my life. I marked it in my brain. *Today I saw a jellyfish. Today I saw a jellyfish.*

I stood near a ferry dock and kept breathing the air in, I could not get enough of that kind of air. The smell of french fries made me look up. There was an outdoor stand where people were buying paper baskets of fish and chips and cups of clam chowder. I had heard of clam chowder. Sometimes people ate it in books. But I didn't know what it was and it did not sound good to me. I got in line and watched the two worker guys, teenagers. The one who waited on me had brown skin and full lips and tilted-up black eyes. He wore his paper hat pushed so far forward

105

the point came down to between his eyebrows.

He said, "What you want?"

I said, "French fries."

He picked up the tongs. "What size?"

"Large."

He lifted a paper basket off a stack. "What to drink?"

"Milk."

"No milk."

I said, "No milk?"

He pointed at the board behind him. "We got Coke, Sprite, Root beer, Orange—HEY, DONITA! HEY!" He started waving frantically and cupping his hands around his mouth. "DONITA! HEY! YOU DON'T SEE ME?"

A girl with dark piled-up hair and a lime green minidress was getting into a car. She waved back and called, "I see you, Romel."

The other worker guy nudged him. He said, "Maybe she see you, but what do she see?"

Romel said, "A stud."

"Shit," said the other worker guy. "You ain't going to get none of that. In your dreams maybe."

I said, "Orange, please. And that girl should go out with you."

"Awwww," said Romel, and he was smiling big. "See there?" He tap-slapped the other guy. "You hear what little man say? Say it again."

"That girl should go out with you."

"Haaaa!" said Romel, and the other worker guy laughed. "Because I'm a stud, ain't it? She look at me and see a stud! Put some extra fries up for little man. Little man, you all right. Who beat you in the face like that? I'll kick the shit out of him if you tell me to. You want me to? Where he at?"

I took my fries to some picnic tables near the water. Seagulls swooped around and I threw a fry, wanting to see how a bird would get it out of the water, but a seagull caught it in midair. I threw a couple more and the birds came swarming. I noticed I was feeling decent. Very decent. I walked to a place with a lot of tall totem poles in front of it. And that's where I found it. YE OLDE CURIOSITY SHOPPE. GIFTS. ODDITIES. SOUVENIRS.

Beside the front door was the bone with the sign underneath it that said WHALE PENIS.

I said the words very softly. I pushed open the door and a bell above me rang.

chapter 19

RAINS. TRAINS in the day are nice but trains in the darkness are another kind of creature. It is a form of tripping to stand on the railroad tracks beside a slaughterhouse in the darkness. To wait in the pitch-blackness with your eyes closed for as long as you can stand as the roaring gets closer and crashes all around you. The groaning vibrations and the metal screeches and the bell going *ting, ting, ting.*

To stay on the tracks with your eyes closed after the twisting bright headlight hits your face, turning the insides of your eyelids white, it will be any second, any second, the mighty engine blasting and its shocking sharp ray of blinding light and then the whistle screaming and you jump, flying to the side, rolling in the stickery weeds and laying flat while the black wind rushes over you. This is what I used to do in the good old days.

"Hey," said Julie. "Want to know what's on *Nightmare Theater* tonight?" She was sitting on the couch eating a second bowl of cereal. I was in the mother's chair smoking one of Vicky Talluso's cigarettes and holding the USN lighter, running my thumbnail across the engraving.

I was wearing Vicky Talluso's hat, and I will admit, some of her makeup. And I had looked through her wallet. And I knew what her address was. And I knew what her phone number was. And the Turtle's stash box was still there. And I was blowing smoke rings and wondering what to do about all of it.

"Let me have one," said Julie, reaching her hand out for the cig pack.

"They're not mine."

"Well, you took one. So I can have one."

"Except she's not your friend. She's my friend."

"Who?" said Julie.

I said, "What's on *Nightmare Theater*?"

She said, "Give me a cigarette."

I tossed one to her and she caught it and got up and lit it off of the stove. I had a lighter but she didn't want the lighter. She wanted to almost burn her face off instead. I kind of understood that.

Then we were both blowing smoke rings. In my restricted life I have had a lot of time to practice and so has Julie. If there was ever a smoke-ring championship we could possibly win it. If we ever had a mantel, there could be a trophy on it.

"I like that hat," said Julie between drags.

"It's not mine."

"Obviously. And your face is dripping blood. It just started. Your nose." She touched her upper lip. "Both nostrils. Never seen that before except on TV. Know what the movie is tonight? It's one you like."

It was just a nosebleed. I ran some napkins under cold water and then tipped my head back and held them there.

Julie said, "It's that hand movie. That outer-space hand one where it has an eyeball on the back and dragging guts are hanging out of it. Remember that one?"

The saggy underwear man started shouting next door. "I am what I am and I am IT!" Julie peeped at him through the side window. "He's just walking back and forth again."

My nose kept bleeding. The sound effects for *Nightmare Theater* started, the wind blowing and the wolves howling and breaking glass and screams and eerie high-voiced singing with no words. The vampire rose out of his plywood coffin and said "Good Evening," and while he announced the night's presentation, I noticed an extension cord running behind one of the plywood gravestones, and I noticed he was standing on a floor that looked linoleum and that his shoes looked Sears, and I was wondering how I could not have noticed this before, I was pointing it out to Julie and she said, "Shut up, OK? He's talking."

I looked closely at the vampire. It was the King's Castle Carpet man. It was suddenly very clearly the guy from the King's Castle Carpet commercials dressed as Dracula. Had the *Nightmare Theater* vampire always been him? How come I never noticed it before?

I said, "Julie, do you know who that *is?*"

When she yelled "SHUT! UP!" her voice was unusually violent.

My nose was still bleeding at the first commercial. I leaned over the bathroom sink and rinsed my face and watched the water swirl pink down the drain. Both nostrils was unusual, like Julie said. In the mirror I saw that my pupils were still fully expanded and that the lightbulb above the mirror had ray-rings around it, the light was expanding out of it in concentric halos. I felt the creeping chills clawing their way up my back and my jaws felt tight and inside my mouth saliva gushed.

"It's back on!" Julie shouted. The haunting Dracula music twirled up the stairs and found me. It was happening again. The rushes, the rushes. I heard the Turtle singing to me.

And then I was heaving, bent over the toilet and heaving, and more than anything, anything, I wanted to see him.

Chapter 20

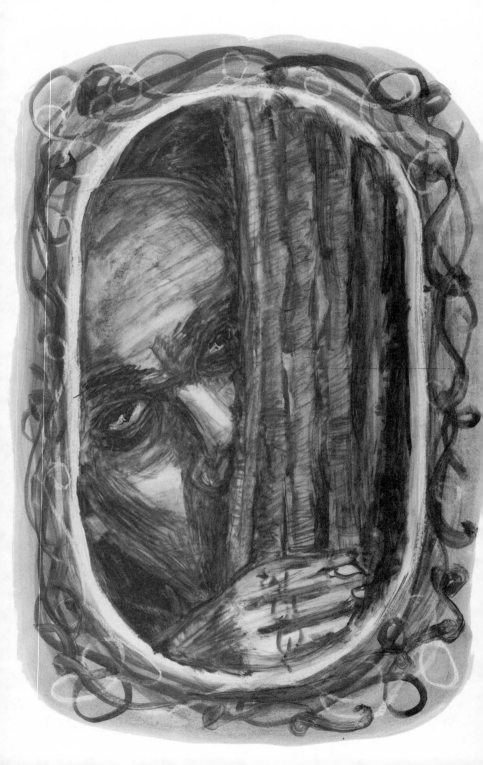

YLVESTER THE nude mummified man at Ye Olde Curiosity Shoppe was not the first dead person I had seen, but he was my most influential one. He had a piece of ancient cloth over his privates but otherwise he was completely exposed.

The sign that explained him said he had been found in the desert. It was the heat and sun that dried him out before he had a chance to rot. You need moisture to rot correctly. Bacteria and certain insects that help the process have to have moisture. But if you croak in the middle of the desert during a hot time of year, all of your moisture can go very quickly and your skin can shrink fast onto your bones and if the blowing sand rolls gently over you it can make you smooth and shiny. Sylvester was smooth and shiny. His eyes were collapsed, understandably, but his mustache was there. His lips were very shrunken but there was no mistaking the reality of his teeth. Very yellow, the front teeth slightly overlapping. His arms were crossed over his stomach and his toes were pointed and the sign said to look for the bullet hole and it was there, easy to see in his chest. The one thing that kept bothering me was that they displayed him standing up.

If it was me doing the display I would have had him laying down. I would have had sand in the case. I would have made it look as realistic as possible and most of all, I would not have covered his vulnerables. I would have wanted everything displayed. In the interest of science. To show what happens to a dead man's pecker in the sun. I thought it even before what happened, happened. But I wouldn't count that as ESP.

At five o'clock I stood in front of the bus station waiting for the father. I watched the black-glass door of the Golden Egg for half an hour and then another half an hour. People wobbled in and people wobbled out but none of them were the father. Finally I crossed the street running and went inside.

It was a very dark place and the air was thick with exhale. A long bar barely lit up, and haggish heads leaning over it, drinking the fantastic booze, sucking it down and tapping empty glasses for more. I examined the faces but none of them belonged to the father. The bartender yelled for me to get out.

A few minutes later a junker car, pink and black and bashed in places with one of the back doors roped shut pulls up next to me and the father leans across the front seat and shouts, "I been circling the damn block. Where the hell were you?" He leaves me in the front seat with the engine running and gets our bags. When he comes back he is happy to report the suitcase still has the tape he put along the edges to make sure, just to make sure no hands have opened it.

The car smelled like old milk and cat pee. The dashboard was cracked open and powdery sponge showed through. Also there were bite marks on it. Teeth marks. Human ones.

We drove up hills that increased in steepness until we were on a hill I could not believe. The street had deep zigzagged gouges for traction. I felt like I was on the first part of a roller-coaster ride, my full weight pressed into the seat back. The father was cussing the transmission. "Shift! Shift! You worthless piece of shit!" The car barely crawled.

All of Dentsville seemed to be nothing but hills, steeper and steeper. When we got to the top of one, there was another, until finally it was time to start down. The father pumped the brakes and got pale. He hated heights. He gripped the steering wheel and said, "This ain't going to—oh shit—oh SHIT!" And we wound around Dentsville like that. Crawling up and skidding down with the emergency brake pressed as far as it would go. And then we came to the neighborhood the father was looking for.

I couldn't believe a place could be so grim. So full of sad yards and boarded-up houses. I didn't see anyone, not a soul except the scrounger trucks driving by with junk piled high and tilty. The father said, "You know what you're looking at here, Clyde?"

I shook my head.

"This is progress."

He rolled the car to a stop and took out a cigarette and handed me one. He pulled out the Old Skull Popper and took a glug and passed the bottle to me. I wasn't really in the mood, but I took a glug because I could tell he was about to lay something on me, a plan was about to be explained, and I learned that in such circumstances a glug of fantastic booze is not a bad idea.

"Clyde. Clyde. Listen to me good." The father was reaching into a paper sack with CRISS CROSS DRUGSTORE printed on it. He pulled out a beige-colored roll of fabric, an extra-wide Ace bandage. He said, "Take off your shirt."

I hesitated, and he cuffed me. "I don't got no time for your shit right now. We partners? Are we?"

I took off my shirt and he wrapped the bandage around my middle. "Don't want it too tight. Want it comfortable. Is it? You can breathe?" He fastened it with three silver-toothed clips.

He reached over the backseat and pulled his knife case out of his duffel. It was a custom-made case. Tooled leather with ancient patterns, saddle stitched, oiled and polished. It belonged to Old Dad. All of the knives had leather sheaths with names embossed on them. There was Big Girl, and Francine, and Cleoma. There was Margy and Lisa and Baby Sue. All of them custom-made with bone handles that had never seen water. They were cleaned only with oil and sharpened so often a few of the blades were quite narrow. Francine was barely wider than a licorice stick. She was Old Dad's favorite. A boning knife he'd been devoted to. The first thing the father did was take Francine out, and slam the pull-out ashtray onto her blade and snap it off clean. He said, "There, you bastard." He threw Francine out the window.

From under the front seat he pulled out a sheath I'd never seen. He said, "You know what this is, Clyde? I about shit when I saw it in the pawnshop. You know what the hell this *is?*"

I had never seen a knife like it. The handle was black and peanut shaped with diamond grooves cut into it like you see on a gun handle. The blade was five inches long, wide and pointed, with razor edges on both sides. The father is right when he said knives are in my blood. There was an involuntary reaching of my hand toward it.

The father said, "That's Sheila."

The father watched me holding her, weighing her in my hand, being fascinated by her balance. Her edges seemed to be sharpened to near transparency. I looked up at him and he nodded. "Ain't she a bitch and a half? And you know what? She has a goddamn sister."

He handed me a similar sheath, saying, "This is Little Debbie."

Little Debbie was even more vicious looking than Sheila. I can't say why exactly, maybe her compact size. Her fit in my hand was incredible.

"You know what these are, Clyde?"

I shook my head.

"Elite Forces. Fucking Navy Special Issue fucking Elite Forces. A hand-to-hand man's dream. Her blade is perfect. You drop her? I'll snap your neck."

He sheathed Little Debbie and tucked her into the Ace bandage where she would lay flat against my skin and had me practice pulling her out, first with my shirt off and then with my shirt on. He showed me some moves.

"Now, remember." He flashed Sheila and his arm arced and

his wrist flicked. "Smooth. No hesitation. Follow through." He pointed to the top of his thigh. "The femoral, OK? That's what you want. Right here. Deep as you can, twist, then rip her down. OK? Just in case, OK?"

I said, "In case of what?"

He hung a fresh cig from his lips. "Believe me, Clyde. You'll know. I won't need to tell you. Partners, right? You in? Ready to stir up a world of shit?"

We turned onto a gravel road that exploded clouds of gray dust behind us. The houses were mostly small, all abandoned, none of them had doors at all. The father said, "Freeway coming through. See here? All of this? Take a good look because it ain't going to be here next week."

The gravel road ended beside a dead-grass play field. The weeds were high but I could see the chalk lines marking the base-ball diamond. The blown-out backstop still stood. Above it was a mostly boarded-up school. Some of the unboarded windows had high scorch marks along the top. Someone had tried to start a fire but failed. Fires can be harder to set than you would think.

The last house on the road had a filthy blue blanket tacked up over the doorway. Parked out in front was a shiny new car with a shiny new trailer attached. The father laughed a high-pitched "Hee-hee!" He slammed the steering wheel with the flat of his hand and said, "We got 'em, Clyde. We got 'em now." He hit the gas and gunned the car into the yard, right to the doorway and laid on the horn.

From behind the blanket someone yelled "Je-mph CHRIMPH!" A corner lifted, and a bald head stuck itself out, looking disoriented and pissed off. The father stepped out of the car very casual, took a last drag off his cig, and tossed it. He said, "Got your love letter."

The bald head said, "Lemme pum my meeph im," and disappeared behind the blanket.

The father flicked his eyes at me and touched his fingers to his lips. L.L.S.S. I nodded.

He said, "What happened to your door, Lemuel?"

"I mphoph im!"

"What?"

The man stepped out, still shoving his top denture in. He had on suspenders and greasy pants, a nude pregnant stomach, wino shoes, and dirty ankles.

The father spit. "I didn't catch that last you said."

"I SOLD IT! Some colored guy come around taking all the doors, see." He gestured at the houses. On his forearm was a smeared-looking tattoo. A lady in a bathing suit with a head too small for her body. "He drive up here collecting doors and I say, 'Hey, you black bastard! You can't just go taking them doors! They ain't for free!' Well, I got my due off him is what I'm trying to say."

"Yeah?" said the father. "What'd you take him for?"

"Fifty cents," said Lemuel.

They both started laughing. The father said, "You ain't changed."

Lemuel jutted his chin at me. "Ugly little shit. Looks like a dogfish. Must be yours."

"No," said the father. "No, he ain't."

Lemuel made a grunting sound and pig-eyed me for a while. He said, "Let's get us something to drink then."

The father said, "I brought you one. Clyde, go get a fresh soldier out of the car for your uncle Lemuel. Get him that one we bought him special. In the white bag. That's right."

"Clyde, huh?" said Lemuel.

"Yup," said the father.

"But he ain't yours?"

"Nope."

"Shit," said Lemuel. "What are you trying to pull on me?"

"Well," said the father. "That depends."

Lemuel's voice got lower. "I heard it was you that found Old Dad."

"That's right." The father rubbed his face with both hands.

"That had to be a shock," said Lemuel.

"A hell of a shock."

I held the white booze sack out to the father. "Not me, Clyde. It's for your uncle Lemuel."

"Clyde, huh?" said Lemuel. "Well, who beat the crap out of you, Clyde? Or did you come out of the box that way."

"He don't talk," said the father.

"No?"

"Faller's disease."

"Faller's," said Lemuel.

"Brain damage," said the father.

"But he seems to understand you fine."

"Oh yes," said the father. "Understanding's no problem for Clyde if you keep it simple. Remembering is what he has trouble with. Can't remember nothing at all. Maybe it's a blessing for him. He's had it rough."

"Rough," said Lemuel.

"He's a stray," said the father. "His daddy come looking for work up to our place one day, and drove off without him. Never came back. Never said boo. I thought, what the hell. Keeps me company."

I need to mention that while this interesting conversation was going on, there was a smell so horrifying that my stomach was ripple-convulsing. Nothing at the slaughterhouse ever smelled as bad. Where was it coming from? It felt like the fumes were coating my eyes. The father and Lemuel didn't seem to notice it, neither of them reacted, but I could hardly hold myself steady. I was trying to breathe through my mouth but I could taste it.

The smell was coming from the trailer. It was so strong the air almost radiated with visible waves. I saw what looked like dried blood on the door. I saw dried brown crusts on the handle and thick spatters on the step-up. There were bottle flies crawling on every crack and crevice. They were going insane trying to find a way inside.

Lemuel pulled the bottle out of the white sack and whistled

low. "Holy Christ," he said. "Whitley's. The Gateway."

"The Gateway." The father nodded. "Many are called but few can get up afterwards."

They passed it and glugged and then the father passed it to me and I glugged.

Lemuel looked astonished. "He drink?"

The father said, "If you had brain damage, wouldn't you?"

Lemuel looked me up and down.

This new booze, this Whitley's, it was very different. It seemed to evaporate off your tongue as you drank it. I felt it go straight to my legs and I began to sway.

The father pointed at me. "Clyde, lay in the grass before you fall and bust your face again."

Then it was quiet. Lemuel pulled out a tin of Copenhagen and untwisted the lid. His bottom teeth came spitting out and he took a honking black wad and pushed it into his cupped lower lip. I could feel a funny crackle in the air between them.

Lemuel leaned toward me. He spat a jet and said, "You're kind of puny, son. Come over here."

The father flitted his eyes at me. The look. The famous go-along-with-it look. Lemuel patted his knee. "I won't bite you."

"Haw!" said the father.

Something about Lemuel put me on alert. When he smiled my stomach twisted. The smell from the trailer was hammering me. In the darkness beneath the trailer I saw a very beat-up-looking cat. One of its eyes was crusty and sunken. It was clawing at the underside, it was trying to find a way up.

I watched the father take out a cig and spend a long time lighting it. He inhaled deep and examined the cig and he exhaled.

He said, "So where's Sugar Dick?"

"Goddamn it, now," Lemuel spat, "Don't start that shit with me."

"Sugar Dick." The father blew a smoke ring which hung in the horrible air.

Lemuel said, "I told you when I called you, I want to see this thing straightened out. I told Leonard the same. You think I like being the man in the middle?" Lemuel spat again. "Fuck all." He picked his bottom denture up off his lap and turned it over in his hand.

"Police involved?" asked the father.

"Hell no," said Lemuel.

"And the suitcase?"

"There ain't no suitcase."

"There ain't, huh?" The father took a drag and pinched his eyes.

"I told you on the phone. Leonard says there is no suitcase."

The father scratched the side of his face. "Gee. I wonder where it wandered off to."

Lemuel pointed to the car and trailer. "There's your god-damn suitcase right there. How much you think that all cost?"

The father snorted. "That ain't a tenth of what Old Dad paid out."

"I heard Old Dad stiffed you," said Lemuel. "Hell, I'd be mad too. When Leonard showed up here crying the story to me, I didn't like it a bit. That's why I called you, you stupid son of a bitch. You got a new car and trailer, full tank, keys are in the ignition. Why do you want to stand there and piss on it?"

"Where is he? Where's Leonard?" said the father. "He inside?" The father jerked his head toward the doorway and called, "Sugar Dick, you in there?"

Lemuel turned his bottom denture upright and rubbed his dirty thumb across the molars. "Let me tell you something, Leonard said—"

"Shit on Leonard."

"Shit on *you*. You going to hear me out or not?"

"Sure." The father glugged some Whitley's and passed it back. "Lie to me, you fat son of a bitch. Go ahead."

The father snatched the denture out of Lemuel's hands and flung it into the play field across the road.

"Aw," said Lemuel. "Why the hell you have to do that?"

"Go hunt it, Clyde. Go find Uncle Lemuel's bottom teeth."

I took my time. Their voices came clearly to me across the road. The story Lemuel told the father went something like this.

Old Dad owed money to Old Man Mottie but Old Man Mottie was dead. Earlis was his grown son and Earlis was a homo, and Earlis tried to cover it up by marrying a lady older than him with huge bags under her eyes and an ass four feet wide. She owned her house and Earlis thought what the hell. Then Earlis met Leonard, who worked at the A&W. He was crazy about Leonard and stories began to spread.

And then the suitcase came.

"You said there wasn't no suitcase," said the father. The light was low and his burning cig end was getting a glow to it.

Lemuel hooked his finger into his mouth and flung his chew-wad. "Leonard said he was *told* about the suitcase but he never *saw* no suitcase. He thought Earlis was shitting him. I mean, it does sound like a pile of crap, don't it? Suitcase with money in it delivered to you out of the sky."

"It didn't come out of the sky," said the father.

"That boy find my teeth yet? Call to him again, will you?"

Leonard was in the middle of his shift at the A&W and Earlis comes barreling into the parking lot, shouting to him about going fishing, yelling come on, they were going after muskie, he had some new bait he wanted to try out, and a couple of people busted out laughing. Leonard threw down his hat and jumped into the car. That was the last time either of them were seen.

"*You* seen 'em," said the father. "You seen Leonard."

"Seen a shadow of him," said Lemuel. "Showed up here in the middle of the night, crying like a baby, wouldn't come in, didn't want me to come out. Told me the whole story through that blanket. Said he couldn't stand for me to see his face. Said he had a gun and he was going to blow his own head off if I tried anything."

"Uh-huh," said the father, sounding bored.

"You want to hear this or not?"

Leonard said they drove to the next county, bought a car and trailer right off the barely used lot with cash and a trade-in, and then they really did go fishing. Lake Marie. Earlis really did have some new bait he wanted to try out. Red salmon eggs, coffee grounds, and mini-marshmallows cooked together in a frying pan. He invented it, and it worked so good the fish were practically begging to be hooked. And then they celebrated with plenty of hugging and a big bottle of Whitley's and Leonard was thinking it was love. Some would call it perverted, he knew that, but for him it was true love at last.

"Cornholer," said the father.

"Goddamn it, man!" said Lemuel. "What do you got for a heart, a cat turd?"

Leonard and Earlis were together all that night and the next. Earlis told Leonard he was wild in love with him, that Leonard meant more than anything in the world to him, but the time had come to move on.

And Leonard said, what the hell did he mean by move on? And Earlis said he was taking Leonard back to the A&W. And Leonard said, "Then what?"

Earlis said, "I'm leaving town."

Leonard said, "Just like that?"

Earlis said, "I shall never forget you."

And that's when Leonard grabbed the gutting knife off the counter and ripped Earlis open clean.

"Gutting knife," said the father. He blew out a jet of cig smoke and nodded his approval.

Lemuel said, "Leonard didn't plan to kill him. He ain't like that. Now, *I'm* like that, and *you're* like that, but Leonard ain't like that."

And Leonard was sorry right afterwards. And Leonard had a nervous breakdown right there and Leonard drove a thousand miles with dead Earlis bouncing around the hot trailer with the piles of muskie until he pulled up to Lemuel's place in the middle of the night and confessed out the whole story through the blue blanket. Leonard said he was killing himself, and there was nothing anyone could do to stop him. He made Lemuel promise to make sure the car and the trailer went to the rightful man. That was Leonard's final wish.

"You," said Lemuel, wiping his eyes. "He wanted you to have it."

"And?" said the father.

"And what?"

"Well don't keep me in suspense here, Lemuel," said the father. "Did that little cornholer blow his brains out or not?"

chapter 21

O-*BER*-TA! RO-*BER*-TA!" Julie's voice was calling me from downstairs. "It's on! You're missing it!" The word is maintain. That is what you are supposed to do when you are high and you don't want anyone to know it. Maintain, maintain, maintain.

"Ro-BERTA! The crawling hand just killed a cow and now all the other cows are freaking out!"

"Cattle," I said, as I came down the stairs. "Not cows. Cattle."

"How are you supposed to know, you're not even watching it." Julie turned to look at me. "Your nose is still bleeding."

I said, "So?"

I got Vicky's purse and pulled out her wallet. *If found, please return to Vicky Tallusoj.* I was looking at the "j" on the end of her name. Thinking it was silent. And then I thought about different silent letters I knew about and if it was possible to put them all together and spell a silent word. A drop of my blood splashed onto the ID card. It was so red.

"Roberta!" Julie's head popped up over the back of the couch. She dangled her hand at me and did crawling motions with her fingers and then pointed at the TV. A lady was standing in front of the dead cattle and screaming. She could not stop screaming. I dialed Vicky's number.

"Who you calling?"

"Nobody."

"You can't use the phone in case Mom is trying to call here."

I said, "She's not trying to call."

"You got blood all over your shirt."

"So?"

The phone rang six times before a man picked it up and started coughing. He didn't say hello. He just started coughing. I got scared and hung up.

I waited a little bit and then I dialed the number again. Six rings, same man. Hack-coughing violently. This time he talks. In an accent. He says "Goddamn!" which scares me and I hang up again.

"Roberta!" says Julie. "Who are you calling?"

"Nobody."

I dialed out the number again. This time the man picks up on the second ring. He says, "Goddamn TO YOU!" and then a sound like he's trying to hang up but instead he drops the phone and I hear another voice yelling in the background. A girl's voice. The phone gets picked up off the floor and Vicky Tallusoj says, "Hello?" and I hang up again.

I don't know why I hang up. I didn't expect to hang up. My finger just automatically pushed the hang-up button when I heard her voice.

Julie said, "Hoooooooo, Roberta?"

I jumped and then yelled at her. "Don't EVER do that to me!"

"Do what?"

"Say that to me."

"Say what?" asked Julie. "Who you calling? That?"

"Shut up."

"Who you calling, Roberta?"

I said, "The time lady."

"Suck," said Julie. Her mouth flattened. "Lie."

For a while I sat on the couch with Julie, sticking napkins with

ice cubes in them against my nose, it had to be Vicky, it sounded just like her. I wondered if her nose was also bleeding. If she was also sitting in front of *Nightmare Theater* with blood on her shirt.

"Come ON, Roberta. Your turn." Julie had been talking but I hadn't really been listening. Something about how I would kill the unkillable hand. She said she would light it on fire. Many squirts of lighter fluid and then a match and then, "Whooooooosh!" she said. "Whooooooosh!" Incinerated. "You, Roberta. Your turn. How would you do it?"

"Stab it. Stab it and pound the knife in with a rock."

Julie scratched her nose and looked at me hard. Could she tell? Was it obvious that a second wave of Creeper was starting to wash over me? She said, "You could stab it, but it would still be alive though."

I said, "It wouldn't matter. It wouldn't be going anyplace."

"But it could still escape and come back after you."

"Not the way I'd do it, it wouldn't."

"I still think burning it."

I said, "But the bones, Julie. Bones crawl after everybody."

I was dialing the phone again, sitting on the kitchen floor with the cord stretched down and I was facing the wall and I was making little fingerprint dots on the wall with smears of blood. I counted the rings. I said, "Come on, Vicky. Answer. Answer."

I did not expect such a hard kick. The back of my eyes tilted out in red explosions from the sudden crack to my back. Julie was standing over me and screaming, "YOU ARE CALLING SOMEBODY! YOU ARE GOING TO LEAVE ME HERE!"

"Hello? Hello? Hello?" said the midget voice from the dropped telephone.

Julie and me were on the floor. She was yanking out chunks of my hair and I was bashing her into the table legs and punching her hard. She started screaming and screaming. I let her go.

She picked up the telephone and shouted, "YOU DIE!" and threw it. She yanked open a drawer and then there was this very weird moment. A weird stretched-out second where everything in the room just expanded. Time expanded. Molecules and the spaces between the molecules expanded. I saw every cell of Julie's arm making the graceful slow-motion arc, and I had time to notice the mother's meat knife cutting through the air, every glinting particle of every single molecule coming straight at my face, and I had time to calmly lean to the side and watch it pass my head and tong into the wall.

Julie. Do you know what the father would have said? He would have said you were a natural. He would have said, "Give that girl a Lucky Strike!" He would have pushed his whole pack of cigs at you and passed you his USN lighter.

Watch out for Creeper. Because just when you think it has all drained out of you, just when you are sure your Creeper experience is over, you will suddenly feel the incredible white explosion shoot up your back, and your fingers will stretch out incredibly long and your mouth will gush incredible amounts of joyful saliva and you'll be hunched over in front of the TV and your hanging drool will look fantastic in the blue jumping light.

And your sister will FREAK. Your sister Julie who just tried to tong a meat knife straight into your face will suddenly FREAK and she will say, "ROBERTA! ROBERTA! WHAT'S WRONG?!" She will FREAK from how you are hunching and stretching out your incredibly long fingers and lifting your lips up and down over your wet teeth and she will keep on FREAKING, even while you speak to her very calmly, saying, "Julie, Julie. Shhhhhhh. Don't talk. Right now just don't talk to me."

And her face will be flickering and it will be wet with streaks of crying and she will say, "Don't die, Roberta. Don't die. Please, please don't die, Roberta."

And you will smile at her and this will be what makes her scream.

Chapter 22

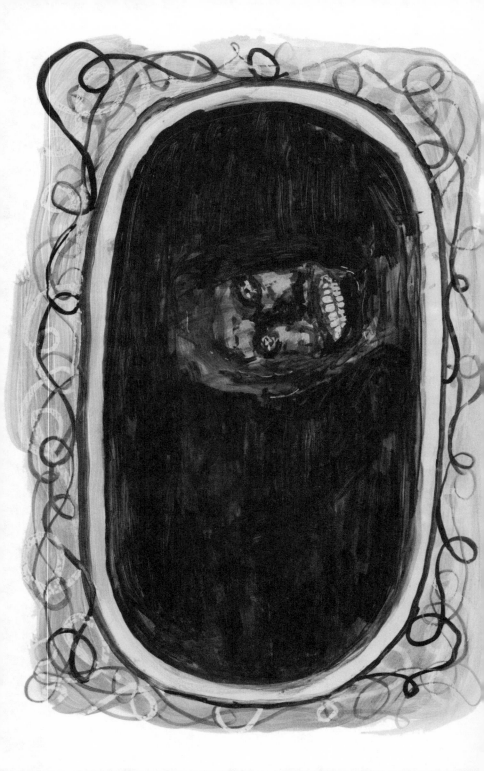

ND THE father and Lemuel finished the Whitley's and wanted more Whitley's and Lemuel needed another can of Copenhagen, and they had gotten jolly and friendly toward each other again, dropping the subject that was on their minds most of all and deciding to go into town.

The father hollered to me through the dusky light. "Clyde! Me and your uncle Lemuel are going to go blow some dust off. You keep an eye on things, you hear me?"

Lemuel finished buttoning a wrinkled shirt and pulled his suspenders up over his shoulders. He said, "How do you know he hears you if he can't answer you?"

The father hollered, "Toss Uncle Lemuel's teeth back this way if you hear me."

From my hiding place in the weeds I gave Lemuel's bottom teeth the hand grenade throw, and watched them bounce twice and land just under the trailer.

"Oh shit," said Lemuel, and he grunted a lot when he bent and squatted to reach them and he made an emission very loudly and then he felt under the trailer and the cat bit him.

"SON OF A BITCH! SON OF A BITCH!"

"We'll be back in a little while, Clyde," shouted the father to the dead play field. "Don't wander." The car with the human teeth bites in the dashboard rolled away down the gravel road.

There was still enough light in the sky to make out the shapes of things. And there was one streetlight that let some light fall onto Lemuel's scraggly yard. I had some questions in my mind. Was dead Earlis still in the trailer? That was the main one. That was the involuntary one. And that was the one that made me decide to take a walk.

All of what surrounded me that evening in Dentsville is gone. Paved over. The freeway did come through. And there are days when I would like to go to Dentsville and see it, make sure of it, because I was not lying when I told Julie that bones crawl after everybody. And that fire can't do a thing about it.

I walked down Lemuel's gravel road toward a train whistle, a loud one. I knew the tracks were close. I followed a steep sidewalk down and down until I came to the edge of a cliff, a sheer cliff that appeared out of nowhere. Trussed up against it was a wooden bridge if a thing that only leads you down and down and down can be called a bridge. It was like a high wooden train trestle that fell down on one side, looking about half a mile long and narrow and rickety with three tight turns to manage before it ended at a flat street.

I stepped onto it and the smell of creosote flooded my nose and it was a relief to smell it. It drove all the ghost smells away for a while.

It was the highest thing I'd ever been on. The drop was about two hundred feet straight down and when a scavenger truck came bumping onto the planks the whole bridge rattled. I saw the man in the truck leaning into his seat. He went slow and the boards beneath him groaned.

Underneath the bridge were the tracks. Bums were in the scrub below, moving in the shadows of vapor lights on high poles. Little bum encampments were farther up the cliff side, with cardboard and old blankets piled up against side-growing trees. Little fires were burning. There were guys sitting on the ground wearing hats and smoking.

The train that whistled me over to the bridge was clacking

away into the distance but another one was coming. The head-lamp twisting and the *ting, ting, ting*. A couple of guys stood and brushed their pants off. When the train came alongside them they took a few quick steps and jumped on easy and graceful. I spent a long time there, just watching the trains come and go. Enjoying my view of them from so high up. Watching the bums. Gripping the wooden guardrail when the whistles blew and the passing trains shook the bridge into nearly swaying. Exhilaration. Exhilaration is the word.

I got back to Lemuel's and faced the mystery trailer again. The father and Lemuel were still gone and knowing the father, I expected them to stay gone for a while. I started snooping. The keys were in the ignition of the car, just like Lemuel said, I twisted them a half turn and the radio came on to a country station and Ned Miller started singing "From a Jack to a King."

On the passenger seat was a partly spilled box of Cracker Jacks with the prize still inside and in the glove box there was flashlight.

I breathed through my mouth and stood on a folding chair to reach the trailer window and pointed the flashlight. The first thing I noticed was the way the miniature kitchen looked in the spin-art of blood, dark flung patterns everywhere, fly highways going every direction. The second thing was on the floor.

I can tell you this. A man who has been dead for a week in a hot trailer looks more like a man than you would first expect. The face bloats out giantly and purple-black, and there are textures, horrifying textures, but it's the mouth that makes you scream. When you see his black crusted lips pulled away from shockingly white teeth, when you see him shining out his special smile, just for you.

I was dead asleep when the car came crawling back up the gravel road. I felt the high beams glide across my eyes and I sat up from my hiding place on the edge of the field. The father drove the car into the folding chairs and there were some metal crunches. He stopped just a few feet from the trailer and the high beams bouncing off of it threw back a strange light on the scene.

The father switched the engine off, leaned across the seat to unlatch the passenger door, and Lemuel poured out rolling.

The father leaned his head on the back of the front seat and stared upwards for a while. He leaned his head on the steering wheel and stared downwards for a while. Then he opened his door quickly and leaned out. There was a sudden waterfall eruption of an intense booze fountain that had many hard pulses and many dramatic splurts before it finally ran out of power. The father pulled himself back into the car, leaned until he fell across the seat, and started snoring.

The car sat like that. Both doors open and the radio static cutting in and out and the headlights attracting bugs. They spun disoriented against the bright trailer, making shadows. The head of Lemuel got miniature tremors and his lips started making disturbing movements, extremely disturbing talking motions and then severe birthing motions and then his dentures did a half roll out of his mouth and into the dirt. The smell coming off of him was flammable.

I was holding Little Debbie. Holding her so tight that my fingers were cramped around her, the cut-diamond pattern of her handle embossed into my palm. I fell back asleep this way and what woke me up in the dimmest rays of morning, the barest gray rays of light upon the damp weedy field, was a soft velvety thing stroking against my lifted head. Stroking and pushing against my cheek, against the corner of my mouth, smelling bad.

I opened my eyes and Lemuel was kneeling over me.

Little Debbie bit him. No hesitation. Little Debbie bit and bit and bit him and if there was shouting, if there was screaming, I didn't hear it. What I heard was a long tone, faint and endless. And the center of my vision was punched out, gone gray, with a hot light scribbling fire at the edges, melting the world from the center outward like a movie burning up on the screen.

"Didn't I tell you?" said the father. "Didn't I tell you you'd know when it was time to use Little Debbie? You're a natural, Clyde. Have a Lucky Strike. Hell, darling, take the whole pack. You earned it."

There is a saying about Jesus. That he will forgive anyone for anything. Anything at all.

Do you know the song by Brenda Lee?

"I'm sor-ry...so sor-ry...please ac-cept...my a-pol-o-gy."

The father was singing it in a jigging cadence as he dragged the blue blanket containing the rotted Earlis out of the trailer and into the shack of Lemuel, singing it jaunty, and leaving a trail of horrible liquid behind him. He had a handkerchief doused in Aqua Velva tied over his nose. His singing was muffled, but it was on key. I think the maddest people in this world are the ones who could have been stars, could have serenaded all people so famously with voices lifting up from spinning gold records. There were so many good things that should have happened to the father. He wasn't your average man. He wasn't meant to live in an average world.

Dead Lemuel was already in the shack. The blue blanket came for him first. The father stood over him smoking a cig. He said, "Jesus, Clyde. You bled him out like a hog. I couldn't have done better." Dead Lemuel received a few last wet crunching kicks and some advice about lying to someone as superior as the father. Because Lemuel had been lying. The suitcase was inside the shack and so was dead Leonard, who didn't blow his brains out after all. His throat was cut.

"See what a shit world we live in, Clyde?" The father took a fortifying glug of Whitley's. "Brother against brother, father against son. Fuck all."

The father bounced back into the trailer and came out with a gray jug of cookstove kerosene. He said, "Hop in the car, sunshine, we got places to go. This will only take a minute."

He disappeared inside the shack and there was the splashing and the distinctive smell of kerosene. I waited for the WHOOMP and the WHOOSH, but all I heard was "Burn you son-of-a-bitch. Take. Take. Shit. Come on." Kerosene can be hard to get going. You'd think you could just throw a match on it and you'd have it made. But it can be a stubborn accelerant. The key is a little Whitley's. BLAM! The doorway glowed bright and the father came leaping out.

The pink and black car with bite marks in the dash got the same treatment. And I was thinking of the teeth that made them. They looked like the teeth of a child. Someone's baby teeth marks melting in the flames.

It started to rain.

"This one's going to blow," said the father, gunning the engine and we were down the road when it did. I looked over my shoulder and watched the brightness through the wet rear window. It started to pour. It was Sunday morning.

"Goddamn!" said the reeking father. "It couldn't go more professional than that. Whole damn street will be on fire before someone calls it in. Fire department won't give a shit. There ain't nothing to save. They'll watch it. Keep it from spreading. Eat candy bars and shoot the shit. But no one is going to go sniffing around back there and if they do? Know what they'll find? A goddamn three-way! Haw! We got us a nice car here, Clyde. The future's looking bright, Clyde." And he went on like that, giddy like that, trying to wipe the steam off the windshield with his filthy hands, rolling down his window, letting the creosote smell curl delicate tendrils into the car and that became stronger and then flooded the air, and as the father tried to find the defroster knob the car slid onto the wet boards of the wooden bridge.

"What the—OH SHIT!" The father hit the brakes and the trailer fishtailed and pushed us farther down. When he was able to stop he tried to back up but the planks were slick and the trailer was too heavy. I heard the oncoming roaring, the *ting-ting-ting* of the approaching bell, not the whistle yet, the whistle would come in a moment, a clear screaming that would shake the world apart.

We were up so high. Up so very high on such a rickety slick

bridge. The father's paralyzed hands were white on the steering wheel. The yellow eye of the train rolled toward us. The bridge was already vibrating. I counted it down. *Five, four, three,* and when the whistle bellowed the father screamed, and the train pounded and screeched and shook at the legs of the bridge like it was going to pull it down.

There are times when a situation is not funny at all. Times when it would be very rude to laugh, but I could not help it. I didn't want to be laughing, but my puppet head would not stop. It was the sound of the father's screaming. Have you ever heard a man scream before? Sounding exactly like a girl?

"You BITCH!" He had me by the head and he was screaming, "YOU THINK THIS IS FUNNY? YOU FUCKING STUPID BITCH!" He punched me very hard then and my teeth hit the dash knobs and broke a short upside-down "V" into my front teeth. I tried to get out of the car but he had my arm and he yank-twisted me back. In a very even voice he said, "I'm going to kill you, Clyde." But when we made it to the bottom of the bridge I was still alive.

Dentsville is a maze, a tangle of curving streets and hills and sudden dead ends. When it's raining and you are pulling a trailer and you are feeling excitable it is a hard place to get out of. Very hard. The father kept trying to go south but he kept getting turned around. Finally he said, "East, then. East. Fuck it."

And soon we were at the edge of the city, rain pouring hard and wipers on high, blood dripping from my nose onto my arms, me not doing anything about it. The road was straight and empty and our tires swished loud, running alongside a junkyard that went on forever behind a fence made of spot-welded tire rims, some of them painted to spell out ANDERSONS ANDERSONS YOU NEED IT WE HAVE IT ANDERSONS ANDERSONS ANDERSONS.

The father twisted the radio dial. The car was a pale green Valiant with black upholstered seats shot through with silver. Bench seats with a divided center so you could lift a lever on your side and lean back to relax if you needed to, if it was possible to relax while the father listed all the thousand reasons why he should kill you and throw you to the crows. You never laugh at a superior officer. Ever. Ever.

We drove out of Dentsville and the world looked empty and green with mountains before us, the road curving gently upwards. Little songs came on the radio the father liked. Sad songs named after towns. Abilene. Detroit City. Saginaw, Michigan. And the father sang.

He could imitate anyone's voice. His Adam's apple went up and down the same as the professionals. So many chances in life just passed him by but all of that was over. There was one more suitcase to go and this one he was going to get without a fight. It was actually waiting for him along with a highball and a loving woman who owned her own motel. Spring was just around the corner.

And so we drove up into the misty mountains disappearing into the conifer forests that are always dim and darkly shadowed, even on the brightest of days. The father had his high beams on and he was driving slow. He was having trouble keeping his eyes open. Too much exhilaration will do that to you. Brings on an aftermath of konking out. I felt it too. He drove up a dog-legged logging road into the lasting darkness of the dripping pines and that is where we slept.

 ULIE SAT on the couch looking at me with the flickering light from the television shining on her eyes. It was still night but all the shows were over and on the screen was the hissing no-picture of a billion insane bees. I'd been watching it, staring at it for a while before I realized my awakeness and my situation. I was in the mother's chair. A blanket from our bed was on me and it was wet with blood and drool. Julie stared at me. "Hey," I said.

She didn't answer.

"What's wrong?" I said. I started to rub my face but the stickiness and crusts stopped me. I kept my eyes off of the TV. There were faces moving in the hissing picture. I'd seen the smile of rotting Earlis there. Of bleeding Lemuel. Of the furious father. The movie called The Life of Clyde was still on but I could not stand to watch it.

"Julie," I said. "You got cigs anywhere? I need one. You got one?"

She said something I could barely hear, I saw her lips moving. *Fuck you, Roberta. I hate you, Roberta. I wish you were dead.* She pulled a blanket over herself and curled up with her back to me and went to sleep. I remembered the cigs of Vicky Talluso. I tried to smoke one but it made me sick.

I showered and dressed and stood in front of the bathroom mirror combing out my wet hair. Looking at myself and trying to decide what I was going to do. Have you ever seen the track a snake leaves in the sand? A skittery track? Bones leave tracks like that when they come back crawling, come tap-tap-tapping dead fingers against your skull from the inside. Earlis was tapping. Lemuel was tapping. Leonard and Doolie Bug were tapping too. My nose had stopped bleeding but my eyes were still blown. Beware of Creeper.

Julie was sleeping when I slipped out the door into the darkness. It was about an hour before daylight. I wasn't sure where I was going. To Vicky Talluso's house maybe. Or maybe to the Trailways station. I wore Vicky's hat and carried her purse and along with her things and the stash box of the Turtle there was a very old friend of mine. The sock monkey named Trina.

I made Trina with the help of the Christian Homes lady who hosed me down in her backyard after the Lucky Chief Motel Massacre. Who wore pink rubber gloves when she threw my bloody clothes straight into the dented metal trash can and who was taking a horrified shower when I fished back into the trash can to retrieve a few things. Little Debbie. A purple cloth Crown Royal bag full of twenties. Trina kept them safe inside of her for five years. It was going to be sad when I tore her head off to get them back out, but Trina knew it was coming.

During my time in the Las Vegas Christian Homes when I was the mystery child who suffered from shock and amnesia, I had a decent life. I had the name of Michelle, the Christians called me Michelle and I enjoyed life as Michelle. I enjoyed making sock monkeys for the Christian Missionaries International Sock Monkey Drive, sock monkeys for disadvantaged children around the world. I enjoyed the Jesus they prayed to, a very different-looking Jesus from the one I was used to. His eyes weren't shocked-rolled high and his mouth didn't hang open in agony and no blood was dripping down his face, or from his slash wound or from his various nailed locations. The Christian Homes Jesus was

a very comfortable-looking Jesus. A strolling Jesus, in very clean clothes. A clean Jesus for clean, strolling people.

I was happy to make sock monkeys in his honor. I was happy to add my sock monkeys to the pile and watch Lawrence Welk's floating TV world and eat green beans and scalloped potatoes and ham made in an electric skillet and drink big glasses of milk and snarf down tapioca pudding and hear the reverend list me in the names of people to pray for. It wasn't the world's most exciting life but I was admiring of the calm that comes with boringness and plenty. Things were going pretty good until the mother showed up and blabbed out my true identity.

I looked at myself in the bathroom mirror and thought of the comfortable Jesus and the scalloped potatoes. I wondered if any of the international disadvantaged children had discovered the hidden prize I sewed into the head of every sock monkey. Twenty dollars of the father's money and a little square of paper written with the nine best words of his advice.

Expect the Unexpected.
And whenever possible,
BE the Unexpected.

You could call it a kind of memorial to the man. If I had an extra knife to sew into each one I would have done that too. Disadvantaged children sometimes need them. They sometimes need them very badly. Inside of Trina, wrapped in layers of twenty-dollar bills and raw cotton, Little Debbie waited.

When I left East Crawford in the dark final hour of that night, I didn't exactly know where I was going. The only thing I knew for certain was that I was never coming back.

I was wrong about that. But as the father would have said, I was still right.

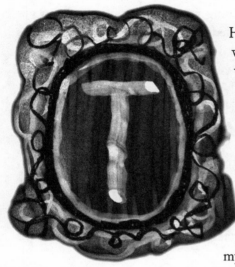

chapter 24

HE FATHER woke me up while it was still dark. He was yawning and said, "Clyde, damn it, I need some help." And what he needed help with was backing the trailer down the dog-leg. Dog-leg is what you call a road that turns like the logging road did, an angle unexpected. I had the flashlight and I did my best even though in the sharp air of the mountains my mind clearly was telling me again to run. Drop the flashlight and run. I looked up through the branches trying to find the sky. I didn't see anything. Not even a star. The back-up lights threw their red glow and the father's face was greenish in the side mirror. I was thinking of what would happen if I did try to run, but I knew it was too late for that. He would never let me go now. And I wondered how bad it would be, really, to die in the forest. To spill out and soak into the fallen pine needles and have it over with.

I ran my tongue along the new gap in my front teeth and remembered the father ramming my face into the dashboard. An inverted "V," rough and sharp and giving a stabbing pain when cold air hit it. It would hurt to die. It would hurt terribly. I'd seen the father with the animals in the slaughterhouse. I'd seen their heads take the face of the Jesus in agony. I will admit I was terrified.

I got back into the car. The father said, "I am tired as shit. Feel like I didn't even close my eyes."

There was a low fog dragging itself through the trees. Fog in motion drifting across the road in the headlights. The father kept yawning and popping his eyes wide and talking about coffee. After a few miles of uphill driving we came to a closed-down gas station and grocery store called Top o' the Pass. The headlights slid over damp old-fashioned walls made of stacked-together stones covered in green-black moss. There was one gas pump and the hose was ripped off and laying in a lazy curve below it. In the window a handwritten sign said HUNTING LICENSES HERE. A larger one said CLOSED FOR SEASON.

The father said, "Shangri-la."

He took the final glugs from last bottle of Old Skull Popper. He said, "Gotta find the crapper," and stumbled around the side of the building. A few seconds later he was back, straddling the trailer hitch and popping open the trunk. He said, "Crapper's locked." He found the crowbar and went back around. I heard the wood splintering.

I rolled down the window and the fog dragged itself in and left a chill inside of me that would not depart. The father was gone a very long time.

I fell asleep and woke up and he still wasn't back. Finally I went looking for him. I found a door that was three-quarters open. I saw the shadow of him on the toilet, leaning against the wall with his head bent in a very weird position. He was snoring.

I considered ways to wake him and in the end I threw a rock. It could have been a smaller rock and I didn't need to throw it so hard and with such good aim but I was feeling moody.

"Ow! Ow!" I heard him holler but he didn't see me. I was back in the car looking asleep before he even got his pants up. He came around the side of the building saying, "It's going to be light soon. We have to haul ass." He stretched his arms out and yawned. "I'm feeling pretty damn good, considering." Then he broke the glass on the grocery store door and called me to help him carry out a couple of armloads of provisions.

There wasn't much to choose from. My flashlight beam moved on piles of mouse evidence. Cobwebs hung from one thing to the next. I opened one of the coolers and a barf-stench clawed out at me, so I shut it. In the end I carried what the father pointed to. All of it seemed dried out and dead. Bulge-top cans here and there.

It started raining again. The road continued downward in gentle looping twists, but even so, the trailer skidded and fish-tailed behind us and the father was cursing it between the words of the story he was wanting me to memorize. The story of our new identities. He said, "Jimmy one of them cans for me, Clyde. All of a sudden I'm feeling hungry. Take the lid all the hell off." I handed him an ancient can of pork and beans and he drank from it, shaking it so chunks fell into his mouth. He said, "Clyde, you know what you and me are? We're just a couple of dumb-asses from North Dakota."

He said "nort" for north. "We're from Milsboro, that's our town. One of the guys on my ship was from Milsboro, North Dakota. North or South, shit, I can't remember which. Don't matter. It's all bum-fuck. So where we from, Clyde?"

I said, "Milsboro."

He said, "Wrong. You don't answer questions. You can't talk. You got faller's disease. Broke your brain. Never get beyond the mental age of five." And he spun out the details, some of them quite fancy. How his wife left him without a warning. How all he had left in the world was a mongolian idiot son who he was trying to spread a little joy to. Taking the boy on a hunting trip, teaching the boy how to shoot. Just drinking and shooting rifles in the woods with a retard to help ease the pain.

"You paying attention, Clyde?" I nodded. I wanted to say that if I was never supposed to talk anyway, why did it matter? There were a lot of things I wanted to say to him but my mouth was not so interested in helping me. It was not going to be hard to play my part of the new identity.

The story he was practicing was for the cops. For if we got stopped. He checked his reflection in the rearview mirror to perfect his look of broke-dick sincerity. "Hell yes, I been drinking, Officer. Don't want to live without her, many a night I come this close, had the rifle barrel in my mouth and my big toe on the trigger. But I got my retard boy to think of, don't I? I can't just turn him loose in the world, can I? So shit yes, Officer. If misery's a crime then lock me up. I don't hardly give a damn no more. Just be good to my boy."

The father inhaled off of one of the stale Old Gold cigarettes he took from the store. "Well, what do you think?" He flashed his wet teeth. "Can't you just see me on *The Movie of the Week*?"

And then for the first time he mentioned the mess in the trailer. How we had to do something about it and he had a damn good idea. He turned onto another logging road, bumped along the ruts for a while, and then stopped the car. He was twitching the radio dial for a station, found one that played his music and said, "Tell me quick, Clyde. Who's that singing?"

I thought, Roy Drusky, but my mouth wouldn't move to say it.

The father said, "Aw come on! You know damn well who that is." His mouth was full when he said it. He smiled at me big through a wet wad of deviled ham. He was feeling jolly. He was feeling optimistic. And he was acting like he liked me a lot.

He said, "Ain't you going to eat? At least have one of them candy bars. I got them for you."

I unwrapped one. The chocolate had gone waxy white. The father took out another ancient Old Gold. He put the lighter to it and said, "Tastes like horse pucky. Want to try?"

I took one. I liked smoking. I was liking it enough to call it love.

He reached over the backseat and pulled up one of the three glass jugs he found behind the counter. They were full of a slightly clouded tea-colored liquid. "Hooch," said the father. "The real deal. Homemade. See what it says here?"

On a crumbling piece of masking tape someone's shaky

handwriting spelled out CORPSE REVIVER.

The father pried off the top and whiffed it. "Hooooo! This shit is a hundred proof. At least. My nose hairs just fell out. Have a snort, Clyde. Come on, son. It'll give you another eye."

I sniffed at the jug. The smell didn't strike me as anything at first and then I saw colored lights behind my eyeballs. I said, "You first."

"All right. Hell." He hooked his finger into the glass loop and balanced the jug on the raised crook of his arm. "This here is how we drink out of a jug back home in Milsboro. Bottoms up." He glugged many glugs and from his eyes rolled burning tears.

He passed it to me and then he started gagging. He started making a wet choking noise and hitting his chest with his fist and then there was an especially creepy sound from the back of his throat. He reached two fingers deep in his mouth and pulled out a rectangular wobbling chunk of fat. He examined it and said, "From that can of beans, I think. Hunk of hog fat they put in the beans." He flung it out the window and said, "Go on, son. Take a pull. You want to learn how to use a rifle? Could come in handy."

I took a glug because I wanted a glug. I was liking the glugs more and more. The swirl they gave me, the curlique slide into nothingness.

He showed me the different features of the rifle he used on Marie Cardall. How to break it down. How to put it back together. Gave a long Navy explanation of the relation of firing pin to the bore axis. Showed me how to load it. Showed me how troubled men used it to blow the top of their heads off, putting the barrel in the mouth, taking aim.

He took more glugs and I took some glugs. It was a strange kind of booze, that Corpse Reviver. It didn't taste bad. It didn't burn. Not in the first ten seconds. And then it just exploded and made you exhale sentimental ignitable fumes. I got wobbly, very wobbly. He got wobbly. He said we ought to drink one to Uncle Lemuel and to any other son of a bitch stupid enough to get in our way. He asked me was it me that pitched that rock at his head

147

when he was sitting on the toilet. I told him yes it was. He told me it hurt like hell but he was glad I told the truth and if I ever pulled a stunt like that again he would mash me like a fly. And he smiled and I smiled back.

The clouds blew away and the sky above us was clear and inky blue. Very clear with sparking starlight and moonlight falling so strangely. We were sitting outside with the rifle. First he was holding it then I was holding it then he had it again.

"Know what we're waiting for, Clyde?"

I said, "No."

He said, "We're waiting for an explanation."

I thought it was strange, him saying that and looking up at the moon. And I was thinking of Ardus Cardall coming home after he buried that Leonards boy under two tons of concrete and telling it to Marie, mentioning how he was hoping the whole thing would just somehow blow over. And right then I felt like I understood Ardus Cardall's logic. Let the past stay in the past. A person makes mistakes. A person has to move on.

After all the things that happened, described and unde- scribed, if I told you I still loved the father would you understand it? How there was a wire of love running inside of me that I just could not find to pull? It was the side effect of being someone's child, anyone's child, whoever God tossed you to.

I was thinking maybe it could work. Maybe we would set up a new life someplace in the yonder and the past would somehow tumble into the hole of forgetfulness. My tingling lips spoke these hopes out loud to the father as the dark conifers rubber-swayed around me. I told him I would never do to him what Marie Cardall did to Ardus. I'd never go to the authorities.

The father laughed a little. He said, "Hell, Clyde, I hate to break it to you, but I'd never give you the chance."

And there in the forest we sat, him with the rifle, sitting very still, waiting for a certain sound, a certain movement in the brush, an explanation.

Any hunter could tell you there were too many smells coming

148

from our way. The father smelled horrible. I'm sure I did too. The trailer alone could clear the area. It wasn't a bad thing to take a glug. It could burn. It could blister. But it kept the thoughts apart, it kept the sweet dizzy tunnel rocking. Any hunter could tell you no deer were coming anywhere near us. Unless that hunter was Navy. Unless that hunter was a Navy man from Milsboro.

An orange flash. BLAM!!! The father's body jerked back hard. It's called recoil. He jumped up and stumbled toward the thrashing with a handful of shells. BLAM! BLAM! BLAM! I told God I didn't care. I didn't care. I was Navy.

The father shouted, "Flip the lights, Clyde. High beams!"

He dragged the creature into the illuminated spill. Blown apart bad. Shot to near disintegration in some places. Dazzle camouflage.

I am someone who can look at certain things without flinching. Certain dead people. Particular dead people. But I cannot look at the creatures. I have tried and tried. In the days of the slaughterhouse I had so many opportunities. And I was whipped many times for turning them loose. Opening the holding pen gates and whispering "Run, run." Even though there was nowhere for them to go. No chance in this world. "Run!" I'd whisper to the cattle. Sometimes they would. Mostly they just bunched together, leaning tighter, and stared at me. But I could not stop trying. Locating the father wire was nothing compared to finding the wire of hope for the creatures. And that is a most dangerous wire. It will make you do things. When you run out of glugs, when you run out of Corpse Reviver and Old Skull Popper and especially Whitley's, that wire is the one that can get somebody killed.

The father had Old Dad's knife case out. Green velvet inside. A blank space where the boning knife Francine used to lay before the father snapped her like stick. He touched the spot with his finger. "That's a wound that will never heal, Clyde. Old Dad owes me. He owes me. He can never pay me back for what he's done."

Glug glug. "Here, Clyde. Drink to the bastard."

"And to her," I said.

"Who?"

I pointed to the steaming creature. "Her."

The father said, "Shit."

The knife the father chose was Big Girl. A twelve inch that would not hold an edge for long and had no flexibility, but for the time she was sharp she was loyal, insane, very strong. The father petted her edge with the side of his thumb. Then he ran her so wrong against the whetstone the hair rose on the back of my neck. He was dulling her. Big Girl dull could take a man's thumb off. Dull knives. All butchers fear them.

The father said, "She's wrong, but that's the point." He started hacking. He made some grunt sounds as he took the creature apart. He said, "Why the hell use a twelve inch for anything I'll never know. All you need to take anything apart is an eight-inch Forsner with a lot of flex. You have a ten inch and a six inch and you got it made. Old Dad said shit on R. H. Forsner but I'm telling you Clyde, to hell with Old Dad. Forsners are the best knives going. First thing I'm going to do when all this is over? I'm getting me a set of Forsners. Complete. Hell yes, I am."

And he told me to open the trailer door, and he started handing me warm chunks of the creature. He told me to throw them into the trailer. He said, "Throw, Clyde. Hard. Don't be a pussy. Fire it." He wanted a mess. Because that was the explanation.

The father's voice was so sadly speaking. Sadly explaining it again to the imaginary cop. "Shit yes, Officer. I've had a few tonight. I'm not apologizing for it. Shoot me. Shoot my boy. She left us. We don't got no reason to live anymore. We'd thank you to do it. We got a deer back there and a pile of fish but I don't know shit about what to do with any of it, don't know shit about gutting, quartering, dressing. I made a mess of things. I'm flying by the seat of my pants here, sir. Jesus God I loved her. She was apeshit half the time but I didn't mind. Had a bramble up her ass and threw squirrels at me, but I lived for her. I don't understand it. I can't pretend to understand it. I miss her, Officer."

The father was crying. Actual tears were spilling down his face. His voice was hoarse. And real tears spilled from my eyes too. I couldn't control it. The sadness of the story. His shaking voice when he told it. The booze. All of it had us both crying over the hacked-apart creature in the middle of the dark woods. Both of us taking more glugs just because.

The father was singing, his voice lifting through the black tangle of trees.

The father wiped his face and smeared blood across his cheek. He said, "What song is that, Clyde? You know it. I know you do." But I didn't.

Above us the sky lightened. The world had spun us into a new day. I didn't look often at the face of the father. But I looked then and saw his wet eyes looking back from beneath sagging folds. And I couldn't help thinking how his eyes were the exact color of the skim mold that floated in the slaughterhouse ham vat. I told God I didn't care.

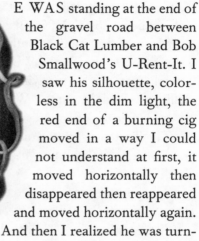

chapter 25

E WAS standing at the end of the gravel road between Black Cat Lumber and Bob Smallwood's U-Rent-It. I saw his silhouette, colorless in the dim light, the red end of a burning cig moved in a way I could not understand at first, it moved horizontally then disappeared then reappeared and moved horizontally again. And then I realized he was turning, spinning slow. And on the other side of Dunbar Avenue the yellow-lit Diggy's Drive-In sign was also spinning slow. They were spinning together. Diggy the bull standing like a man with a chef's hat on, offering a hamburger made from his personal meat and the Turtle blowing clouds of the ancient smokeable into the beginnings of the morning sky. I was thinking, *Is he waiting for me?* A little thrill ran up my spine and sparked in the back of my throat. I lifted my hand. "Turtle. Hey, Turtle."

A dark car pulled up next to him. The guy driving said, "Turtle. What it is. I'm late, guy. I'm sorry, man."

The Turtle leaned into the car and said some words. The guy driving said, "Where?"

The Turtle pointed in my direction. The guy said, "Hell yes!" He turned his car into the Diggy's parking lot and parked beside the Dumpster. Pigeons ran out of many hiding places to meet him. He was tall and thin with a Diggy's uniform on. Black slacks and a yellow shirt that said, HAVE YOU DUG DIGGY'S?

The Turtle made a come-on motion with his arm before he crossed the street. I felt the miraculousness of us finding each other again drain away. He didn't seem surprised to see me. I was thinking, is it because he's a hippie? Is it because no hippie is ever surprised by anything? People show up, people disappear, and people show up again because it is all so cosmic. Maybe the Turtle was just being cosmic. It was possible.

Some of the pigeons split off from the Diggy's guy and walked over to the Turtle. When I got to the parking lot, I heard him talking to the birds, saying, "What it is, what it is, what it is." Calling the birds by name. "What it is, Stump Foot, Greasy Wing Dragger, Greasy Wing Dragger Junior."

The Turtle gestured from the pigeons to me, he said, "Meet your Queen. You will love her. Her motto is, 'Cold french fries for all.'"

The Diggy's worker wore a plastic engraved badge that said DANNY, but the Turtle introduced him as the Monkey.

The Monkey said, "This is her? I thought you said she was very horny looking."

The Turtle said, "That is the Violent One. This is the Hillbilly Woman."

"Oh." He lifted a hand and said, "Hey."

"Hey," I said.

He looked at the Turtle. "So, is she coming? The violent girl-whatever? She part of this?"

I almost said "Part of what?" But the Turtle put his arm around me and said, "Let's go inside and roll a fatty."

The Diggy's worker said, "Man, there's no horny-looking violent girl-whatever. It's just more of your psych-out bullshit, man. She's just another psych."

The Turtle said, "The Violent One is not just another psych. She's *the* psych. She is watching you this moment in her cyanotic ICU2 TV set. She is leaning forward and hooting her magic horn. We will get the Hillbilly Woman very very high and she will lead us over the smaragdine mountain to a quiet pool where the Violent One awaits you."

The Monkey said, "It's just more of your bullshit so forget it, fuck it, it don't matter."

I said, "Smaragdine?"

The Turtle said, "From '*Increase Your Word Power*.'"

"Vocabulary," I said.

"Absolutely," said the Turtle.

"Piss on it," said the Monkey.

He jingled some keys, unlocked some locks, and we followed him through the side door into a narrow hallway, stepping over brooms and dirty mops and then into a storeroom. I was still waiting for the Turtle to say something about how incredible it was for us to find each other again, and to ask me what happened after he dumped his stash and ran away from the rolling cop, and then to ask me about the fate of his stash, and then to have me blow his mind by reaching calmly into Vicky's purse and handing it to him.

I looked at him expectantly but all he did was nod and gesture to the stocked shelves and say, "Hungry? Can I interest you in anything? Buns? Sweet relish?"

I was wondering if it was the presence of the Monkey that kept the Turtle from bringing up all the bulging questions. I was watching his eyes but they were giving no clues. The irises were showing and I was surprised by the color. A tiger color, orange-yellow flecked with brown.

"Tray," said the Monkey. "Tray."

The Turtle nodded. The Monkey said, "Sec," and left the room.

"Hillbilly Woman," said the Turtle.

"Turtle," said I.

And then he kissed me. Hard. Very hard. Mashing his mouth against mine. When he pulled away I saw his gums were bleeding. The Monkey came back with a smaller version of a lunchroom tray. The Turtle pulled out a bag of the ancient smokeable and dumped it on the tray and proceeded to roll a few fatties.

The Monkey said, "So, Turtle. You got something for me, right?"

"There has been a complication."

"Fuck."

"Yes."

The Turtle pushed a paper twist at the Monkey who stuck it in his mouth and lit a match.

"Fuck," said the Monkey, and then he took his inhale.

"Indeed," said the Turtle. We passed several circles of Sir Fatty. I was getting very stoned. I reached into Vicky's purse and said, "I got a surprise for you, Turtle. Guess what I have of yours?" His tigered eyes flickered the smallest warning flare and I stopped.

The Monkey blew out a cloud and said, "What is it?"

The Turtle's eyes flickered again and then went out.

I said, "This." I pulled out Trina.

The Monkey started laughing.

The Turtle reached for her, saying, "Lost, and by the wind grieved, Ghost, come back again."

After many different subjects were brought up and commented on and dropped, the Monkey said to me, "Were you like, in a car accident?"

I said, "Car accident?"

"Your nose and your teeth. What is the deal? No offense, OK?"

I can be very sensitive about the various smashed aspects of my face but Sir Fatty got me feeling free. My teeth have certain benefits. I can whistle ear-splitters. I can shoot unbelieveably precise jets of water across a room. I shot one out for the Monkey. He seemed like the kind of person who would like it. He fell against the cooler scream-laughing. I had a new friend.

The Turtle said, "And now tell us the story of your finger."

"Finger?" said the Monkey.

Instinctively I closed my left hand into a fist. When it is in a fist, my finger situation is hard to detect. People almost never notice it unless I want them to. But the Turtle had noticed it.

"Please," he said. "Show us." And I hesitated but the father's voice did not scream at me for the hesitation. When it came to my finger situation I do not think the father had anything more to say.

The Turtle set Trina on the condiments shelf and took my hand and opened it.

The Monkey said, "Whoa."

My left index. Called the pointer. I only have half of it. Tough crabbing scars cover the middle joint and creep down the sides, giving it a melted candle look. They're called keloid formations. Some people are prone to them.

I watched the Monkey slowly hide his hands. I have noticed that people will do this. He said, "Accident?"

I said, "It was removed."

The Turtle said, "Violently? Purposely?"

"Both."

The Monkey said, "Wait, man, whoa. Someone like, *cut* your finger off on *purpose*? Like, not a doctor? Like, just an average *person*?"

I started laughing. It was the word "average."

There was a knock on the side door. A man saying, "Danny? Goddamn it, who you got in there with you?"

The Monkey jumped, freaking. "Fuck! FUCK! Uncle Myronto!" He clawed at the air to try and break up the cosmic clouds.

"He wants my head on a spike," the Turtle said. "We must depart."

I grabbed Trina and shoved her in Vicky's purse.

The Monkey said, "Other door, other door. THAT door! Go! Go!"

We slipped out, keeping close to the cinder-block walls, listening to Uncle Myronto scream at Danny from the other side. BLAM! BLAM! BLAM! "Open the door!"

A cop car skidded off Dunbar and into the parking lot.

The Turtle ran, tearing up the street, diving into the first bushes he came to.

The Monkey put his calm paper-hatted head around the side door. "Hey, Uncle Myronto. What's going down?"

The cop car did a tight turn that brought it my way. I freaked and got the Turtle's stash out of Vicky's purse and dropped it into the Dumpster.

The cops hit the siren and the lights, and floored it back onto Dunbar. They were using Diggy's parking lot as a turn-around.

Uncle Myronto went berserk. "IT'S NOT A RACE-TRACK! IT'S NOT A FRIGGING RACETRACK!" He ran inside and in a few seconds I could hear him screaming into the phone.

"WHAT?! HELL *YES* THIS IS AN EMERGENCY! YOU PEOPLE THINK MY PLACE IS A GODDAMN RACE-TRACK! WHAT?! *NO*! HELL NO! DON'T YOU PUT ME ON HOLD! DON'T YOU—GOD*DAMN* IT!"

I heard the Monkey saying, "Whoa, Uncle Myronto, your blood pressure, man. Danger."

I boosted myself up the side of the Dumpster to retrieve the stash. A rotted-meat smell drifted and the yellow jackets swarmed. I saw what I thought was the top of the can laying low in clotted grease. The Monkey came up behind me and I instantly jumped down. In a low voice he said, "Turtle in there?"

"No," I said.

"Because he does sometimes hide in there."

"He got away."

The Monkey rubbed his face. "I'm so fried. Are you fried? You look fried."

"I'm very fried."

"The Turtle burned me. He thinks he can fuck with me. Do you know when he got out? He wouldn't tell me. He won't tell me anything."

"Out?" I said.

"Of Barbara V. Hermann. You know, the home."

"Oh yes," I said. "The home."

He looked at me from the side of his eye. He said, "You don't know about him do you? I bet you just met him."

"No."

"Lie. He ask you to go to New Orleans? That's his first question to everybody."

"No."

"Did he tell you he's Canadian and he knows Neil Young?"

"No."

"His parents are rich as fuck, man. They own Channel Three. He won't tell you that though, because it's true. They're looking for him. I'm thinking of turning him in."

He pulled out a pack of Salems. "Fag cigs, I know. Want?"

I took one and he lit mine and his off the same match. Uncle Myronto was still yelling into the phone. Someone on the other end seemed to be listening.

The Monkey said, "The Turtle does got the good drugs, though. That part's for real. And he gets the girls, man. Ugly little dude, but he always has the women. He's always telling me he's going to get me laid. And I'm always stupid enough to believe him."

I blew a smoke ring. He said, "Is that girl, that violent girl-whatever, is she real?"

I said, "Vicky?"

He said, "That her name? Because the Turtle never calls anybody by their actual names. Like I don't even know your name. What is it? Because I know it's not Hillbilly Woman."

A yellow jacket did a tight circle by my face and I swatted at it. The Monkey said, "Don't, man. That just pisses them off. What's your name? You know what is super weird about you, and I'm not saying this just because I'm high, OK? Your face, you know, it's—"

I looked away.

He said, "No, man, listen, it's good, it's good, I mean your face is totally fucked up, right? But it is totally amazing, I'm serious. I should be thinking you are like, very ugly, you know, but I am just getting very blown away by you, and like, are you a virgin?"

chapter 26

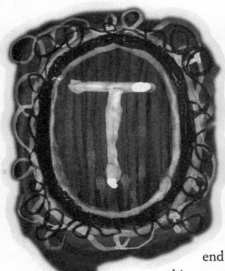

URTLE? TURTLE? Turtle?" I whispered to every bush in the vicinity but could not find him. I was thinking I should just try to get cosmic. I should just try to get cosmic like a hippie and expand to the natural flow but that didn't work either. It was my ear-splitter whistle that did it. The Turtle appeared at the end of an alleyway. I followed him to a garage. He twisted the T-shaped handle. The garage door lifted about two feet and then stopped. I rolled under and the Turtle followed and the door fell shut.

There was one window, clouded with grime and an old car with flat tires. Everything was covered with layers of drifting dirt.

There were peat moss bags stacked against the back wall. We made ourselves comfortable on those. I didn't know how to tell the Turtle I dumped his stash and how I was too freaked to crawl into the Dumpster to get it back. Turtle wanted to kiss. His breath was rasty, but I noticed I did not mind his arms around me. My biting urge was weak and then weaker and then it was gone. There was some frenching before he pulled away. He said, "I just dropped two hits of Windowpane and I—wait, wait." He reached in his pocket and unfolded a piece of gold origami paper.

He said, "Open your mouth. Lift up your tongue. Sublingual is the way. Sublingual is the only way. I'm in love with you, Hillbilly Woman. You need to be with me."

He sounded very sincere. I was thinking about the warning words of the Monkey but they shriveled away in the new lushness of touching; I was shaking from it. Looking into his eyes and watching the tiger irises melt away into expanding black.

He took my left hand and examined my finger again, touching the hard-ridged scars. He turned it over and traced the Tiparillo scar. "Tell me. Tell me everything." And my rushing feelings were strong. When he ran his hands over me I did not flinch. He lifted my shirt and I put my arms up to help him.

I am not a developed person. There has been almost no development. And I thought I would not be able to stand it, being looked at the way he was looking at me, letting his fingers circle my places. He touched the inside of my arm where the words are. He traced the small raised scars spelling out the words, *I'm sorry*.

He looked at me without blinking. "You did this?"

I nodded.

He said, "You're perfect."

There was something I should have told him then, a little bit of information he could have used, but I didn't want to interrupt the picture he was seeing of me. Or the twining captivation curling in my throat, making me lift my chin until my head fell back. And too there was the sublingual addition of the Windowpane. One hit or two hits. He never told me.

He said, talk. Talk and keep talking and do not stop talking because it was so good that way. Close my eyes and keep talking while he kissed the places, keep talking, keep talking while he touched every part of me.

chapter 27

HEN WE rolled out of the wet mountains, there was a shock waiting. The land suddenly went flat and dry except for irrigated fields with high jets pulsing, and canals of violently swift water. It was a place of scrubby orchards and reservation Indians and migrant Mexicans and tumbling white trash. And there were miles of stockyards on either side of the potholed road, full of groaning cattle standing together around low muddy hills of feed. And there was a place where you could see it all from a single bar stool. Have you ever heard of a place called the Knocking Hammer?

The father found it in a very cosmic way. He finished the first jug of Corpse Reviver and instead of knocking him down, it made him precise and activated. He was just rattling with expanding action, taking smaller and smaller roads, looking for the right place along the irrigation canal to kill me on. He was so happy to see the canal. Not the culverts, not the corrugated half pipe that carried a bit of water here and there. It was the concrete canal that fascinated him. Dry and empty until the sluice gates opened. He was calmly explaining how perfect it would be because he could kill me right in the concrete ditch itself and when the water came it would gush me and all of the evidence away.

He said he was sorry, but it just wasn't working out anymore. He wanted me to know it wasn't anything personal, nothing I did or didn't do. The problem was the hundred complications a kid couldn't help but bring along. That, and the possibility of me breaking down and saying something that would put him up shit creek. He said he'd had enough of shit creek. He told me he knew just how to do it, he'd use Sheila and it wouldn't hurt at all, and he would go to hell for it, if that made me feel any better. And while he laid out his plan I stared out the window with an old sentence he threw out once, repeating in my brain. *"Freight cars are empty, that's why she bounces."*

He followed the concrete canal until he came onto a road that was hardly more than two ruts through the dirt. It took us to land so bare it looked like it had been burned. Beside the road were train tracks and beside the train tracks was the dry canal bed. He pulled up close to a low berm, called a berm, a stretch of fortified earth built up from the ground a little so that the train can run free and clear on the flat tracks that disappeared into infinity. And I was remembering how the father told me that anyone could derail a train, a five-year-old could do it with a tablespoon. You just had to be patient. It could take you a couple of months but there wasn't any magic to it. You just dig away at the berm. Dig it out from under the tracks, dig away and dig away and the day will come when you have pulled away the right number of spoonfuls. It was mathematics. And the one thing your average man does not know about train tracks in a derailment is that they will spear right up through the cars like a knife through a box of animal crackers.

The father opened the second jug of Corpse Reviver and passed it to me. I didn't want any. In my mind I saw my name added to the list that included Doolie Bug and Uncle Lemuel. That started with Marie Cardall. Or maybe the Leonards boy buried in the foundation. Or maybe it was Old Dad. Or maybe it was that certain ancient monkey. The monkey with the most meat wins.

The father and I crossed over the train tracks. I was wonder-

ing if he forgot about Little Debbie or if he remembered Little Debbie and what I was going to do about it either way.

It was full afternoon in the middle of nowhere. We were in plain sight if anyone was looking. Dazzle camouflage. Very Navy. We stood on the edge of the canal together. He told me again that he'd make it easy on me, to lift my chin and let my head fall back and look at the sky, I wasn't going to notice a thing.

I stabbed my arm backwards and Little Debbie bit into his leg. And then two things happened. Two things came thundering straight for us. The first was the water roar-rushing, it came with such a sudden groan and churning furiousness that it froze the father's action. And then came the scream-whistle of the black train, a train really hauling, if you have ever seen one hauling, if you have seen them speed when the land is open and the light is good and the track is a straightaway. When the conductor and the engineer just look at each other and say, Why the fuck not?

And the whistle screamed and screamed and screamed because the father parked the car and the trailer so freakishly close to the track, very close to the knife-shiny rails, and the conductor and the engineer were saying, *the stupid son of a bitch, the stupid little bastard, the stupid son of a bitch, the stupid little bastard*, and I saw the father step back and stumble and his face was very white. It was too fast, too much like falling, everything rushing at him like that. He lost his balance and grabbed on to me, I was thinking we could fall either way, water or train, water or train, and I wished train. Train. I'd rather explode.

But I didn't explode. And when the last car shot away down the track flying, there was a new element in our situation, someone watching us from the driver's seat of a car parked alongside ours, and the car had a big yellow star on the door with COUNTY SHERIFF painted in a half circle in black. Behind the wheel, there he was.

He spotted us on the way to the Knocking Hammer for his usual afternoon binger, driving slowly through land so open he always had an excellent view of the local goings-on of nothing, because nothing is what there usually was, so you could say we stuck out.

I said, "Cop. Cop."

The father hissed me quiet.

The sheriff leaned his head out of his rolled-down window and shouted something our way. I felt Little Debbie get wrenched out of my hand and I felt her sharp point in my back. The sheriff shouted something like what asshole parked his car so close to the track?

The father said, "Wave at him." Little Debbie gave a little nudge, just a paper-cut nudge.

I waved.

The father called out, "My boy here, he was feeling a little sick. Let him out to puke."

Barely moving his mouth the father spoke low. "He's County, Clyde. He's just half a turd."

The sheriff got out of his car. You would expect him to be fat. Fat with a gut hanging over his confused pants and a big double-wobble chin and a bullet head with tiny eyes peeping out. But this man was made out of whip wire. Slender and hard looking with eyes barely blue; they were the color of cigarette smoke.

We didn't have any choice but to shamble back to where he was standing, he was obviously wanting to strike up a conversation, whiffing at the trailer, saying, "Who died? That'd scare the stink off shit. And you two look like you been attacked by the goddamn Mexican ho-dag. Looks like blood, hell, looks like you're still bleeding there on your leg. What the hell's going on?"

The father's hand on my shoulder gave me a squeeze and our new identities rose on this command. It was a freakish sensation to feel them come to life so naturally, to witness the father drain away and the brokenhearted barber from bum-fuck take his place. We walked toward the sheriff and he put a hand to his hip and drew his gun.

chapter 28

ET US cuT youR MeaT We WiLl DReSs YouR meAt wE WilL bUy YOur MEaT we Will PAy CAsh BeSt PricEs tHE BesT nOnE bEttER cuStoM HousE ButCher hoUSe louNgE gRocERy CamPinG this is what was written on the side of the long sagging building that was part of the Knocking Hammer. It was painted in a variety of letter sizes, smalls and capitals mixed, looking random, looking distracted, looking half out of the bag.

The Knocking Hammer is where the sheriff took us after he looked in the trailer and finished hearing the father's story, which the father told without ever looking directly at the gun the sheriff kept pointed at him in an almost casual way.

"Milsboro," said the sheriff. "You'll have to show me on a map."

The father said, "If you got a map that shows little pinprick towns, sure."

"Barber, huh?" said the sheriff. "You take a drink?"

"Oh yes," said the father. "I'm not going to lie about it."

They were getting along even though the sheriff kept his gun out for the whole conversation. He had the star and all the father had was a stinking trailer and a mongoloid son. How shitty. That was the sheriff's comment. How shitty, and what will happen to the boy when he gets older?

They were getting along but they were circling. The father told me later he knew he was in fine shape from the start because he never met a county sheriff yet who wasn't a lying bastard. "It's an elected position, Clyde. You scratch his ass and he scratches yours."

The sheriff was sniffing out potential. Right away the father knew the sheriff was dangling a possibility in front of him because of which questions he asked and which questions he didn't.

The sheriff said for us to follow him. He knew a place where we could get cleaned up. Get ourselves together. Campground with hookups for the trailer. Bar. Grocery. Whatever we needed. The lady who ran the place was a cousin of his, a widow, Pammy. She took over the whole operation once the Original Swede became the Dead Swede. And she liked new faces and she loved children.

"What they got to drink up that way?" asked the father.

"You heard of Whitley's?"

"Lead on!"

In the car on the way to the Knocking Hammer the father went over the rules and regulations of being the mongoloid son and I stared out the window and watched the land change like it had a mental illness. Dead and barren became spinach, chard, and cabbage glittering with the pulsing spray from long-wheeled irrigators, and then a dead stockyard with knocked-down fence posts and a collapsed ramp and then a dumping ground for junk cars and raw garbage with turkey buzzards circling overhead and then sudden low orchards, peaches it looked like, with migrants reaching into scraggly trees with dirty pick-sacks slung over their shoulders.

And then it was barren again, looking quite scorched, and then we came to the Knocking Hammer.

The smell from the feedlot was instant and strong. A nose-twister of super-heated cattle pee and the further nose-twister from the cull pile behind the slaughter shack. More turkey buzzards. The sound of a meat saw buzzing. The familiar flies rising up in greeting. It was a dilapidated operation, small and ratty, but the father's face lit up when he saw it. He patted the steering wheel and said, "Well, I'll be a son-of-a-bitch." He looked over at me but I turned away before our eyes met. He never mentioned what happened at the edge of the canal. For the father it was another world ago. The balance didn't carry over. He said, "This lady, this Pammy, she likes kids. I want you to honey-up to her, Clyde. And the sheriff too. Come on then." He got out of the car.

There were some barefoot kids with slept-on hair and dusty legs wearing raggy shorts and tank tops watching us from in front of one of the Knocking Hammer entrances with "Gro STORE" painted above the door. The kids were licking their tongues into the tops of empty Fanta bottles and picking their faces and jumping up onto the sagging porch to try to see into our car. One ran up very close to my window and the sheriff cuffed him. They scattered around the side of the building.

I looked at myself in the wing mirror and saw my eyes looking back through holes in a horrible head, my face was swollen and bruised and there was a pounding pain behind my forehead that was getting louder. The father said, "Quit dragging ass, Clyde."

There were a couple of cars parked cockeyed out front. The sheriff was late and the regulars who gathered to hear his afternoon wisdom were watching for him. When they heard him haw-hawing so loud outside, they came out of the door marked LOUNGE. They were rubbed-out men. Looking like old hard erasers.

The sheriff was standing at the open trailer door. Around him flocks of new flies were rushing in, attracted by a scent, a new drift of promising molecules. "HAW-HAW!" brayed the sheriff. Then his smile dropped away and he turned to the father, pulled out his gun and said, "You're under arrest, you bastard."

The father jerked so slightly, the movement was hardly visible to the human eye. A fly would have noticed it. The compound eye makes even the most minuscule motion seem huge. And I was thinking that maybe the sheriff was part fly because he saw it. He saw it and he kept his hard-faced expression for a few more seconds and then laughed harder. He said to the men, "You see his face! HAW HAW." He tapped the father with the gun barrel. "Got ya, Milsboro! Haw haw haw!"

The father saw the men with eyes and ears open for a show. It was just a show. The sheriff called them over to have a look inside the trailer. He jerked his thumb at the father. "Do you know this joker tried to sell a county sheriff deer meat off-season?" And I watched the sheriff lie and the father follow.

The sheriff said, "And look at how he fixed it up for me. Don't it just look mouthwatering?"

More haw-haws. The father played to the sheriff. He said, "Now where's this Pammy?"

"Ho!" said the sheriff. "You'll know her when you see her. Somebody call to Fernst. Somebody call Fernst to help with this mess."

One of the men loped back inside. I heard him holler "Fernst? Fernst?"

A woman's voice shouted, "What do you want with him? Don't you go in there. He's on the job! Goddamn you, get your dried-up ass back on the other side of the bar. Who wants him?"

There was some low-voiced conversation and then the man loped back out and the sound of the meat saw stopped. The sheriff said, "You go on inside, son. You tell Pammy I said for her to give you a red soda pop."

"Well," said the father. "He don't exactly talk."

The sheriff said, "Oh, shit, that's right." He looked at the men and said, "Mongolian idiot. Genuine."

"Boy's pretty busted up," said one.

The sheriff said, "Faller's disease. Brain troubles. Thrashing spasms." He talked like he'd known about me for years. "He'll never get beyond the mental age of five."

"Like Fernst," said one of the men.

"Yup," said the sheriff. "He's a little spooker, just like Fernst."

I didn't look at the father even though I felt his eye rays on me. He wanted me to throw him a look, to let him know I was cooperating. The sheriff was adding his own bits and pieces to my story and the father was counting on a good trade-in for it. I could hear him in my pounding head, *Look at me Clyde, look up at me.*

The sheriff touched my shoulder and my teeth exposed themselves and I fought to put my lips in a smile around them. He said, "Go on inside, son, Pammy's a natural mother. She'll know what to do with you."

The father said, "Go on, Clyde. Don't be shy." He was still hoping I would look at him. I didn't.

I walked though a screen door that was more chicken wire than screen. Flies could come and go as they pleased. My eyes were adjusting to the dimness, I walked a few paces and a voice said, "Freeze!" It was the same lady's voice. "Don't take another step, you little shit."

She was a big pinch-faced woman with hair that was crispy-fried blond, like old doll hair that had been rubbed all day on the sidewalk. Her eyes were squinting mean and she was blowing snorts of cig smoke at me. She said, "Get the hell back outside. Don't filthify in here."

I didn't move. She didn't insist. She leaned to look out the doorway. "That your old man?"

I nodded.

"Where's your mother at?" I shrugged.

She heaved the bar rag at me. "Wipe your face. You know what little boys like you grow up to be? Do you, huh? Ask me because I know."

With my eyes I said, "What?"

She said, "Assholes. Can you spell that?"

Through a row of small rectangular windows along the far wall I saw a tall man carrying chunks of the hacked-apart deer on his shoulders. He was dressed in butcher clothes stiff with blood. The father was saying something that made everybody start wheeze-laughing. Pammy regarded him and I watched something like thinking going on behind her eyes.

I thought my smell glands were dead from all the overload but the bar rag stank so bad it brought them back to life. I wiped my face, thinking honey-up, honey-up to her and felt the transfer of the filthy smell of a horrible thing that never dried out.

Pammy watched the father. "He don't fool me. Your old man? He don't fool me at all."

She had a dead front tooth. A blue front tooth. And when she came from around the side of the bar to get a better look at the father I saw her huge stomach fat folds hanging over pink stretch shorts, hanging flatly like she had been deflated. Her boobs hung flatly too under a pink sleeveless blouse. And her bare legs were a horrible white with knotted humps of veins under the skin looking blue and mold green and twisted. She wore sling-backs with sad little bows sagging at the toe line. She rocked her dead tooth with her thumb and watched every move the father made.

From the ceiling above her hung hundreds of yellowed rolls of flypaper, some ancient, some recent, all looking like horror party decorations and loaded with flies. When one got full, Pammy just got the step stool out and hung another one. They stretched in every direction all the way to the corners. The bar was a horseshoe shape with the open end pointing toward a doorway that opened into a long hall. At the far end a back door to the outside was wide open.

Through the door I could see the butcher man pass one way and then pass the other way and then pass back again, like he was pacing. He was very strange looking, earthworm looking, is the only way I can describe it. His posture was in constant motion, going from question mark to exclamation mark and back again, and all his extremities, including his head, seemed to flatten and retract and then extend and sharpen. He was chomping on something while he paced. Eating something in his wiggling bloody hand. From the colors on the dangling wrapper I was thinking it was a Three Musketeers bar. He stepped up into the hall and I looked away. A door opened and closed and a locking bolt was thrown. The meat saw started up again. That was Fernst. And he didn't talk either except when he went, "Hoooo-hoooo."

Hanging on a wall behind the liquor bottle display was a calendar. In big letters it said DON'T MONKEY AROUND. ASK FOR WHITLEY'S! Underneath was a picture of a chimpanzee dressed in a nurse's uniform and holding a huge hypodermic needle. She was sticking her lips out. The caption said, WHO ORDERED A SHOT?

The sheriff stepped up and spoke to Pammy through the screen. "You think we could get Grandma-ma to clean out this trailer?" Pammy started to open the door and the sheriff said, "You don't want to look. It'll make you puke, I guarantee it."

Pammy said, "I've never puked in my life."

The sheriff said, "Well, this could be your lucky day."

And they talked about it some more and a dusty Fanta child was sent with a message to Grandma-ma that there was fresh deer meat waiting if she wanted to earn it. The sheriff called, "And you tell her Pammy'll throw in a couple pounds of tripe if she's fast about it."

Pammy said, "The hell I will."

The sheriff said, "What do you think of Clyde?"

Pammy said, "Who?"

The sheriff nodded his head at me. "His name's Clyde. I think a red pop and a bag of chips would put him right. That sound good to you, Clyde? He don't talk."

Pammy said, "What brand of shit are you trying to stir up here, Arden?"

The sheriff said, "Well, that depends on you."

The father and the men came in and rounds were poured. I never got the red pop and chips. I didn't care. What I wanted was a cigarette. I noticed the father pinching at his thigh. Trying to keep some blood-stopping pressure where Little Debbie got him. I went over and did a Helen Keller tug at his arm. I made my fingers into a scissoring "V" and met his eyes with sincerity.

"Naw," said one of the men. "He don't smoke!"

"Oh yes," said the father, tapping out a cig for me. "Keep an eye on your smokes and your lighters. He can be quick."

He lit it for me and I gave him the same clear-eyed look of co-operation. The man said, "Now all he needs is a shot to go with it, haw-haw."

The father said, "He'll drink you under the table, I ain't shitting." He handed his shot of Whitley's to me and I downed it, stuck my lips out and knocked the glass against the bar for more. Everybody laughed. I was honeying-up. I wanted the father to believe that.

The sheriff tilted his head at me. "He's so damn ugly he's cute. You know who he reminds me of? That little humped over Ee-gore from that movie, what the hell was it, that horror one? Come on over here, Ee-gore."

The father said, "He bites."

"Haw," said the sheriff.

"I'm telling you," the father said. "He bit our minister in the gonad one time. Talk about embarrassment."

HAW HAW HAW

The sheriff swept his hand over his privates. "Mine are so big he'd never get a grip."

HAW HAW HAW

Pammy kept her eyes on the father. She refilled his shot glass without him making a move toward it. The father lifted it and nodded a thanks to her and held her eye while he drank it down.

Behind the Knocking Hammer was the campground and it was divided into two parts. One had hookups and one was primitive. The hookup section was where they unhitched the trailer and propped it steady with cement blocks. The primitive section was farther back past the scrub hedge and it was all migrants. Pammy said she didn't give a damn where they camped as long as they paid their five dollars a week and stayed out of her line of vision.

The father said we might as well clean up and the sheriff

showed us to the shower stalls and stood around and lingered, acting like he wanted to stay, but the father told him I was hellishly shy and finally he left.

The stalls had warped plywood doors and no hot water. The wooden floor turned slippery slick when the water hit it. The father soaped up on his side and then threw the soap over the top to me. Some of the dusty kids were circling. They closed in and an eyeball came peeping on the father's side and he popped out naked and dangling. "I'll kill you little fuckers! Get away from here!"

He pulled my door open and pointed a finger at me and then pointed to his leg, to where I stuck in Little Debbie. He made half of a laugh noise but he wasn't smiling. He went back to his stall.

After the shower the father felt like a new man. He walked up to find Pammy to see if she had a needle and some thread. When she asked him what for, he told her he was such a dumb-ass he stabbed himself in the leg trying to open a can of beans and she got out a big first-aid kit and offered to stitch the father herself. So he sat on a chair with his pants down and a bottle of Whitley's to take some of the sting out and she kneeled on the floor and made serviceman-sized stitches.

I had a cut too. I got bit on the finger when Big Girl slipped during the gutting of the deer. It was deep but not horrible, only about half inch long, but it was a crossways cut on the joint right below my fingernail and it wouldn't stay closed. It was a little swollen and there was a little bit of throbbing, but I wasn't thinking too much about it. There were other things to think about. Like where was Little Debbie?

The Knocking Hammer had a dip vat for the cattle, called a dip vat because it's what the cattle land in after they are taken up a ramp and shock-prodded to jump. The vat is full of strong liquid, insect killer, and it has to be deep enough for the steer to be completely submerged for a few seconds before it makes it across the vat to the ridged ramp where it can climb out. The Knocking

Hammer had a dip vat but it hadn't been used for a while. The liquid bug killer was still there, although evaporated down to a certain soupiness and this was what the grandma-ma used to clean the trailer. She sent a dusty Fanta child running with a yellow plastic bucket through the barbed wire of the stockyard fence. He came back carrying it two-handed and it was sloshing on his legs.

The grandma-ma took another bucket and stretched an old T-shirt over it and poured the liquid slow to strain it. The Fanta children bent and watched the black gushball of hair and dead insects forming. She pulled up the T-shirt and squeezed around the wad to wring it dry. And then she dropped it in the empty bucket and told the Fanta children to leave it alone.

She was a tiny woman wearing old clothes that were too big for her and too warm for the weather. A sweater over a shirt over a dress over some pants and then just a pair of fifty-cent flip-flops. I was surprised by her feet. They were so delicately shaped. She wore her thinning hair knotted at the back of her neck and a blue farmer's handkerchief tied like a headband with the knot on top. She kept untying it and retying it, trying to get it tight.

I sat watching her go in and out of the trailer, and every once in a while she'd look up and show me her teeth. They were strange teeth, like fish teeth, pointy and unevenly spaced and the way she showed them off made me laugh a little bit and she seemed to like this.

While she cleaned, the Fanta children ran around the bucket with the horror wad in it, daring each other to touch it until they got bored. Then they dragged each other around on a big piece of cardboard for a while and one of them kept shouting "Ho-ho-ho."

When the grandma-ma finished, she gathered her rags and her buckets and she was eyeballing me hard. She had found something in the trailer besides the smaller chunks of deer and the putrid mound of muskie. She dropped it into the bucket with the deadly macaroon and called to the children to help her carry the seeping newspaper-wrapped packages of deer meat Fernst set out on the back steps for her. I watched them disappear behind the scrub hedges, walking in the direction of the primitive area.

The dip vat fumes coming off the trailer were so strong, flies that tried to land were dropping off the sides. I looked in through the door and was amazed by the cleanliness.

Pammy and the father came down the back steps and I noticed he was wearing clothes I never saw before. Out of style but looking new. And Pammy had a little velvet bow clipped into her sad version of hair, and there were curling emissions of a perfume preceding her that did immediate combat with the fumes radiating off the trailer.

I moved away and they looked inside.

Pammy said, "What y'think?"

The father said, "I would not have thought it possible."

Pammy said, "The grandma-ma is a sour little bitch but she is hell on cleaning. I'll give her that. Cute little place here." She stepped in and the whole weight of the trailer shifted. "Real cute. I always wanted a trailer. Every since I was a little baby girl."

She had a plastic cigarette case with a special place for a book of matches. She had a pint of Old Skull Popper. She had a knife and a hunk of special blood sausage left over from the days of the Dead Swede, hand ground and packed in hog intestines. She was wearing tangerine-colored lipstick and when she and the father closed themselves inside the trailer and I was left to wander I found the lipstick tube laying in the dead grass. Orange Pucker was the name of it. I opened it and swirled it up and saw pale tufts of mold growing near the bottom.

The sun was going down and I thought I'd walk over to visit the cattle, to smell them and listen to them chuffing and making low moans. And that is when I found the railroad tracks. My own personal railroad tracks, glinting in the last of the sun's rays. And far in the distance with its pale eye rolling, I saw my own personal train.

In the night when the moon is large, the world spreads blue in every direction. In the night the creatures in the feedlot are sometimes asleep and sometimes they stand at the edge of the fence watching you with heads nodding, *go ahead, go ahead, go ahead.*

The line that runs past the Knocking Hammer is freight only. No passengers. The creatures in the feedlot are used to the engine and the racket of ventilated cars. Sometimes the cars are full and sometimes they are empty but it's a smell that alerts the creatures and stirs them in a terrible way. Trains heading to Rapid City and Kansas City and Chicago. Trains heading to any packinghouse town.

I have heard that certain vibrations can move through bones, move up through the ground and alert your bones. Train vibrations are strong. Vibrations moving though the rails cool and very smooth under my hand.

I crouched low in the sharp dead grass of the berm. I didn't want the engineer to see me. Sometimes the engineer is observant but mostly at night his mind is in the nowhereness. Drifting and dreaming. The rocking motion and the rolling engine and the hypnotic shine of the headlamp on the tracks. The night train. The night train. There is something different about them, especially when they are all freight and black, black, black. If I do it just right, he'll never see me, he won't blow the whistle, maybe he'll feel it and think a deer or a dog, a deer or a dog, maybe he won't think anything. Here comes the freight train, here comes the freight train, roaring and screeching and twisting a yellow eye across the blue flatness, lighting up the scribbles of scrub, here it comes here it comes here it comes NOW.

I couldn't. I wanted to so bad but I couldn't. My involuntary systems wouldn't. My involuntary systems threw me flat on the berm with the roaring above me but there was no exhilaration. When the train passed and I rolled onto my back and looked up into the night sky, I knew there was nothing looking back. Twinkle twinkle little star, you are nothing. You have been dead for thousands of years.

chapter 29

HERE WAS the crunching of tires on the gravel, someone was driving toward the Knocking Hammer with their headlights off. The father and Pammy had already crossed from the trailer to the house, a light came on in Pammy's chambers, a tiny buckling apartment above the lounge. Her window was open and a curtain fluttered. Music corkscrewed out of a hi-fi. The light went off. There were some cow sounds. And then it was quiet for a long long time until the shadow car rolled out of the blackness.

Two men were inside, two cigarette ends burned. From the deep black alongside the far end of the building came another man with a wheelbarrow. It was the spooker. It was Fernst.

There were hissing whispers and car doors opening and the quiet popping of the trunk. And from the trunk something was lifted, a man curled into a ball. Fernst wheeled him into the blackness and the men rolled back into the night.

I woke up when the shadow of the sheriff passed over my face. He was reaching down, about to lift me, but I crab-scrambled away. He said, "I'm not going to hurt you, Ee-gore, what in the hell are you doing out here? You didn't sleep out here, did you? Son? A freight train could come and cut you in two as neat as an ax. Let's go inside. We'll let Pammy make us breakfast."

The meat saw was going and the flypaper waved a little when the sheriff opened and propped the door. He'd been trying to walk with his arm around me but I pulled away. The father wouldn't have liked that but the father wasn't there.

"PAMMY!" The sheriff stood in the hallway hollering up some stairs. "PAMMY!"

For breakfast I had the terrible red pop and an ancient bag of Fritos. Pammy wanted me to sit on the floor near the screen door and I did it. The sheriff kept looking at her and wiggling his eyebrows up and down and smiling. She leaned with her back against the bar and one arm crossed over her stomach flaps and the other arm moving up to her face with a cigarette in the fingers. She said, "What?"

The sheriff said, "You tell me."

The father came down the stairs tucking in his shirt. He was barefoot and his hair was sticking up. He nodded to the sheriff. "Morning."

The sheriff said, "Pajama party?" He wiggled his eyebrows at Pammy again, and she threw the bar rag at him.

They made conversation. Pammy twirled a finger in the father's hair. I saw her clip-on bow hanging off the side of her head. At one point she smiled, looking like a backyard puff-fungus that had blown out all its spores. My life at the Knocking Hammer had begun.

There was a round of eye-openers. Pammy called the father Mils. The sheriff had introduced him as Milsboro and she thought that was his name. Mils Boro. The sheriff laughed until he got a groin cramp and had to stand up and shake out his leg, but he didn't correct her.

I forced down the pop and the Fritos, half gagging.

The father held up his cigs to me with a question mark on his face. I shook my head. He held up the bottle they were drinking from. He said, "Breakfast snorty?" I shook my head again. He said, "You ain't going Episcopalian on me are you?"

184

A Fanta child burst through the screen door shouting and jumping and pointing toward the canal. There was a commotion of more shouting outside. Pammy said, "Goddamn it." She shouted, "FERNST! YOU, FERNST! BRING THE POLE HOOK!" The meat saw stopped.

I looked out the door and saw the grandma-ma running fast with her flip-flops in her hand. Pammy said, "Sit your ass back down. This don't have anything to do with you."

The father said, "You heard her, Clyde."

Pammy's feet came stomp-crunching back across the gravel. She was wet up to her terrible hind end with chunks of mud and unidentifiables clinging to her legs. I heard crying. Wailing.

She dripped a trail across the wooden floor and sat on the stool beside the father. She lit a cig.

"And?" said the sheriff.

She blew a jet of smoke out of the side of her mouth and then turned and gestured to the doorway. "The grandma-ma would like a ride to the orchard. She wants to be the one to notify."

"Shit," said the sheriff.

A Fanta child had fallen into the canal.

chapter 30

HE FATHER said, "It ain't such a bad place to lay low for a while, Clyde. I can think of worse places. And hell. How many kids you know can say they got their own trailer?" He was laying across the plastic-covered mattress with his arms behind his head. I sat on the bench seat at the miniature kitchen table, smoking. The father said, "Want me to teach you smoke rings?" He demonstrated. Told me to practice. He said the more stunts I could do the better off I would be. He said, "Pammy has a stack of cash up there. And I mean a STACK. In her dresser. Why the hell do women hide everything in their underwear drawer? Any man knows it's the first place you look once they step into the shower. Big bills, Clyde. And I know she ain't getting it from running the bar. Hell, I'm getting the feeling nobody comes to the bar. Nobody showed up last night. We were in here shooting the shit and at about dark I say, 'Who's running the bar?' She says, 'The bar's running itself.'"

A blue smoke ring drifted upwards and broke apart.

"It sure as shit ain't cattle. Only man working here is that goddamned Alice the Goon on the meat saw. The stock out there in the feed pen are mostly culls and there's but a handful of them. Stack of bills six inches high with a rubber band around it and one just like it underneath. Got any ideas, Clyde?"

Later that afternoon I was sitting on the trailer step looking at my finger. It was throbbing and looking very swollen. My fingernail was lifting away at the sides and the cut itself was a wet yellow-green. Fernst stepped out the back door with a candy bar, unwrapped it, and paced while he ate it, making soft *hooo-hooo* noises.

A truck pulled up driven by a man with very bad skin and a very purple nose. Fernst shoved down the end of his candy bar and hopped up the back-door steps. The truck man did some steering wheel maneuvers and backed up almost right against the door. It was a refrigerator truck but old and dented with rust stripes running down the sides. The man got out and opened up the back and set a ramp from the truck bed to the back door. Gagger smells emanated instantly.

He was wearing grime-shiny pants and flies swirled around him. When he stopped moving they crawled on his face and he didn't brush them away. This was Mom. This was the rendering plant man. He looked over at me. He said, "You Clyde?"

I didn't move.

He said, "I heard about you, Clyde."

The open back door blocked my view but there was the sound like a dolly or wheelbarrow rolling. Rolling in and rolling out and rolling back again. Then Mom pulled in the ramp, shut the back door, and Fernst jumped in the cab with him. They drove a short distance to the cull pile and the ramp came back out and they loaded culls. The truck drove away.

The father was right about no one coming to the Knocking Hammer lounge at night. The old men came in the afternoon as usual, but they left before dark. That night the sheriff showed up with dinner, Chinese food from the next town. It was cold by the time he set it on the bar, but I ate it gratefully. Pammy and the father also wolfed. The sheriff said, "Pammy, why do you make Eegore sit on the goddamned floor to eat?"

"Hey," said the father. "It's her place."

Pammy's fungus smile shot some spores his way.

She'd taken a break from her chomping to pull out a ladder and hang a few more rolls of flypaper. Black dried-out exoskeletons cascaded wherever she bumped, coming off at the legs. A couple bounced off the bar but no one seemed to mind. The father especially. I've seen him keep drinking with one swimming in his glass. Once when I said something about it, he said, "Butt out, Clyde. This is between me and the fly."

The sheriff said, "You know, I have connections with a private institution that takes Ee-gore's type."

"The Home," said Pammy. "Call it The Home. It don't sound so bad."

"Vocational training," said the sheriff. "Fernst is fostered out from there. You never seen anyone better on the meat saw."

"Fostered?" said the father.

The sheriff explained that it was like taking care of a foster child only it was a foster spooker.

"Don't call him that," said Pammy. "Don't use that word."

Spooker was another word for mongoloid. As far as the sheriff could tell, I was one. Pammy thought so too. And they were telling the father about the great spooker home just up the way, just outside of the town where the sheriff picked up the Chinese food.

"It's real nice," said the sheriff. "Hell, they live better than most of us and they learn a trade at the same time."

When the father asked what kind of trade, the sheriff said, "By-product processing."

The father asked, "By-products of what?"

The sheriff mooed.

"I'll be jingled," said the father, pouring himself another.

When Pammy said she was ready for bed and the father said good night and followed her up to her chambers, the sheriff said, "Let me walk you to the trailer, son. It's pretty dark out there."

chapter 31

SUDDENLY I was shivering. "I assure you," said the Turtle. "I promise you, the sleeping giant will wake." The whole day had passed. I could see the sky darkening on the other side of the grimy garage window. I felt around for my clothes and started putting them back on.

The Turtle patted around for his shirt and pulled a paper twist out. "Wait, wait, we'll have a fatty and I'll try again. It's the Windowpane. Shouldn't have dropped two. Hillbilly Woman, sit back down."

"I'm freezing," I said. My teeth vibrated against each other. "Let's go," I said. "Let's get out of here."

We walked down the alley and I felt the confusion of wanting his arm around me and hating his arm around me. His breath had gone back to rasty again. I felt freaked by what we did. As the Windowpane drained away my jaws kept clenching until I could feel my teeth springing. The Turtle passed me Sir Fatty Bone III and I was thankful for it. It slowed down the murdering shocks that were shooting through my mind. The question of did it count. What we did in the garage. Did it count without the word, that word, *penetration*. Did it count without that? He tried but he couldn't. He was ready, but the sleeping giant was too wasted.

He squeezed me. He said, "Hillbilly Woman, I have yet to hear about your finger. Yes. Absolutely. We must do it all again. I must hear the rest of the story. We will find a place and you will keep talking."

I said, "What happened to my finger is that it got infected and the father cut it off, OK? The End."

He said, "I sense an irritation." His voice had a hurt tone. "I sense there is a thought which you are having about me."

The sky was streaked with the marks of sundown. A jet trail glowed in the ugliest pink. My eyes felt raw. The Windowpane had twisted time so badly. The day had seemed a minute long but in that minute my life uncoiled.

We were at the end of an alley and I was trying to decide what to do. The Turtle was looking very sad. His eyes looked dark and large with the barest rim of tiger-colored iris. The Turtle said, "I sense you will leave me. I sense our love has died."

He sounded so sincerely troubled. I was thinking, what if it is love but I just can't tell? I never kissed anyone before him. I never anythinged with anyone. It could be love and I could be wrecking my chances. And this made me freak and put my arms around him. He smelled sour. I thought about the power of love and tried to ignore the smell. He kissed me very hard, moving his head in circles and his teeth scraped against mine. It smelled like something was rotting inside of him. I couldn't help pulling away.

"Hillbilly Woman, what is it? What has gone wrong between us?"

"Turtle," I said, "I'm sorry."

He said, "Hillbilly Woman, please lay it on me. Truthfulness at all times. Absolutely."

I couldn't say anything.

He said, "It's because I'm Canadian, isn't it?"

"What?"

"Canadian. Yes. I confess it before you."

The Monkey at Diggy's had warned me. He had told me.

I said, "Do you know Neil Young?"

"Hillbilly Woman. Absolutely! Would you like to meet him?"

And that's when I started the crying.

And half an hour later I was still crying. I did not know if I would ever stop crying. I was laying in somebody's front yard and I could not stand up. The Turtle said, "Hillbilly Woman. I did not think you would take it so hard."

He said, "Hillbilly Woman, it's the Windowpane. You are very sensitive to acid."

He said, "Hillbilly Woman, please, you are very loud for this time of day in this sort of neighborhood. The lady has just come out onto the porch. The lady has gone back inside and I fear she is phoning the authorities."

He said, "Hillbilly Woman, rise. I cannot stay here much longer."

He didn't. By the time the cops arrived he was gone. An officer came out of his car, squatted beside me, asked me was I on drugs. I said my boyfriend just broke up with me. He said I was too young to be taking it so hard and that I would have another boyfriend in the future. The other officer was looking through Vicky's purse. He opened her wallet. He pulled out her "If Found, Please Return To" card.

They were both very kind to me. They were very understanding. They said, "Come on, Vicky, we'll give you a ride home."

Vicky Talluso's porch light was green, and even though her house was in a decent area it was in very skagged-out condition. There were things in the yard. Like chunks of old carpet and some tires and an armchair on its side barfing out its stuffing. I was still crying. I was actually feeling normal but my face kept on crying. The officer stood beside me on the wooden porch. He rang the doorbell and a man's voice inside said, "Shit and goddamn! It is door!" And then he started his horrible hack-coughing. The door swung open and when Vicky saw me and the cop, her mouth hung open. She was eating a piece of white bread spread with bright mustard. Behind her a television light flickered. She didn't say anything while the cop explained the situation, beginning with "Your sister" and ending with some encouraging words about my future.

The door closed behind me and Vicky whispered, "Shit, Roberta!" and then there was the sound of feet pounding down the stairs, a guy who looked about seventeen, very very fine, wearing jeans and a T-shirt. Brown hair falling to the back of his neck. He said, "What did the cops want?"

Vicky said, "It's not really your business is it?"

"Shut up and tell me."

The hacking man said, "Shit and goddamn, I welcome to you this house!" He was old and laying on a plaid recliner and he was wearing a woman's pink chenille robe. That was Susy Home-maker.

Vicky yanked me away by the arm. She said, "Don't look. Don't talk to him."

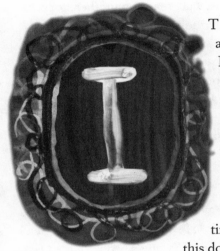

I AIN'T nothing, Clyde. Just a little blood poisoning, Clyde. I've been through it a hundred and fifty times. You take a shot of Old Skull Popper, you chew three aspirin, and in an hour your troubles will be over." This is what the father said when he opened the trailer door and set the aspirin and the Old Skull Popper on the tiny kitchen counter. "You lock this door behind me, you don't let the sheriff in here, Clyde, no matter what he says to you. He can't get off the subject of you. He wants me to sign you in to that spooker home. Says you look trainable. Trainable, my ass. I'd say he's tantalized. There's some weird shit going on around here, Clyde, but it could work out good for us. Hey, what do you think of these slacks? Fit me good, don't they? They're Italian." The father shut the door and left.

I was so sick. I was shaking and sweating on the plastic-covered mattress in the clean, clean murder trailer. I was freezing, then I went burning hot. I felt my insides turn to foam. My finger was killing, killing, killing. It was so swollen you could hardly see the nail. My teeth were vibrating and then my jaws would catch and clench.

I pulled myself up, locked the door, and brought the aspirin and the Old Skull Popper back to bed. Every once in a while a Fanta child's head would rise and stare into one of the windows, wobbling for a moment and then falling away when the person boosting them lost their hold. One of them was watching when I threw up so hard the aspirins I swallowed tinked out whole onto the floor.

The father said blood poisoning was nothing to worry about until I dried out. If it was tetanus, well, that was another story. Either way, when I couldn't pee anymore, I was in trouble.

I fell asleep and dreamed about the father in the Dead Swede's Italian pants. The Dead Swede's Hush Puppies. The Dead Swede's delicate blue socks. The Dead Swede's Arrow shirt and his precious bolo tie. Pure silver. A little dancing man holding a rattle and a weed. And the Dead Swede's cologne, plentiful imported fumes that singed the inside of my nostrils. I dreamed of the father saying, "You know, I don't think I ever looked so good. When's the last time you took a piss? When's the last time you took a piss? Clyde. Clyde."

It was all true. The father was wearing the Dead Swede's clothes and cologne and his bolo. He was drinking in the Dead Swede's bar and sleeping in the Dead Swede's bed with the Dead Swede's widow who was feeling the fantastic love flutterations, who was transforming before everyone's eyes. No one had seen her smile since the days of the Dead Swede. And she was wearing the tiny high heels again. She hadn't had those out since the night she did the dance that gave the Dead Swede the cardiac.

There were more details about how Pammy was coming along, and the father laid them on me whenever he stopped by the trailer, but most of them I couldn't hang on to with my gummy brains. At night certain music blared from the Dead Swede's hi-fi, melodies came through the trailer walls. "The Three Bells" by The Browns. "Come Softly to Me" by The Fleetwoods. Smooth blended singing with no edges, horrifying in its perfection. I was losing my hair. Chunks of hair fell out onto the plastic mattress every time The Browns or The Fleetwoods sang. The music stuck in my mind. Brain congregations singing little parasitic melodies.

The father came and went making different assessments. "The streaks up your arm, see there? There is no way around it. Goddamn. It's going to have to come off."

There are certain dangers in homemade booze, and the second jug of Corpse Reviver must not be forgotten. There can be chemistries like firing pins sending perfectly calibered visions, there is such a thing as the bore axis of the mind. The father felt something funny and wonderful when he drank from the Corpse Reviver. He didn't want to share it. He kept it in the trailer and took a glug whenever he visited. And then he showed up and took several glugs and I saw he had his knife case out. He had his whetstone out.

Time had fallen apart for me. I lost the order of days and nights and conversations. I know the sun was either coming up or going down because I saw the golden rays falling upon the metal-seamed walls. The father said, "It's got be done, Clyde. I can't take you to no hospital. You understand that. At least you know I'm the best possible man for the job. Sit up here, drink, again, and one more."

His worn whetstone was oiled and he was making the motions. The knife he was honing was her, Little Debbie, he said she had just the right sort of point for small-joint separation. I listened to the soft circular whisper of the sharpening and the familiar promise that I would not feel a thing.

The father was strapping my arm down and tying my wrist tightly and jabbering on, he was laying out his Corpse Reviver–fueled plans about how to make the gold mine that was the Knocking Hammer his. He held the jug up to me. "Take a drink, take another. I'll tell you what, you feel anything? You can take off one of mine. That's a promise. The only reason I'm putting this rag in your mouth is for just in case. Now, turn your head, Clyde. Look out the window for the sandman."

The sandman. The sandman. The sandman.

And then the father owed me a finger but he did not want to pay.

I have read enough of *Stedman's Medical Dictionary* and other medical books of information to know that cutting half of my finger off was not what saved me. At that point the poisoning was in all of my bloodways. Even if the father had taken my whole arm off it wouldn't have mattered.

What saved me was a midnight tap on the trailer door and the grandma-ma's voice. What saved me was a soup she made from the bones of the murdered deer. That, and a few little other things she ran back to get after she saw my situation. A soothing paste she brought for my finger, that smelled like lemon and mint and Clorox, and her delicate stitches in place of the ones made by the father. She used low-test fishing line, she said she found it in the trailer on the day she cleaned the horribleness away. She said she found other things too.

One of the Fanta children sat on the edge of the bed watching me with quiet eyes and holding a flashlight for her. Another stood guard at the trailer door. Before she left she pointed toward the Knocking Hammer with bared teeth and said, "No good."

Chapter 33

GOT BETTER. And when I was well enough I went looking for the grandma-ma. I found her near the cull pile squatting by the bodies, doing something with a spoon and what it turned out she was doing was digging out a cow eye. She stood up and tilted her head toward a plastic bucket. She said, "Carry it for me?" It was half full of eyeballs and walking flies.

I followed behind her thinking she was going to the campground area but she turned down a little trail zigzagging through thicker scrub and kept walking. She said, "Everybody's packing up. Apple season's early. Beats peaches. I'm leaving out of here too."

She said, "Your daddy has a flat ass. Flattest ass I've seen on a man. I don't like men with flat asses."

She said, "Do you know what hoo-doo is?"

We came to a shed. Flies swarmed around a set of yellow buckets arranged in a semicircle. I smelled the dip vat fumes.

She said, "Some people think I'm in with that hoo-doo, they come to me for things. I tell them to their faces, you can give me your money and I'll make you a Custom Creation, but it doesn't have any powers beyond what's in the intended's mind to begin with. But I *can* make things that will scare the face off a man. Since

199

I was little I liked to make such things. I was raised by an auntie that used to whip me with an extension cord. It started with her."

She said, "I'll make one for you if you like."

There was a loop of string hanging out of the dip vat liquid. She pulled it and up came a headless chicken carcass, its raw wings raised like a marionette. She said, "It doesn't look like much, but neither does a hand grenade."

She said, "A man lost his life in that trailer of yours. I know it for a fact. He left behind what no man leaves behind unless he's dead. You want to see it? I sun-dried it but it will get its shape back once it soaks awhile."

She pulled out some waxed paper and in the waxed paper was a dried-up thing looking like a very old hot dog with a helmet on.

She watched me looking at it. She said, "You want to help me scare the living hell out of a couple of people? They're people you know."

chapter 34

E WERE up in Vicky's room. She had a canopy bed with severe dust-chunks hanging. There were bowls and plates of half-eaten crusted food laying around and the drawers of her dresser were half shut with clothes hanging out. Piles of clothes were everywhere. Some had the price tags still on them but they were balled up anyway. There were pictures taped to the walls of models with insane amounts of eye makeup doing pissed-off poses, and there were models who looked like they were flowing free in fields of tall dandelions, and there was a hot pink chipboard sign that said THE SWINGING CHICKS ALL GO JAY JACOBS!!! It was a bus sign. Stolen, obviously. So many things about Vicky were stolen. Even the cross that hung from her neck was shoplifted. She said she was very glad to have her purse back because it was her trained purse, the best shoplifting purse ever made. All she had to do was lean against it a certain way and it opened and then when she leaned back it closed. She was going through it, an unlit cig hanging from her mouth.

She said, "Where's the stash box?"

She said, "Where's my lighter?"

She said, "What the fuck is the deal with this sock monkey?"

The super-fine guy stood at the doorway staring at me. Her brother. This was the Stick.

She said, "Get OUT of my ROOM!"

He pointed down at his bare feet. They were on the other side of the threshold. "I'm not in your room, am I?" He was eating from a bag of Oven Joy bread. Just mashing pieces of white bread into his mouth. He said, "What's wrong with her, Vic?"

Vicky got up, slammed the door, and hooked the lock. She said, "Where's the stash?" She dug around her bedroom for another lighter and I told her what went down at the Diggy's Dumpster.

She said, "Is the stash still in the Dumpster?"

I shrugged. "Probably."

She said, "Well, we have to go get it." And then she told me my crying was really getting on her nerves and I needed to stop before she got violent. I wanted to stop. In my mind I had stopped, but my eyes stayed wet, wouldn't stop spilling over. She never asked me why I was crying and I was thankful because I didn't know if the answer had words and if it did have words I doubted that she would listen to them.

A ruler poked up into the door crack and knocked the hook out of the latch-eye. In he walked, in he strolled. The Stick. His jeans hung low on his hips and his eyes were brown and his nose was a little bit smashed looking and his mouth was full and all of him looked the way suede feels. He said, "Who are you?"

Vicky said, "GET OUT!"

Downstairs the hack-coughing began. "Vidjki! Shit and goddamn! VIDJKI!"

The Stick said, "Susie's hungry. It's your turn."

Vicky said, "I don't care if he eats."

The Stick said, "Yes you do."

She said, "No I don't."

Louder hacking. "VIDJKI! SHIT AND GODDAMN, YOU KNOW!"

The Stick looked at me. "Who are you? Seriously."

"VIDJKI! SHIT AND GODDAMN I DIE!!"

Vicky said, "Don't talk to him, Roberta. Don't say anything to him. And don't give him anything. I'll be right back." Then she told the Stick to fuck himself and walked out the door.

He had a boy-smell coming off of him that made my stomach undulate. It was making me lean toward him and I could not stop it. He said, "Can I talk to you about something? Let's go out on the roof. You scared of heights at all?" He was staring at my face with the usual curiosity. I turned away. He said, "You ever seen a satellite? You should come out on the roof."

I followed him and my eyes spilled harder. Everything was blurred and mixed together. We went into his room. The boy-smell was very strong and it made my legs wobble a little. The walls were bare and painted brown, a chocolate brown, and his mattress was on the floor and the floor was covered with piles of clothes and books and papers and there was a truck-tire inner tube inflated. It had a lamp beside it.

He told me to take off my shoes. That it's easier to walk on the roof barefoot and he went out the window first, and then turned and waited for me.

The warm composition shingles felt good on my feet. I hadn't climbed anything in so long. I followed him up around the dormer to the peak of the roof. We sat for a few moments without talking. Vicky's house was nearly at the top of the hill that was opposite mine. I looked across toward Dunbar and saw the yellow Diggy's sign lit up and turning. I knew that right across the street was Black Cat Lumber, although I couldn't see it, and I knew that behind Black Cat Lumber, life was going on in the mud of East Crawford.

The Stick gave me a cigarette. He lit his and then lit mine. He said, "So what's the deal?"

I shrugged. I was grateful for the cigarette. My eyes spilled harder from the gratitude. I blew a smoke ring and it hung in the still night air. Above us were the random pale stars.

He said, "Seriously."

I said, "I'm a fucked-up person."

He said, "I mean with the cops."

I heard Vicky screaming, "ROBERTA! RO-BER-TA!" The Stick said, "She won't come out here. She can't take the roof. If you want to get away from her this is the best place." I heard her shouting my name from the dormer window. And then in a few moments I saw her backing up in the front yard and spotting me and having an instant fit. The Stick started laughing a little and I started laughing a little too, and I thought about jumping, wondered how bad it would be, and wished there was concrete around the house instead of bushes and grass.

Vicky shouted, "You're STUPID, Roberta! STUPID! He's a USER, Roberta! My brother's a USER!" I couldn't think of anyone who wasn't.

A little bit later Vicky left the house with her trained purse hanging from her shoulder. She was dressed up. She had her crinkle-vinyl boots on. She hollered, "I'm going to get it. Because obviously I'm the ONLY ONE WHO CARES! You're going to keep your promise to me, Roberta. When I come back you are going to keep it or I am going to KILL YOU!"

"What promise?" said the Stick. "Where's she going?"

I said, "How come you're talking to me?"

He said, "What do you mean?"

I stood up and walked the roof ridge with my arms out until I came to the very edge.

I looked up at the dead pinholes that barely glittered. I said, "You ever think about killing yourself?"

He said, "All the time."

chapter 35

HAT THE hell smells so bad?" said the sheriff. "Pammy farted."

"The hell I did," said Pammy. "When I fart, you'll know it."

"Sheriff's been drinking Blatz," said the father.

"What's wrong with Blatz?"

It was past midnight, and hot. Outside the night insects clicked and whirred and the ones that were too big to get through the wide-gauge screen on the door to the lounge, bashed their heads against it trying. But there were lots of bugs who fit through fine and Pammy watched with some satisfaction when they found the flypaper. "See there? It isn't just for flies."

Every time she looked up, I freaked.

The father said, "Why do you keep that meat saw room locked?"

Pammy and the sheriff hesitated. Pammy said, "Mexicans," and the sheriff said, "We've had trouble."

The father said, "Well, that sure explains it."

There was an uneasy silence and then the sheriff started in again on me and the spooker home. He had the sign-over papers on the bar.

I'd seen the shadow car three other times. The shadow men rolling in quiet with no headlights on and unloading rigor mortis cargo. I'd seen the rendering man called Mom come and go.

During one of his extended Corpse Reviver trailer visits, the father reached in his pocket and pulled out a gold pocket watch, with four diamonds marking the quarter hours. He said, "Look at this. She gave it to me this morning. She told me, 'Don't let Arden see it.' I said, 'Why not?' When I ask questions, she gets French on me." And what he meant by getting French was that instead of answering him, Pammy started kissing him violently. "It's effective," said the father. "I'm thinking her and Arden are running some sort of fence, but some of the shit I stumble across don't fit."

For example, the lighter he was using. He handed it to me. It was the familiar steel rectangle with USN engraved on one side. On the other side, it said, CV HOT PAPAS-PTO-1944-SEMPER FI.

"Marines, Clyde," said the father. "You know what the Hot Papas are? Goddamn ghosts is what they are. White asbestos suits from top to bottom with just a little peephole for the eyes, them are the ones that run into the wreckage and drag your ass out of the fire. Know where I found this? Laying out front in the dirt. And here, look at this."

He reached in his shirt pocket and handed me a heavy gold ring studded with diamonds. A man's ring. He said, "She gave me that too. It'd look about right on a pimp, wouldn't it? Arden ain't supposed to see that neither." He glugged on the last of the mind-bending Corpse Reviver. He said, "I could drink a bathtub of this, here. It just gets better."

I turned the ring over in my hands.

"You know why she gave me that, Clyde?"

I shook my head.

"She wants me to marry her." Glug, glug. Glug, glug. "And I'm thinking of doing it." And the Corpse Reviver spun his mind into an excited and vicious trance, pinwheels of possibility whirled. He said, "Vegas. That's the place to do it. It's so goddamn perfect. I can go by Doris's motel and get Old Dad's last suitcase, me and Pammy can get married. This place is in her name, the Dead Swede signed everything over." His face was dripping sweat and he was turning very red and his lips pulled away from his teeth in an uncontrollable smile that was not a smile, more like something you see on a dead person's face. Rictus. It's called rictus.

He was getting emotional, he was talking about Old Dad. He was pointing at the light fixture and saying Old Dad was trying to make him understand. Old Dad guided him to the Knocking Hammer to carry on the tradition that began before man could hardly stand straight and still had ten pounds of hair on his ass. "You know what I could do with a place like this? I could kick the shit out of Chicago. The name Rohbeson would be right up there with Swift, Armour, and Hormel."

A salty tear rambled down his craggy face. "Old Dad didn't turn on me, Clyde. A father's love is eternal. And when I think of how I stood up at his funeral and called him a lying sack of shit—"

I looked up at the light fixture and watched a trapped fly jerk around in the last stages of buzzing itself to death. "Old Dad," he said. "Please forgive me." Glug glug. "Old Dad, I swear to you—" Glug glug. More salty tears. Some shaking sobs. And then his arms reaching out for a certain kind of comfort. "Clyde. Clyde. I need you."

The sheriff had tried to get some comfort from me too. The night the father and Pammy left me to him. The night the sheriff said, "Let me walk you to the trailer, son. It's pretty dark out there." He tried to get some comfort and ended up shouting, "OW, OW, YOU SON-OF-A-*BITCH*!" and the father leaned his head out of Pammy's bedroom window, calling, "He bite you? I warned you."

And the sheriff had been trying to get me into his car with offers like, "I'll let you blow the siren, Ee-gore, I got twenty-six candy bars, Ee-gore, I'll let you shoot my goddamned gun, Ee-gore."

The father wanted me to keep playing him, but I didn't know how much longer I could play him without help. I needed Little

Debbie but the father's knife case was locked in the trunk with the suitcases.

"Pammy farted," said the sheriff.

Pammy said, "Goddamn you, Arden, I did not."

"There's no shame in it," said the father. "I farted once myself, in Korea."

I was sitting on the floor of the bar playing with a tiddlywinks game the sheriff bought me. Pammy kept telling me to get to bed but I was not about to leave. The grandma-ma had done her part and I had to do mine.

I shot the tiddlywinks, trying to see how many times I could hit Pammy on the back of her legs before she freaked on me. I wanted to distract her from her natural inclination to check the flypaper.

The father and the sheriff were plastered. Pammy was too. She turned and hissed, "You hit me again and I'm going to pull those Dumbo ears right off your head."

"Oh, now," the sheriff said. "He's just playing. Don't you think he looks cute sitting there?"

"If I *thought*," said Pammy, "I'd blow the perverted brains out of your head."

The sheriff started talking up the spooker home again, telling the father how good it would be for me, the father could visit me anytime, and when I learned my vocation, Mom had agreed to let the father be first in line to foster me back.

The father said, "Hey, Arden. You want to see something I learned in the Navy?"

The sheriff said, "Not especially."

The father set the lighter on the bar, and concentrated on it. He did something quick and one-handed, the lighter flipped into the air and bloomed into flame before he caught it. He said, "How'd I do that, Arden? Want to see it again?" He flipped the lighter so he caught it close to the sheriff's face and there was a flinch. The reflected flame moved weirdly in the sheriff's pale eyes.

The father said, "Try and blow it out."

The sheriff said, "How about if you just shave my ass instead?"

The father leaned in and blew on the flame as hard as he could. It went sideways but didn't lose strength. Then he slung it hard across the room and it hit the wall, fell, and kept on burning.

"Golly," said the sheriff. "Ain't that a thriller."

The father said, "Get it for me, Clyde."

It was hot to the touch. I flipped the lid open and shut a few times, liking the action. When I handed it back to the father, he lit a cig and passed the lighter to the sheriff. "See what it says on it?"

The sheriff held it away to get focus. "Let me see. 'Property. Of. A. Dumb-shit.'"

The father said, "See that there? PTO. Nineteen Forty-four. Know where I found it? For a nickel I'll tell you." The sheriff looked up at him.

A train roared by and the booze in the bottles trembled.

The sheriff said, "You going to sign them papers or not? Mom's got a bed vacant N-O-W and I could take him tonight. Vacancies there don't last. You drag ass on this and you may not get another chance."

Above the bar, hanging from one of the rafter ribs, something was attracting certain night insects, carrion feeders. Something about the size of a head was crawling with shimmer-butt flies in ecstasy. It was all I could do to keep myself from looking up. The waxed paper loops and special trusses were about soaked through.

Something fell against the father's neck, caught in the back of his collar. The father hopped off his stool and swatted it out. It bounced on the floor. "What the hell is that?"

The sheriff leaned down to pick it up and flung it as soon as his hand made contact. "It's a goddamned EYEBALL!"

Pammy threw the bar rag over it. She stepped on it. There was a sick wet popping sound. They all stared at the bar rag like it was going to move. The sheriff pig-squinted his eyes at the father.

"What kind of trick-shit are you trying to pull?"

The father said, "Me?"

Pammy whispered, "It's the Swede."

The sheriff snapped. "Don't start, Pammy. It ain't the goddamned Swede."

And that is when the rest of the paper loops gave way.

There were some thin shrieks and violent shouts and a scramble to get to the door and then the three of them were outside half hopping in the gravel.

"Oh shit," said Pammy. "Oh goddamn, Arden. I told you we should have—"

"Shut it, Pammy." The sheriff had taken some direct hits and was panic-brushing putrid slime chunks and sopping hair wads off of his shirt. "Oh, Jesus," he said. "Don't anybody talk to me for a minute here, I'm next to puking." And then he roared such a gush that he stumbled backwards.

The father said, "I need a goddamned drink and we left the goddamned Whitley's in there, Pammy."

Pammy said, "I'm not going in there."

The sheriff said, "Shit, I ain't scared."

The father said, "I ain't scared."

Pammy followed them back inside. A dozen eyeballs lay on the floor in assorted positions. The rotting smell was horrendous.

Pammy whispered the Swede's name when she saw the carcass on the bar. Out of the gape of its horrible hind end, long pale hair hung dripping with slime.

"It's a chicken," the sheriff said. "Some wise ass is playing tricks." He was looking at the father.

chapter 36

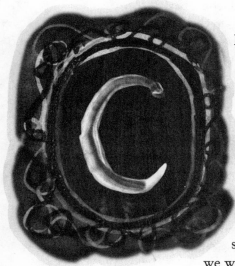

LYDE," SAID the father, gesturing out the trailer window. "Some day all of this will be yours."

"Clyde," said the father, "I signed the papers on you."

He laid out his plan, drawing pictures with his fingers on the Formica table between us, little strategy maps showing where we were now, where he was going and where I was going and then he drew some lopsided circles about what was going to happen in the future. He said, "You won't be in there long, when me and Pammy get back from Vegas I'll come and bust you out, Clyde. Promise."

I just stared at him. I'd planned to leave with the migrants to pick apples but they were already gone. The grandma-ma was gone. All that was left in the campground was trash and torn tarps. I didn't see them go. Nobody did. The father said he and Pammy were packed and ready. He said we would look back on this time someday and laugh. When they wrote the book about how the Rohbeson's meat empire rose again, it would be the first chapter.

His brain was corroding. At the time I thought it was the work of the Corpse Reviver. Making his talking and his thinking so confident and insane. But I think his brain would have corroded anyway because he was a naturally corroded person. There are people like this. There are people like the father everywhere. Now you see them, now you don't.

When I spoke, he jumped a little. I think he'd forgotten I still could.

I said, "Can I have Little Debbie back?"

He said, "Do you promise to be good?"

I said, "I promise."

I was so thankful to have her back. I laid low in the scrub feeling her edge in the darkness while I listened to Pammy cursing out Fernst. They were half looking for me. The father and the sheriff had hollered my name a couple of times. I thought of the grandma-ma making the sign of the cross over me the last time I saw her, saying, "Not that this is going to help, but what the hell."

I could see Pammy upstairs in her chambers, getting ready to fry some potatoes and a couple of hamburgers in her little tiny kitchen. She'd been bragging about cooking all day, she was doing it for the father. She wanted him to know she could.

The father and the sheriff stood out on the porch. The sheriff said, "Think he ran?"

The father said, "Not Clyde. It's not in him."

He whooped out my name a couple more times and the sheriff said he was going to check the trailer. It was a moonless night and stars glinted over the Knocking Hammer. I guess it was then when I first noticed I was thinking about killing the father. It's hard to say when premeditation begins. Laying there in the scrub watching his jug-eared silhouette with Little Debbie in my hand, the idea of killing him seemed very practical. On that night it seemed like a good idea to kill them all. Afterwards I'd take a walk, a stroll in the dark on the railroad tracks with my back to my personal train. I'd take a walk and then explode.

I am also a corroded person. Extremely corroded. I knew Pammy didn't have a sense of smell. I heard her talking about it. She told the father she doesn't miss it because she never had it.

Who squirted the lighter fluid all over Pammy's hamburger meat? Who poured out her corn oil and replaced it with kerosene?

chapter 37

DON'T THINK jumping is such a bad way to do it," said the Stick. "But there are better." With my feet still on the rooftop ridge, with the night sky above me, I said, "I saw a guy jump once."

The Stick said, "Head-first? If you're serious you go headfirst. You dive. Hey, there it is, there's the satel-lite."

At first I couldn't find it. And then the Stick was behind me, his head bent close to mine but not touching, trying to show me. And then I saw it. It looked like a faint star, but it was moving.

The Stick, "It's tumbling. They tumble. Who did you see jump?"

I pictured Cookie biting the mother as the mother lifted her over the railing of the Aurora Bridge and let go. Let go and walked into a candy store and bought a pound of candy stars.

I said, "Where's your mom?"

He said, "You need to see the attic."

I followed him over a narrow shingled ledge that had to be walked sideways before we got to the oval attic window, a window without glass and a cloudy piece of plastic hanging over it from the inside.

It was easier to do than it looked and I have to say I enjoyed it. The hardest part was going headfirst through the window into the

blackness. The Stick lit a match and then he lit a candle and then he set the candle on the floor beside a cracked mirror propped against the slanted roof and the candlelight doubled.

It was a good smell, the smell of the attic. The smell of wood very ancient and unpainted. Pine. The slanted walls had long pine-board cladding. And above the candle in the flicker light I saw a sentence written in pencil, in a child's handwriting. *I hope you die. I hope you rot. I hate you all. 16 September 1919.*

The Stick watched me read it. He said, "She was locked up here because of him."

I said, "Who?"

He said, "Well, he was obviously some asshole."

"No. Who is *she?*"

He said, "Who are you?"

We sat by the window. I told him all of my names. Roberta, Clyde, Ee-gore, Mystery Child, Michelle, then Roberta again, and recently Hillbilly Woman. I told him the story of meeting Vicky and the Turtle and dropping Creeper.

He said, "Creeper?"

I told him it was in the stash box Vicky went to get. I told him the whole story except for what happened with the Turtle in the garage. Loose Lips Sink Ships and I was wanting to sink ships very badly, but I could not talk about the Turtle's motions against my bare legs in the garage.

The Stick said, "What's it like, Creeper? What's it feel like? Is Vicky bringing it back here? Is there a lot?"

I said, "Is that guy downstairs your dad?"

He said, "Fuck you, OK? Don't talk about Susie."

I was trying to think of a way to explain the feeling of Creeper. I said, "It makes everything significant. Even trash. Even flies." I told him about the Washeteria, the lady with the shadow of a "W" falling on her face and her freaky beige moles, how when I turned and looked at her I started screaming and could not stop. "That's Creeper," I said.

"Would you do it again?"

I said, "Yes." I told him about the exhilaration. How to me, even horrifying exhilaration is incredible.

He said, "When Vicky comes back will you drop with me?"

I was wondering if he really was a user like Vicky said. I saw him looking over my face. I saw him notice my finger. I saw him staring at the raised letter "y" scarred into my arm, showing just below my sleeve.

The Stick looked at me and the flame from the candle moved in his eyes. Normal pupils. Brown eyes.

I said, "You know that guy I saw jump?"

He said, "Yeah?"

"His name was Fernst."

chapter 38

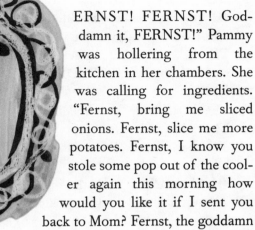

ERNST! FERNST! Goddamn it, FERNST!" Pammy was hollering from the kitchen in her chambers. She was calling for ingredients. "Fernst, bring me sliced onions. Fernst, slice me more potatoes. Fernst, I know you stole some pop out of the cooler again this morning how would you like it if I sent you back to Mom? Fernst, the goddamn pilot light is out. Fernst, that flame is too damn high, Fernst, watch that oil. Fernst—"

Bright flash. WHOOOMP! Pammy screaming. Screaming she was on fire.

The sheriff and the father were shouting back and forth and Fernst scrambled out the window with his long arms in flames, fire leaping from his clothes, he was hopping and flapping and then he jumped.

The sheriff and the father got ahold of Pammy and rolled her. They got her to the outside shower and sprayed her down. The father said, "Hell of a grease fire." And then the sheriff saw the broken Fernst in a heap, twitching, smoldering, and he said, "Oh shit."

He walked over to look at him. Foaming noises were coming from Fernst's throat. The sheriff bent down, stuck the gun in Fernst's mouth and then it was over.

In the bar they were all taking drinks. The sheriff kept his eyes on the father. "I bet you didn't have a thing to do with that fire."

The father said, "Damn it, Arden. No."

Pammy was pig-eyed, pacing the bar and smoking. She said, "It's the Swede." Her skin was bright pink under thick layers of melting Vaseline. "The Swede, Arden. He set that fire."

"Horse shit," said the sheriff.

"It's the Swede, I'm telling you. He's goddamn walking."

The father stood at the screen door and cupped his hands around his mouth. "CLY-YDE! THIS AIN'T FUNNY NO MORE!"

The sheriff said, "He ran, Milsboro."

The father said, "Not Clyde."

The sheriff said, "I'm not the type of man that puts up with shit like this."

"He'll come back," said the father. "CLY-YDE! CLY-YDE!"

"Well," said the sheriff, cracking a new bottle of Whitley's. "If he don't come back, we're going to have to hunt him. Mom don't wait for no one."

Pammy said, "The Swede got him."

The sheriff said, "The Swede has better things to do with his time." He poured a round. They drank.

The father kept looking toward the screen door. Watching for me. Pammy was digging some pills out of a brown jar and downing them with a half tumbler of Whitley's. Horse tranquilizers.

The sheriff said, "Those ain't for people."

She said, "I know it, and I don't give a goddamn."

The father said, "I don't mean to intrude but what should we do about Fernst out there?"

The sheriff said, "You read my mind, Milsboro. Got a job offer for you."

"Yeah?" said the father.

"Can you face a meat saw?"

"Which end?"

The father stuck a cig in his mouth and pulled out his USN lighter. The sheriff slammed his hand on the bar. "Wise-ass! Always have to be the wise-ass, don't you, Earlis?"

"*Earlis?*" said the father.

The sheriff said, "That's your name isn't it?"

"Naw, naw, Arden, I ain't Earl—"

The sheriff pulled out his gun. "Go ahead and lie to me. I ran your goddamn plates. I know all about you."

Pammy said, "Ear-less? Who?"

The sheriff picked the father's lighter up off the bar, lit a cig, and hurled the lighter against the far wall of the barroom. "I do it right? Huh, Earlis? Navy my ass."

The father and Pammy were looking at each other. The sheriff said, "Our meat saw man gave out on us and we got a job waiting."

He downed his glass and poured again but the Whitley's was pouring funny, and then it wasn't pouring at all. And the sheriff saw something like a ragged hot dog was hanging out of it. "What the shitting hell? A FINGER!" He glared at the father. "You stupid-son-of-a-bitch. You think you can scare me? You think I'm afraid of a GODDAMN FINGER?"

The sheriff yanked the fleshy end and held it up in a one-second display of courage before he got a good look at it and sent it flying. "It's a COCK!"

The father said, "Now *that* is goddamn eerie. What the hell is going on? Why don't you just tell me?"

Pammy's hands shook as she fished two more horse calmers out of the bottle. "He's coming back in pieces, Arden. The Swede wants his revenge."

The sheriff leveled his gun at the father. "You put that cock in there."

"That bottle was sealed," said the father. "It was you that cracked it."

The sheriff eyes narrowed. "And then you slipped it in."

The father said, "Arden, where the hell would I get a man's

cock? Why the hell would I ruin a full bottle of Whitley's? Put your gun down, Arden, you're making me feel bad."

The sheriff aimed at the father's forehead. "Let's go outside, Earlis."

Pammy said, "Arden, IT'S THE SWEDE MAKING YOU DO THIS! He's turning us against each other. Shit, Arden. Goddamn it, Arden, DON'T YOU SHOOT HIM, ARDEN!"

The sheriff walked the father out to where Fernst lay. There were deep shadows all around. It would have been nothing for me to get the sheriff. Little Debbie was wanting to. Little Debbie was straining in my hand like a dog seeing a rabbit. It would have been nothing to do a fast slice that would cause the sheriff a surprising intestine cascade.

But I wasn't in the mood to do the father any favors. I was enjoying the terrified look on his face, I have to admit I was enjoying it very much.

If Pammy hadn't spotted me, who knows how wonderful that night could have turned out to be?

chapter 39

HERE ARE certain creatures in the ocean called sessile creatures, creatures permanently attached to one place, like the barnacle and the anemone and the feather-duster worm. And there are also drifter creatures, attached to nothing, carried places by the current, and at night some of them will glow when disturbed. At night they can leave a phosphorescent trail five miles long behind a ship, a trail clearly visible from the air. That could be hell on a Navy man. Dazzle camouflage is useless in the dark.

I was shut into the blackness of the meat saw room. Shut in there by the sheriff. He shoved me in, said, "Don't turn on the light unless you want a surprise," and bolted the door.

It was a cold room but there was a smell of spoilage. The refrigeration unit gave off the smell of a washcloth gone sour. There was the smell of disinfectant and fresh sawdust. And twisting around all of it was the high scent of blood, bitter and metallic. And a much heavier odor I recognized. The complicated smell of a sliced creature. Complicated because sliced hide smells different from sliced fat, and sliced fat smells different from sawn bone, and internal organs each have a particular smell, and then there is the raw odor of the divided meat itself. All of these smells were fresh.

My hand found the light switch. Did I want a surprise?

"YOU DO NOT KNOW WHO YOU ARE DEALING WITH, YOU STUPID SHIT!" That was the sheriff shouting

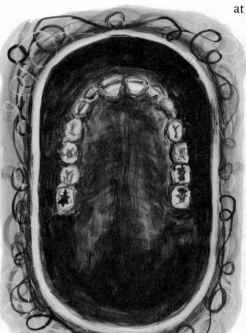

at the father. I could hear his words but not the father's or Pammy's. The sheriff was shouting that he was big, very big. He had big connections in Chicago, with the BIG boys in Chicago. Did the father understand the legal implications of habeas corpus? No body equals no murder equals peace in the valley for all concerned. Was the father starting to get the picture? It was the sheriff who oversaw the final steps required to turn an important somebody into a scattered nobody of bone, blood meal, and cat food.

The father asked a question but I couldn't hear what it was. The sheriff said, "That's THEIR business. I keep out of it. I don't want to know, you understand?"

There was more conversation but it was getting too mumbly for me to follow it. Voices low, making deals, making plans. The sheriff saying, "So you in or out, Earlis?"

The father saying, " I'm in."

I heard their footsteps coming down the hall. The sheriff saying, "You got a strong stomach?" and then the sound of the lock and the sliding bolt.

The sheriff rapped out some knocks. He said, "If you're by the door, Ee-gore, you better back up."

In a low voice the sheriff said, "You ready?"

The father said, "I was born ready."

The sheriff pushed the door open. He said, "Goddamn it, Ee-gore, you switched the light on."

What I saw before my vision disintegrated was a double sink, very deep, a metal table with a drainage trough around it, heavy hooks for hanging, and a job someone left in the middle of. And the job's head was severed from its body and the head didn't have a face or a lower jaw. It had a horseshoe of human teeth, and some of the teeth had gold fillings. And that was what I stared at until something like ash began to fall inside of my eyes, an obscuring gray ash, a blinding that comes. An incineration of vision.

I heard the father and the sheriff. Words, words, words, and someone was walking me outside, fingers pinching tight around my arm, a voice whispering, "Be good, Clyde. We struck gold, Clyde. See you next week, Clyde."

And then I was in the sheriff's car, in the grated-off backseat. From the sticky upholstery came an old puke smell very strong. I could smell Old Skull Popper, I could hear the sheriff sucking down long pulls from a bottle. I felt for Little Debbie. She was there.

The sheriff said, "Ee-gore, right now you need a friend in the worst way, don't you?"

We were on a dirt road, possibly a field road. There was the fragrance of hops. If you know the smell of fields of hops at night. It can be a calming smell. A very kind smell. I heard the hissing of the irrigation devices. The stutter of the water jets. A spray welted hard across the roof and the sheriff rolled up his window. He turned onto a smaller wheel rut path and then he stopped the car.

It was a hot night but he wanted the windows up. Sound travels so easily over flat fields. But even with the windows shut I could still smell the hops, and I fought to hold on to that smell, to concentrate on it. The molecules of it. The sheriff took another pull off the bottle and got out of the car. The back car door opened and he squeezed himself in. He said, "We can make this easy or we can make this hard. If you try to bite me, you won't have a mouth left. Understood?"

He wanted me to take a drink. He passed me the bottle. I took a glug and passed it back. I wanted him to know I was being cooperative. There was the sound of him unbuckling his belt, and the unzipping and the rearrangement of pants. He put his hand on the back of my neck and pushed my head downward. I didn't resist. I didn't hesitate. Never hesitate. Move fast, follow through, let the blade do the work.

My first swipe was a reach-around. Little Debbie was so sharp I didn't know I truly cut him. I felt something like a knife passing through a hard-boiled egg but that was all.

The sheriff froze in the shock of it, and in that instant I took my second swipe. The neck, always the neck in one motion, get the carotid, the jugular, the windpipe if possible, then GO! GET! Jump away from his grabbing hands, jump out of the car flying because he has a gun, insane pop-pop fire power giving flashes brief and bright, the smell of hops of hops of hops and then the smell of the wet earth itself.

His car engine revved, he was driving wild, I looked up to see his headlights swinging through the blackness, and then a sick crunching and everything stopped. His taillights were high and uneven. He was in the culvert. He had driven into the culvert.

The dome light weakly illuminated his body laying strange, half in the car and half out, his face down, the red draining slow into the corrugated half pipe.

I followed the culvert back to the main canal, stopping once to wash his blood off my face. I was looking for the train tracks. I was praying for the train tracks. And I cannot describe the relief I felt when I heard the distant roaring and saw the beam from the twisting yellow eye of the night train.

chapter 40

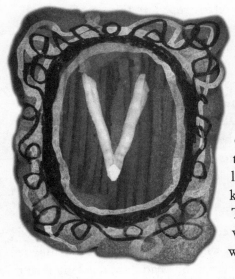

ICKY'S BACK," said the Stick. Through the oval window frame I saw her cross over a pale pool of a streetlight, throwing a shadow first one way and then the other. She was walking like a successful person and I knew she'd gotten the stash. The Stick said, "You still want to drop, right? You still want to trip with me, right?"

I did.

We climbed out onto the ledge and made our way back through the Stick's bedroom window. Vicky was in the hallway calling my name. When she saw me she held up a Diggy's paper bag bloomed over with grease stains and shook it. "I called Dane. He said we should come over at eleven. He says for me to bring you for sure. I'm going to do the most incredible transformation on you, Roberta. You will not have one inch of skag left after I'm done."

She noticed the Stick in the shadowed doorway behind me. She said, "No one is talking to you. No one is interested in you." Vicky pulled me into her bedroom and locked the door.

"You need a cig, Roberta. You need a cig and I especially need a cig because I did something. And now you need to do it." And what she'd done was dropped two caps of Creeper as soon as she got the stash back.

She pointed at Trina. "What's the deal with that thing? Are

you giving it to me? Because if you are I don't want it. Sock monkeys freak me out. You need to know that about me. Sock monkeys can make me very violent. You need to make sure there are no sock monkeys ever around me when I'm high. You going to drop? Because I think you need to drop. Two this time."

I could smell the rank grease of the Dumpster. Vicky fished out two caps. I told her I needed water to swallow them. She said, "In the bathroom," and got busy setting up the vanity, called a vanity, with three mirrors and a low curved top and little drawers crammed with shoplifted makeup. She said, "Wait, wait a sec. You need to take a shower, OK? And you need different clothes." She started digging through her closet and pulled out a sleeveless yellow minidress covered with chocolate-colored flowers.

I said, "I can't wear sleeveless."

"Yes you can."

"It has to be long sleeves."

And we argued for a while. She never asked me why I wanted long sleeves and I didn't know what I would say if she did. Maybe she wouldn't even notice my scars. She hadn't noticed my finger situation or my nose and teeth. Vicky wasn't the kind of person who looked hard at anything. Her eyes flitted and kept flitting except when they came to a mirror.

Finally she found a dress for me. It was crimson crushed velvet, with half-ratty white trim of some kind of fur, looking very lady Santa Claus. There were accessories. A bra was one of them. And two pairs of socks was the other. And the socks were for the bra. Because I was too flat for the dress otherwise. And she did not know why I was taking the sock monkey with me to the bathroom. What was I going to need it for?

"I'm going to get rid of her for you," was my answer.

"Don't try to flush her, OK? Because our toilet clogs very easy."

I tapped lightly on the Stick's door and whispered his name. I reached my hand out and showed him the caps. "You're cool," he said. "Very cool." We took them.

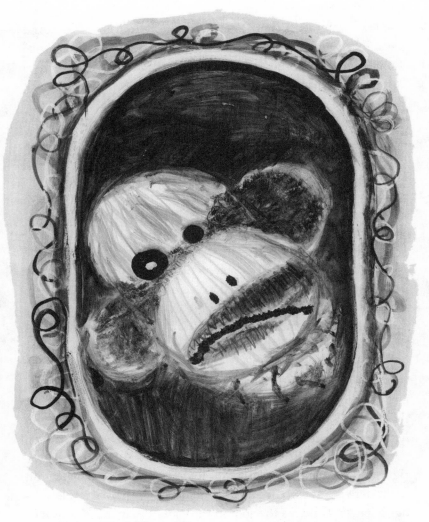

I showered fast and kept the water running while I took Trina
apart, loosening the stitching at her neck. Taking apart the seams
that ran up the insides of both her legs, and peeling her inside out
over the raw cotton. My heart was pounding. In my head, pictures
very vivid were displaying themselves, the day I made Trina, trying to make her as ugly as possible so no one would want her but
me. The Christian Homes lady picking her up and looking disappointed. Trina was too stiff. Who could hug such a stiff sock

monkey? Why did I choose two different buttons for eyes? And the stitched mouth line was sideways. She told me I should take Trina apart and do her over. I made mentally disturbed noises that made her hand Trina back. Who could hug such a stiff sock monkey? I could. And I have every night since then.

I peeled away the cotton batting. My hands were shaking at the thought of seeing her again. Little Debbie. My savior.

Under the batting was my Ace bandage, stained and slightly powdery. There is a thing people say about elastic. That it has memory and that it can lose its memory. The Ace bandage was expanded and could not shrink back down. The tiny elastic threads had crumbled.

Under the bandage was the Crown Royal bag and inside the bag was the money. I had stomach jolts when I saw it. In the time of the father I became very used to seeing wads and wads of cash. But it had been a long time since my eyes saw so many twenty-dollar bills. Five hundred dollars worth tightly rolled around Little Debbie's flexible leather sheath.

What would she look like? I'd taken the steps every knife person knows about. I'd oiled her and wrapped an oiled piece of cloth around her blade and folded a piece of waxed paper around that before I put her into her sheath. I did not want to see rust on her. I prayed not to see the tiniest bit of rust on her.

She gleamed. Seeing her made my eyes wet. The father was right, I am a knife person. Knife-loving blood circulates within me. There is a symbol for infinity, a line that describes a sideways figure eight. X marks the spot in the center. X marks the spot of recirculation. That is where you should plunge the knife to stop the blood of time past from infecting the blood of time future. I held her. It would be so easy. Slicing up from the wrist toward the inside of the elbow.

According to the mother, all emergency room doctors hate people who cut short-ways across the wrists. It's a secret not well known outside of hospitals, that all medical workers despise the people who cut and fail. Even the ambulance drivers can't stand them. It was the mother who showed me the way to do it. Who said water will keep the blood flowing. That very warm water was the best, not because it was more comfortable, but because cold water would constrict the vessels and water that is too hot would be hard to stay in. These are not the only instructions the mother has given me on how to cut one side of time away from the other. She has seen the inside of my arm, she has read the keloid letters and she actually believes the carved words of apology are for her. I didn't disabuse her of this notion, called disabuse when you let someone know they are incredibly wrong, even hilariously wrong. I could tell she was flattered.

"RoBERta!" Vicky was banging on the door and then twisting the doorknob. I turned the water off. "RoBERta, come ON! Open!"

"One sec," I said.

"Open the door. I have to pee so bad."

"One sec!"

And so I had to move very quickly. And so behind the toilet went the deflated body of Trina. And so the money and sheathed Little Debbie were tucked in at the center of the bra, the crushed velvet Santa Claus outfit was in place. I opened the door.

Vicky pushed past me and sat on the toilet. I started to leave and she said, "Prude. Can't you be in the same room as a person who is peeing?"

I stepped into the hall and saw the Stick standing in his bedroom doorway. He looked at my dress and drew a backwards question mark in the air with his finger.

I drew an exclamation mark.

He started laughing and Vicky heard him. "Don't talk to him, Roberta! You need to keep away from him." The toilet flushed and the Stick stepped back into the darkness of his room.

Vicky sat me in front of the vanity. I noticed a weird burning smell, kind of an electrical melting smell. Vicky had her hot curlers plugged in. She had two bottles of Sun In and she planned to use both of them on me.

"Normally you spray this on, OK? Normally you spray this on and go in the sun and you magically get highlights. But I have to do my own method. I swear I am going to have my own salon someday."

She bunched the towel around my neck and poured. Rivulets of Sun In spilled down either side of my nose. The smell was harsh and it stung. I said, "Ow! Ow! My eyes!"

Vicky said, "Keep them shut."

She combed my hair hard and rolled in the first hot curler. It was spiked and molten and it branded my scalp. "OW, VICKY!"

"Quit being a baby. This is only going to take a—GET OUT OF HERE!"

The Stick's voice. "What are you doing to her?"

"SHUT UP AND GET OUT!"

From downstairs, "SHIT AND GODDAMN! MY PRO-GRAM!"

The Stick said, "You're pissing off Susie. His show is on."

The theme music of *Rat Patrol* came shooting up the stairs at full volume.

The Stick said, "How long does it take to work?"

Vicky thought he was talking about the Sun In. She said, "Roberta already has a boyfriend."

The Stick said, "I mean before I feel it?"

And then the truth came out and Vicky whapped me hard on the side of the head and some of the curlers flew off. "YOU GAVE HIM DRUGS?!!"

The Stick said, "How long?"

I said, "Any minute now."

chapter 41

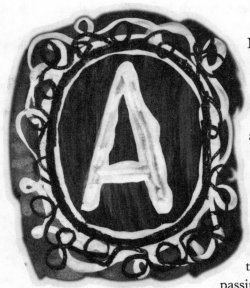

ND SO I crossed through the dark field of fragrant hops with the sheriff's blood sticky on my shirt in the hot night air, and there were about a million bugs hitting me in the face as I crossed to the berm. I was there when the train roared up on me, shot by just above me. Exhilaration. Distraction. When a train is passing a few inches above your head you can't really think about anything else and there are times when a clear head is something I am most thankful for.

And when the train is gone, there is a kind of silence called a ringing silence. Something like the negative shape of sound. People call it a ringing but this word isn't quite right. I think it's more like the sound you hear when you are drowning, when water encloses you and keeps air away from you and sound moves differently to reach your ears. Would drowning be so bad? The canal was right on the other side of the tracks. How bad would it be to wrestle for a few minutes and then be done?

This ringing, this high-pitched sound was something I heard during my fever. My fever time in the trailer. The father told me to look for the sandman. Told me if it hurt at all I could cut a finger from his hand. He made so many promises to me.

I didn't know how far I was from the Knocking Hammer. I

only knew to keep the canal on my right as I walked the tracks. There was a hot wind and the insects were plentiful and loud, and these things comforted me as I made my way back to the father with Little Debbie in my hand.

It wasn't very long before the drifting smell of the cull pile came my way. It wasn't very long before I was in the shadows of the Knocking Hammer again, watching the father bouncing back and forth between the car and the lounge with armloads of things he was going to need on his trip. Clothes, booze, cigs.

Pammy snored in the front seat. She was in a muscle relaxer dreamworld. Her head lay tilted on the seat back and her fat arm protruded from the passenger window like she was giving blood.

And a little farther off, the shape that was Fernst rested in its final heap. I felt bad about Fernst. Very bad. I wanted to cover him with something but there wasn't time. The father was almost done packing.

I lay hidden in the backseat as he drove the dark road away from the Knocking Hammer. I heard the slosh of booze and the satis-fied inhale of a cig and the words of congratulations he spoke. He said, "I got barbed-wire balls and a cock of steel. Goddamn. I sure do."

I didn't mean to fall asleep. I actually thought falling asleep would never be possible for me again. But after all exhilaration comes the crashing. Wakefulness breaks apart.

And then it was light out and the father was panic-screaming and the car was weaving all over the road and the sun was bright bright bright and hot on my face. The father slammed the brakes on and jumped out of the car. I sat up and watched the dust clouds fly around his feet. He bent over and did some dry heaves. He was staring at the car.

Pammy was snort-snoring and her head had vibrated its way over to the open window. Around us the land was gray and emp-ty, dust and flatness. Some low weeds covered with stickers. I caught sight of my face in the rearview mirror. My hair was stiff with dried blood. It was caked around my nose and streaked on my neck. My shirt was covered with the brown stiffness. Blood was caked on my hands, on my fingernails.

Pammy released a very relaxed emission and I got out of the car. The father straggle-ran a few more steps when he saw the car door open and made more panic sounds. He looked very bad in the hard light. He was thin and slope-shouldered and scared. And I have to say it was not a bad feeling to realize what he was scared of was me. Me appearing so suddenly in my Night of the Living Dead aspect.

After a while he hollered, "Clyde, Clyde, is that really you?"

He said, "GODDAMN YOU, CLYDE! SCARED THE LIVING SHIT OUT OF ME! THOUGHT YOU WERE A SON OF A BITCHING ZOMBIE! ABOUT GIVE ME A HEART ATTACK! GODDAMN YOU TO HELL, CLYDE! GIVE A MAN SOME WARNING!"

He said, "All that blood. Where you cut? You're cut somewheres, show me."

He said, "Son of a bitch, Clyde. If it ain't *yours*, whose blood is it?"

I never said any actual words to the father. I made my disturbing noises combined with various nods and shakes of the head and just let him make up his own story. He figured that after the sheriff dropped me off at the rendering plant, I got loose from Mom and hid in the bleed-out room, until I made it to the road and hitched a ride with some Mexicans.

He said, "Missed me that bad, huh? I bet Mom and the sheriff are going apeshit looking for you."

We rolled on, the father following the wires to a place where we could get some gas and he could get some smokes and I could wash up. He kept looking at me in the rearview. He called me one tough buzzard but he seemed unsettled. He asked me to search out a fresh bottle of Whitley's for him. He invited me to take a glug. What a strange strange kind of booze. Sharpens the edges of all things, but dulls the centers.

"I saw that blood on you, see, and I thought you were some kind of goddamned I don't know what. When I seen it was you I thought Arden had cut your throat and meant to pin it on me. Got me nervous there for a minute. Haw. Haw-haw. Almost had me there, Clyde. I'm glad you decided to sign back on. Partners, right? Goddamn partners all the way. Fifty-fifty from here on out."

We came to a half-dead town. Half dead, half palsied, with a boarded-up main street and crooked telephone poles with wires hanging. The gas station had one pump and the gas man didn't say a word to us. The father told him to fill it and asked where the bathroom was. He jerked his thumb toward the back. I scrounged some clothes out of the pile and went around the back of the station to a tack-on shed with a horrifying toilet and just a trickle of water coming out of the faucet. I washed off what I could, rewrapped the Ace bandage around my middle, tucked in Little Debbie, and left my bloody clothes on the floor.

When I got in the car, the father said, "He look familiar to you, Clyde? Fellow pumping the gas? He strike you as familiar in any way? Looks like Earlis, doesn't he?" I didn't know what

Earlis looked like alive but the face on him dead has never left my mind. The smile in the middle of the black rot of his face. Rictus.

I looked at the man. He sat in filthy coveralls on a cast-off kitchen chair just staring straight ahead and sucking his bottom lip in and out. Is that what Earlis had looked like?

The father leaned his head out the window and said, "Hey! Which way's Vegas?" The lip-sucking man didn't look at the father but he said something out loud. The father cupped his ear. "I didn't catch that."

He turned his horrible eyes onto the father. "There's a man in my belly wants your company, son."

The father floored it and Pammy's head lolled and bounced hard as we curbed the corner. "GodDAMN!" He was scared. "Strange shit lately. A *lot*." He kept checking the rearview. He was wearing down.

The time had come for me to speak. What I said was, "That man back there? I think he recognized you."

The day spun overhead and the road went shiny and sent up heat wiggles and Pammy's head hung out the window all the way to the Nevada border. She got the worst sunburn.

As the light began to fail I watched the father's cooked-liver eyes in the rearview. He was on Whitley's and Snore-Not and the Snore-Not made him jumpy and talkative. Made him come out with different provoking sentences. One was, "You know Clyde, I've been meaning to tell you, I'm not really your father."

chapter 42

OU GAVE HIM DRUGS?!" Vicky was screaming at me. She was screaming about the Stick's condition and the Stick was telling her to shut up, just shut up.

Susie yelled from downstairs, "I DRINK TO YOU, CAPTAIN! GODDAMN! WHITLEY'S SPEAKS IN A WHISPER. SHIT AND GODDAMN! I WHISPER!"

Vicky yelled, "SHUT UP, SUSIE!"

The Stick was getting the rushes and so was I. It was making us freely ask and answer questions. I said, "Why is his name Susie?"

The Stick said he gave himself that name after seeing the E-Z Bake Oven commercial and grooving violently on its song.

I want to say more about the mysterious Susie Homemaker. Horrible fumes came from him. He was a cigar person, a Swisher Sweets person. He was also a don't-touch-my-rotting-food person, and a pee-in-a-Gallo-wine-jug person with bad aim. He was a twenty-four-hour person in love with his swivel TV. And he wore women's clothes, and every time I asked either the Stick or Vicky if Susie was their father they told me to go fuck myself.

"THE STICK CAN'T HAVE DRUGS!" screamed Vicky and she moved like she was going to hit me and then she shivered. Her rushes came late. Her rushes came late because she dropped the Creeper with a Diggy's milk shake. My stomach was empty and so was the Stick's. We began to raise.

I said, "You want to hear a story?"

Vicky said, "No."

The Stick said, "Yes."

I said, "Once upon a time in a deep cave, a dry cave, a certain spectacular cave among the thousands of caves in the area of the Moapa Indian reservation and the Valley of Fire in the state of Nevada, in a location about to be swallowed up by Dreamland, called Dreamland by the military, called Area 51, a secret testing place for spy planes and nuclear bombs, very near the Dam of Damnation, once Boulder, now Hoover, which insults a huge river called the Colorado, in this cave a three-headed dog sits in the blackness upon three Samsonite suitcases and the suitcases are full of money and the dog has six swirling eyes as big as saucers."

"How much money?" asked Vicky in a very blasted way, her eyes gone black from the dilation.

"Thousands," I said. "Thousands and thousands. And it's still there. And anyone who finds it gets to keep it. And I know exactly where it is. And if anyone wants to get rich, all they have to do is ask me to take them there."

Vicky raised her hand very excitedly. "Me! Me!"

The Stick started laughing.

I said, "But can you face the six dreaded eyes of the three-headed dog? Many have tried and all have failed. The money is covered with blood."

Vicky said, "Don't freak me, Roberta, OK? Because I don't want you to freak me so just don't, OK?"

"I'm not trying to freak you, Vicky."

"Then don't say the dog has six eyes and the money is covered with blood because it wrecks the whole oh oh oh oh oh oh." The double rushes shook her and her needle stuck on the word "oh."

I said to the Stick, "What condition? What was Vicky talking about when she said your condition?"

The Stick stood up and stretched. He said, "I'm going to take a walk outside."

Then Vicky started laughing very hard. She said, "You? YOU?" Because it turned out the Stick never went outside. He hadn't been outside for several years. And I was thinking this was the condition because I had heard of this condition where a person is not able to go outside without having a massive flip-out.

But the Stick went down the stairs and I followed him and Vicky grabbed her purse and followed me saying, "I have to see this. I have to see this." And we walked past Susie Homemaker, who held a yellow Tupperware tumbler full of booze up to us, saying, "Shit and goddamn. I need to get organized." And around his lounger the clear glass of empty Whitley's bottles was so plentiful that it looked like he was on an island of ice.

And with no hesitation the Stick went into the kitchen and opened the back door and went right out. "Roberta," whispered Vicky into the back of my neck. "You just saw history."

We were in the backyard and the Stick was staring at average things around him. He pointed to the glass-domed electric meter and said, "Whoa."

He kept stretching and I admired the way he looked against the peeling paint of the collapsing garage. I admired the blue shadow thrown by him. He said, "Let's go."

Vicky said, "Go? Stick. Stick. Wait."

But he was already out of the one-hinged gate. He was already in the alley. He told me he didn't feel it, feel anything from the Creeper and I could tell he didn't know it, but the Stick was very high. He was gazing at me. It was different from watching. Different from looking. He was gazing. And I was gazing back. And he said, "You have such a fucked-up nose. And your teeth and your finger. All of you is so fucked up. I have never seen such a fucked-up person and it makes me so sad."

"Don't listen to him, Roberta," Vicky said. "He doesn't really mean it. He's not sad about how skanky you are."

To the Stick she said, "OK, you need to go home now because Susie is alone and Susie can't be alone and me and Roberta have to go someplace, OK?"

"OK," said the Stick. And he turned around and went back to the house. And then it was my turn to be so sad.

Vicky said, "Don't start liking him, Roberta. He's a user."

I said, "How? How is he a user?" But she wouldn't say. She started talking about Dane and his amazing brother and interrupting herself with Creeper revelations like, "Electricity. It's in the wires," and, "You should never feel bad about being a skag because for you being a skag is beautiful." She said she felt like she was in a HeavenScent commercial and she started doing slow-motion running in the middle of the street and flipping her hair up and saying, "Who am I? Who am—I TOLD YOU TO GO HOME!"

The Stick came up behind me.

Vicky yelled, "YOU CAN'T COME WITH US!"

"Hey," said the Stick, and his hair was falling in his eyes and I was thinking the word "palomino" and the word kept circling in my head *palomino palomino palomino* and the boy-smell of him was making me lean close.

"GO HOME!" shouted Vicky.

"OK," said the Stick, and he dropped back into the shadows.

And the whole way to the house of Dane and his amazing brother I was certain the Stick was behind us, following us, and I was very happy about this until I realized it wasn't true. We were at the gate of 11 Circle View and the long road behind us was empty. Big big trees and some streetlight shadows but no one with hair falling in his eyes.

"What," said Vicky. "You're not chickening out on me, are you? I mean, Roberta, *look*." She gestured at the house behind the tall wrought-iron gates. It was huge and very brick and very royal in its details. We crossed the curving walkway to the front door. I heard a piano playing inside. Vicky rang the doorbell.

An eyeball looked at us through the peephole. A voice said, "Yes. Absolutely." The front door swung wide. It was the Turtle who greeted us.

Vicky said, "What the fuck are *you* doing here?"

The Turtle said, "Please. Come in. The Great Wesley is leaning forward in anticipation."

Vicky said, "Who the fuck is the Great Wesley? Where's Dane?"

I kept my eyes down. I did not expect to see the Turtle and I had not wanted to see the Turtle. He said, "Hillbilly Woman. Is it love? You have returned to me."

Vicky pushed past him. "Dane!?"

A harsh voice answered, "What?"

The Turtle said, "My love." His eyes were pink. He was extremely high. I followed Vicky into the living room.

The furniture was modern. Big leather couches. Black leather swivel chairs. A huge glass table in a paramecium shape. On it was a tall brass water pipe with personal smoker tubes for everyone. The Ancient Substance was piled high and glowing. There was a gargling sound. A guy was huffing on one of the smoker tubes. It was the amazing Dane.

He looked about seventeen and was decently foxy, although not in my style. He had blond hair and Sir Lancelot features. His eyes were large, with lashes so long I have to say he looked slightly like a girl. He wore in-style clothes, looking new, very hip, but even so, something about him looked lame. When he saw us he looked really irritated.

Vicky lifted her hand. "Hey, Dane."

He blew out a huge exhale and said, "What the fuck are you doing here?"

Vicky said, "We have chocolate mesc."

The person playing the piano was a fat and pale person in a blue bathrobe. His face was babyish and his hair was scraggly and he was sweating hard. He looked up at Vicky and me and nodded calmly. His expression was friendly. He had a look of kindness.

He rocked back and forth as he played and the music kept shifting, melodies strange and ancient turned into the music for "Marvel the Mustang," which turned into "Winchester Cathedral." No song ever finished, one just turned into the other. He said, "*Adagio con molto sentimento d'affetto*," and "Junior Samples leads me through worlds of wonder."

Vicky smiled at me. She smiled the smile of "Didn't I tell you it would be incredible?" She whispered, "That's him. That's his brother. Didn't I tell you he was perfect?"

She handed the Turtle's stash box to Dane. He said, "This isn't mesc. This is that mental-house shit. Wes. Wes." Dane held up a cap. "It's that psycho shit you guys stole from the nuthouse, right?"

The piano player nodded.

"The preferred term is *pharmaceutical shit*," said the Turtle.

Dane said, "Fuck off, fuckhead."

The Turtle said, "Are you familiar with the work of Dr. Peter Mark Roget? He understood that to dump sewage into the river you drink from is to no one's advantage. He would be very happy if you would open up his thesaurus and quit saying 'fuck.'"

"Don't fuck with me, man. I can fucking turn you in. Your parents got a reward out, fuckhead. Five thousand bucks. One phone call. You fucking better watch it."

Vicky said, "*Reward?* What reward?"

The Turtle said, "Ladies, will you stone?" He offered us smoker tubes. We took in the water-cooled clouds. Dane stared at Vicky for a while and then stood up. He said, "Come on." She followed him down some stairs.

"Violent One," called the Turtle. "Reconsider!"

After a while there was the sound of splashing. I went to the window and in the turquoise swimming-pool light I saw Vicky and Dane in some naked positions. The Turtle stood beside me. He said, "He will conjugate her verb. He will use her in a single sentence and punctuate her and there is nothing we can do."

He leaned onto the piano and said, "My dear dear Wesley. Your brother is the Sultan of all Ass-heads."

The Great Wesley nodded sadly.

chapter 43

I MEAN, TECHNICALLY," said the father, "I might be your father. There's a resemblance, but—" Glug, glug, glug. He never finished the sentence. Glug glug glug. There was severe slippage. The Whitley's was shrinking his mind.

"All I'm trying to say here, Clyde, is that, except for possibly technically, I'm not your father. I want us to be clear on that. It's partners, fifty-fifty, partners all the way. If you're in, you're in. You in?"

"I'm in," I said.

"Her." The father pointed at Pammy. "Fat-ass here. When we hit Vegas I mean to get a powerful buzz on and then I'm going to technically marry her. But it's not technically going to mean shit to me at all. Technically, I'm still married to your mother, which also don't count because I never let technical shit constrict me. My philosophy is live and let live or kiss my ass." Glug glug glug.

"Maybe I'll go back up to the Knocking Hammer, maybe we'll just say fuck-all. Maybe I'll shove her out on the way to goddamned Tijuana. Maybe keep rolling 'til I hit the Panama Canal. Park my car, take my pants off, go wading in my skivvies. What I'm trying to say here, Clyde, is there's a reason God made roads that lead in every direction. What I'm trying to say here,

Clyde, is I think it's time you learned to drive."

We were on an unpaved road marked PRIVATE, then we passed through a barbed-wire archway marked NO TRESPASSING, and then we went past signs with red skulls on them saying DANGER RESTRICTED AREA and that is where he gave me my driving lesson. On the shockingly white desert flats between ranges of dried mountains and sudden rock formations so peculiar.

"Straight," said the father. "Go that way, south, south, until I tell you to turn." And then he stretched out in the backseat, closed his eyes, and he tumbled into snoring.

I liked driving. I liked it very much. And I liked the weird landscape. It seemed like I had been there before and that was a mysterious feeling.

Pammy stirred. In her oblivion she mumbled some words I couldn't make out. I tried to keep us going straight on the forbidden road, which was getting fainter in the blowing dust. The place was looking so familiar to me it made some chills run up my back. Pammy mumbled again and I looked over and saw she had wet her pants. Her face was looking quite boiled. Her dried-out lips were moving.

The white flats before me had a shimmer rising. Looking like water up ahead. Looking cool in the wiggling heat. I was feeling so thirsty.

The blowing dust was alkali, called alkali, a mineral in the dirt that the wind kicked up and made you taste it. It was bitter and metallic. But the whiteness it gave to things was beautiful and I will admit I became enchanted and I found out I could feel even more enchanted if I smoked a cigarette and did some graceful curves with the steering wheel and then I had to try a circle and then I had to try a spiral and then I went back to peaceful serpentines. I had some quenching little sips of Whitley's and then my mind jolted. There was a reason I knew this place.

The Horror of the Blood Monsters. It Came From Outer Space. Them! The Blob. The Mummy. The Amazing Colossal Man. I was in the valley of the monsters. I was in the middle of the location where so many of the world's greatest movies were filmed. I was right where the plane did a sudden nosedive and crashed and blew up on fire and an innocent man ran to help, he jumped into the flaming wreckage to pull the pilot to safety, but BLAMBLAM! There was plutonium on the plane and the radioactivity burns him crunch black. He ends up very bald but he lives. The radiation has caused a change. He starts growing. His body becomes huge and he can't stop wanting to destroy everything, he hurls a bus full of people over his head. They all die. The furious emotions of the Amazing Colossal Man are real.

I kept thinking, "*I am driving right where he was formed. I am driving right where he walked.*"

I took another little sip of Whitley's. I thought about how there actually were moments when life was good and decent. I kept driving and sipping. I can't tell you exactly when I lost the road. At some point I just noticed there were no tire tracks to follow anymore and then a jet came flying so low and silent followed by an explosion so loud that my mind just went white. Then came another and another and another. "Fucking hell!" shouted the father.

Pammy was roused. She unlatched her door, fell out and rolled. I opened my door, walked around the car and leaned on the back bumper. Radiation transformation. I puked silver heaves.

chapter 44

HE AIR above the white desert flats was so still after the jets passed over. I heard the tobacco on the father's cigarette burning on every inhale. He was leaning on the hood of the car, surveying the four directions. "We are lost as shit."

Pammy said, "Hepme, hepme, I canna mo mah les." She was wiggling in the alkali.

I heard a slight vibration in the air. Like the sound of wind whipping over something hollow. I said, "They're coming back."

"Shit on it," said the father. "It's just the Air Force."

Pammy said, "Tha lilbassart tahks! Ah jassherd hi! Tha lilshid tahks!" The father propped her up. He said, "You're dreaming, fat-ass."

The planes came at us.

The father yelled, "INCOMING! INCOMING!" We were all flat on the ground. The stillness returned. We loaded Pammy into the backseat and the father took the wheel. He drove randomly. He laid on the horn, saying, "Somebody is bound to hear us."

Pammy said, "Imma keel yuh yuh bassart!"

The father said, "I guess that means the wedding's off."

"Wha??" Pammy said. "Wewwing?"

"Take a look, baby-doll! We're in Las Vegas!"

Pammy made many rubberized movements before she was

able to lift herself up enough. What she saw made her lay back down and say, "Imma keel you dahd."

In the distance a white cloud was rolling toward us. In the middle of the cloud was a Jeep. In the Jeep were two soldiers with helmets and two rifles.

The father glugged deep from the last bottle of Whitley's. He said, "Shit on the Air Force." He quick lit a cigarette. "I can handle the goddamned Air Force."

The Jeep stopped some yards away. One of the soldiers stood up and said through a bullhorn, "THIS IS A RESTRICTED AREA. YOU ARE IN A RESTRICTED AREA."

The father cupped his hands and shouted, "NO SHIT, SHERLOCK. WHICH WAY'S VEGAS?"

The two soldiers jumped out of the Jeep with their rifles. They trotted toward us in high black boots laced tight at the ankles.

The father said, "Which one of you clowns is going to point me to Vegas?"

"You need to leave the area immediately, sir."

"My wife is drunk out of her mind and my kid has diarrhea."

"Sir?"

The father tapped me on the shoulder. "See there, son? That's an Air Force man right there." He pulled a long drag on his cig. "My boy is crazy over the Air Force. You wouldn't consider giving him a little ride in your piece-of-shit Jeep would you? Turn a couple brodies in the sand? It would mean a hell of a lot to him. He don't got long to live."

"Sir, you need to leave the area immediately."

"Can my boy have a ride?"

"I can't do that, sir."

"Aw shit, why not?"

Pammy said, "Hep me."

"Shut up, honey. I'm talking." The father made a drinking motion with his hand. "She's topped out."

"We'll escort you, sir."

"Just tell me who in the hell is going to give a shit if you give my boy a ride in your vehicle there?"

"I'm sorry, sir."

"Well, you tell me, what am I busting my nuts to pay taxes for then? I paid for that Jeep."

The two soldiers exchanged looks.

The father rubbed his face. "Shit, boys. I'm sorry. Guess I'm wound a little tight. I got the piles so bad I'm about to have a nervous breakdown."

"Vegas is that way," said the bullhorn soldier.

They led us to a dirt road that turned into an old severely cracked paved road and the father waved. He said, "Goddamn it was hard not to kick their asses, Clyde. Goddamn I hate the goddamn Air Force."

Along the road there were some old signs advertising attractions in Las Vegas. Some had a few silver sequins still wiggling on the nails. The expansion of Dreamland had killed the road we were on. It wasn't used anymore.

If you look at a map of Nevada you'll see a place called Nellis Air Force Range just east of the Funeral mountains and Devil's Hole. Dreamland won't be marked. But it is there, underground, at the center of a world of tunnels as wide as highways. Tunnels and certain cave passages.

We came to a crossroads. The father said, "I know right where I am."

In front of us was a hand-painted billboard. It said, SEE THE LAST LIVING POWDER MONKEY! HE IS FANTASTIC! SEE THE MAN WHO BUILT THE DAMN! HE DEFIES GRAVITY! HE DEFIES DEATH!! HE IS FEARLESS!! THE POWDER MONKEY INVITES ONE AND ALL TO ENTER HIS SPARKLING CIRCLE! THREE SHOWS DAILY!! THE POWDER MONKEY WILL THRILL YOU AS NEVER BEFORE!! UNFORGETTABLE!!

Underneath the sign was another sign. In faded-out cursive words it said, *The powder monkey is dead.*

chapter 45

FEAR THE Sultan of all Ass-heads has already betrayed us." said the Turtle. "I fear the arrival of the authorities. He frolics with the Violent One. We cannot save her from his power. We must depart at once. Yes. Absolutely. North to Canada. North to the sweet homeland."

"My dear, dear Turtle," said the Great Wesley. "I am in the mood for fruit. Will you join me in the kitchen?"

In the kitchen was a huge bouquet of rotted flowers tied with a black bow. Wesley said, "My father and mother. How sad for me."

I said, "What happened?"

"They have gone the way of all parents, I'm afraid."

"Dead?"

"Switzerland. I counted on them remaining in Lausanne for at least a month. Unfortunately the news of my escape and unexpected homecoming has somehow reached them. They are due back tomorrow."

"DEATH TO THE SULTAN OF THE ASS-HEADS!" said the Turtle. "They won't take us back alive, my dear Wesley. This I swear."

In the kitchen a plastic bag of apples lay on the counter with a stretched hole ripped into the side. The Great Wesley took one apple and began opening the drawers. "I am in need of a small cleaving instrument."

"A knife?" I asked.

"Exactly."

I produced Little Debbie. The Great Wesley admired her. "It has been a long time since I have seen anything so sharp. At the home we were not permitted such things. And yet we managed, did we not my dear, dear Turtle? Barbara V. Hermann could not dampen our love for adventure."

"Down with Barbara!" said the Turtle.

I said, "The home?"

Wesley carved a careful hollow into the apple. "The Barbara V. Hermann Home for Adolescent Rest. Yes. This is a fine knife. Quite a fine knife."

With some careful cutting and boring and a bit of foil and a few pinpricks the Great Wesley transformed the apple into quite a pipe.

"Oh my dear Wesley. How I long for sensational smoky-smoky."

"To hear is to obey, my dear Turtle." Wesley drew a metal canister from his robe pocket.

"My dear Wesley! You old fox!"

We smoked.

I said, "Tell me about the home."

The Great Wesley exhaled a great apple-scented cloud. "The Barbara V. Hermann Home for Adolescent Rest is quite exclusive and the membership requirements are stringent. For suicidal and psychotic youth from distinguished families, it is top tier. International. Discreet beyond words. Nestled in an obscured location adjacent to the Lolo National Forest. Triple-fenced and gated. But still the Turtle and I managed to escape with quite a valuable bundle of medications. Great quantities stolen from the Barbara V. Hermann drug treasury. We left in search of sensational smoky-smoky. Most of us preferred the combination of smoky-smoky and ample television to the antipsychotic pharmaceuticals we were given. A majority of the residents at the home were in agreement on this and we petitioned Barbara V. Hermann to include smoky-smoky on her vast roster of drugs but she refused. It was a simple concept," said the Great Wesley. "But you know Barbara."

"Death to Barbara," said the Turtle.

"Yes," said the Great Wesley. "Perhaps I overreacted when I killed her." He inhaled another cloud.

"My dear, dear Wesley," said the Turtle. "It was I who killed Barbara. Let the truth be known."

Wesley said, "My dear, dear Turtle. There is no need to confess to a crime you did not commit. It was I who strangled her."

"My dear, dear, Wesley. You are kind in your wish to protect me, but I alone am guilty of this crime. As proof I offer you her last words. She said, 'Turtle, no.' I said, 'Barbara, yes.' She said, 'Turtle, you strange psychotic fucker.' "

The Great Wesley shook his head. "My dear Turtle! But those were not her last words at all!"

"My dear Wesley, but they were."

"No, as I choked the life out of her body her last words were, 'Make my skin into drumheads for the Bohemian cause.' "

They gently argued for a while and then the Great Wesley turned to me. "Hillbilly princess, it is rumored you can drive. Is this so?"

And when I told him it was, he stood and carefully straightened his bathrobe around himself. From his pocket he produced two keys on a golden ring.

chapter 46

HE FATHER actually did have a destination. He did have a location objective. It was off the beaten track. It was about fifty miles down a rock-filled road barricaded by a sign that said DANGER! ROAD OUT! The father drove around it without even touching the brakes.

The horse pills were wearing off and Pammy was feeling better. She was leaning up from the backseat and using her lardy fingers to do twirlies in the father's hair. The father had given her a ring. She said, "Ish betafol."

It was a man's ring, fat with a low setting, and the stone in the ring, the jewel, was peculiar. I didn't know what it was. The color of butterscotch candy and catching the light in a way that was hard not to stare at. Shooting little flitting sparkles around the car when the light caught it right. Where was it from? What was it?

Pammy reached over and tried to do a twirly in my hair. She said, "We're ganna be a family."

I jerked, and said, "Quit."

I got an instant whack on the side of the head from the father, who slammed on the brakes and made me and Pammy change places. "Don't be rude to her, Clyde. She's your future mother and she's still half tanked on muscle relaxers."

Pammy kept turning around to look at me. Her burned and blistered face was freaking me. Her horrible dead tooth was freaking me. The rolls of fat on her neck were freaking me. She had a fresh change of clothes on, her peed-on Bermudas were on the floor of the backseat. The father was messing with the radio, trying to get a station to come in but all he got was a violently loud hum. He said, "We're almost there."

He said, "Clyde, I ever mention Auntie Doris to you?"

I said, "No."

Smiling, Pammy said, "Ya talk. Why ya sneaky little turd. Say something. Say a little rhymey-something for me."

I concentrated on the scenery. The radio was off but the hum was still detectable. The sound of power lines. Of hydroelectricity blasting through power lines.

The father said, "I never mentioned your crazy Aunt Doris to you, Clyde? The one with the two green W's tattooed on her ass? Bends over, spells WOW. Stands on her head, spells MOM. She's Navy. But Navy don't begin to describe her."

The road began to wind upward through rock formations, we headed into the dry jagged hills. The sun was setting and the sky was flaming out colors in that spectacular desert way, combinations that didn't look actual, didn't look possible. Gold and violet and blood-red. The father stepped on it a little, fishtailing around the rock-slide bends. Wherever he was going, he wanted to get there before dark. He and Pammy finished off the last drops of Whitley's and the bottle sailed out the window. The hum was so loud my teeth were affected. They started itching from the inside.

We made a couple more turns and then hit a stretch of black-top, very smooth, it went on for about a quarter mile and then dead-ended in the big black parking lot of the Lucky Chief Motel.

There were many signs nailed onto a wooden post. They said CLOSED FOR SEASON. CLOSED FOR REPAIRS. EXCUSE OUR DUST WE'RE REMODELING. GUARD DOG ON DUTY. THIS PROPERTY PATROLLED BY RADAR. YOU'LL GET MORE THAN AN ASS CHEWING IF YOU TRESPASS HERE. THANK YOU. DORIS HORACE, OWNER, OPERATOR.

Two things happened right away. A stick-skinny woman with

a big lower jaw and overcurled hair came running in a flapping flowered housedress screaming, "No! Stop! Goddamn it!" That was Auntie Doris.

Behind her a shadow-shape of a tall man took off running. The father threw the brakes on long enough to jump out and he tore after the shadow-man, both of them vanishing into some rock formations. Caverns and caves. They were all over.

The car kept rolling and Pammy was trying to hit the brake but was having a hard time getting her big leg to cooperate, we plowed along the natural dip in the parking lot with Auntie Doris chasing alongside us, grabbing on to the door handles and trying to drag the car to a stop, and this was my first real view of her, screaming her head off and trying to stop an entire car with her bare hands. The parking lot had just been re-topped that very day. The high bitumen content gave it a glassy surface. We rolled into it, rolled right through it. Came to a sticky stop. Auntie Doris stood at the edge of it with one hand over her mouth.

Pammy got out of the car. She said, "I'm Earlis's fiancée."

Auntie Doris said, "*Earlis*?"

"He asked me to marry him."

"*Earlis* did?"

"Surprise wedding."

"I'll say."

The father came huffing and wheezing back over the rocks. Auntie Doris shouted, "YOU DICKLESS PIECE OF SHIT! SEE WHAT YOU JUST DID TO MY GLOSS ASPHALT?"

The Lucky Chief Motel was long and low with orange doors and cement-block windows. It was built right into the rock face. There was a theory that attaching directly to the rock would keep it cooler in the hot season. Some of the rooms had actual rock walls, and there was an awning over a cave opening that descended to a shallow underground stream. Water for anything but drinking came up from there. Over the cave entrance was quite a fancy sign. It said THE LAIR OF THE SEQUINED GENIUS. As the light faded down to the last shreds I looked for bats to come shooting out, silent and swift. I like bats very much. They are the most incredible creatures. But none were in the Lair of the Sequined Genius.

There wasn't much else to the Lucky Chief. Some truck-tire planters with zigzag edges and a couple of concrete picnic tables. I figured I'd seen everything there was to see. And then I saw her.

She was sitting on the bench of the picnic table closest to the door marked OFFICE. A very intelligent-eyed little dog staring straight at me. Studying me. Scraggly haired and dirty looking. A whitish-grayish dog.

The desert is famous for certain types of hallucinations. Mirages they can be called. Always in the distance, the thing most hoped for appears, like cool, cool water or the ice cream man. The superheated air rises in wiggles and reflects back your last wishes. There are a thousand movies that end with the main character crawling through the desert toward something that does not exist. Often this happens when treasure is involved. When one guy cheats another guy and won't pay what he owes.

I walked toward the dog.

Auntie Doris said, "Careful. She bites."

"Haw!" said the father. "Them two could have a contest."

Pammy said, "Earlis, honey?"

The father said, "What, dolly-baby?"

Auntie Doris said, "*Earlis?* Shit. I need a goddamned highball."

Darkness in the desert is so quiet. There weren't any of the usual sounds, there were no train tracks, no sounds of cars, nothing to break the stillness except for a cracking explosion that had everyone but Auntie Doris diving to the ground.

"Testing," she said. "They're just testing is all." She had the yellow bug lights on but I didn't hear or see any of the usual night insects. I didn't see any bugs at all except for small gatherings of midnight flies.

Pammy drained her third highball and ran her finger in the dripped condensation. We were sitting at the concrete picnic table. I was holding Cookie, then Peanut, née Snarla. It was Auntie Doris who named her Snarla, the Sequined Genius who named her Peanut, and me who named her Cookie.

I had my nose on the top of her head and I was inhaling her calming fragrance. The fragrance of dogs and the feeling of my face against their fur puts me in such a relaxed mood. A comforted mood. The father and Auntie Doris were glugging and re-glugging and re-hashing old times. On the table was a plastic container full of melting ice and an assortment of bottles and an ashtray that said STOLEN FROM LOU'S EFFICIENCY APTS. SPARKS, NEV.

Auntie Doris said, "Goddamn it, quit shooting your butts all over my asphalt. The ashtray is six inches from your elbow. You say he hung himself?"

The father said, "You know he hung himself, Doris."

"Well. You scared the living crap out of Gy-rah."

"I just wanted to give him a little half-brotherly kiss is all."

"He don't want to know you. He said you're a pollution."

"Pollution?"

"Don't ask me. He's the genius."

"What do you think about it?"

"Me?"

"Uh-huh."

"I could give a French shit."

"Well, that's good."

Pammy was staring at her engagement ring. I was starting to feel sad for her. I knew all about trying to hang on to certain words said by the father. She wanted the words to be true. And I could tell she loved him. And although she was an evil fungus growing on 200 pounds of irritated lard, her feelings were real. It wasn't her fault that the father wandered into her life. Chance blew the father in a lot of directions. He rolled around this way and he rolled around that way, deforming everything he brushed up against.

"Earlis, what kind of stone is this?" Pammy held her hand up and touched the ring. "Daddy-baby, what's this type of jewel called?"

The father lit another cig and threw the match onto the asphalt.

Auntie Doris said, "God*damn* you."

The father said, "Dolly-baby, that right there is the genuine Eye of the Idol. Worth a pile."

Auntie Doris snorted the word "*Earlis*" into her highball glass.

Pammy hung on.

 ICKY CAME up the stairs dripping wet and her mascara had run black streaks down her face and her missing eyebrow area was looking very waxy and prominent. "Roberta. Come here! Come here!" Her whisper was urgent.

She pulled me over to her and put her face against my ear. Some of her dripping soaked into me. She whispered, "We did it. We did *it*. Oh god. I am SO in love."

The Turtle and the Great Wesley stared at her.

Vicky said, "What?! Mind your own! Fuck."

No one knew what to say.

Vicky pinched her eyes down into suspicious lines. "How come everybody stopped talking? What's going on? You guys were talking about me, weren't you?"

The Turtle said, "My dear Wesley. Let us return to the piano. You will play a dirge. I shall sing."

And so the Great Wesley played and the Turtle sang, "*Daaane...is such...a fuh...ker...He...is...such...a fuh...ker...*"

Vicky's smile shined when she saw Dane come up the stairs with his wet hair combed back. I saw him avoiding her eyes.

"Alas," said the Turtle. "Alas and oh fuck. The Sultan of Assheads lives."

"Fuck you, fuckhead. I need to get high, man." He picked up the carved apple. "What a wicked fucking pipe, man. Matches.

Matches." Vicky scrambled to get him some. He took them without looking at her. He was acting like she was not in the room. Every time she sat closer, he moved away.

The Turtle said, "Observe. The Sultan knew her and now he knows her not. The Violent One has become a banished and broken filament in the world's saddest lightbulb. Play, Wesley. Play the mournful tune."

The Turtle sang to Vicky and threads of drool hung from his lips. He was looking very pale, and even when he sank to his knees he kept singing and in between vomits of watery pinkness into the shag carpet he kept singing and crawling toward her and she scrambled backwards, shouting, "Fuck! Fuck! Get away!"

The Sultan thought it was hilarious. He coughed out his apple cloud and said, "You two are fucking *perfect* for each other!" Vicky slapped the apple pipe out of his hands. The Sultan flipped her the finger.

The Great Wesley closed the piano cover, stood up and readjusted his bathrobe and said, "Brother, it is time I inform you that I am leaving and I will be taking the car."

"The FUCK you ARE!"

The Turtle crawled to the apple pipe and was trying to get a hit off of it when the Sultan kicked. The apple pipe flew and hit the wall and the Turtle rolled onto the floor holding his jaw and the Sultan was about to kick him again but was stopped by a sudden cut on his arm, a slice, very clean and very deep and instantly gushing. Little Debbie gleamed in my hand.

"FUCK!" shouted the Sultan. "What the fuck ARE you people? I'm FUCKING calling the COPS!" And he ran to the telephone and we ran for the garage. All of us piled into a very sleek car and after a few false starts and some violent jerks we were rolling, rolling though the deep shadows of the dark boulevard, listening to Vicky crying and saying, "He used me. He used me. He used me."

chapter 48

LYDIE? CLYDIE, honey?" This was Pammy talking, looking yellow in the bug light. A little spot of light in an ocean of darkness. We were at the concrete picnic table. She kept trying to make conversations happen with me. Talking out her little comments and observations. Asking me for mine. Freaking me with her friendliness. It was so sincere and horrible.

The father and Auntie Doris were inside the office settling out some private things. It was Gy-Rah the Sequined Genius who had received the final suitcase. Gy-Rah, half brother of the father, son of Auntie Doris and Old Dad, sired by a slaughterhouse man and not the Sensational Powder Monkey. This was news Gy-Rah could not accept. This was news he refuted through a bullhorn from his hidden location in the rock face above us. He did not want the money, he wanted no part of the pollution, he wanted the defiling elements to leave his surroundings.

"Clydie," said Pammy. "Why don't you run go knock on that door and find out what is taking your daddy so long in there." She lit a Salem from the charity pack Auntie Doris tossed her like an apple to a hog. "Son of a bitching menthol. Can't taste them." She was lighting up one after the other, smoking them down, stabbing them out, lighting one up again.

"YOU WILL EVACUATE THE AREA IMMEDIATELY!" said the insulted amplified voice.

"Clydie," said Pammy. "Could you run up that hill and find that screechy little bastard and tell him his voice is giving me a headache?"

Cookie was asleep on my lap. She was wiggling her feet slightly and making little noises. Dreaming. I didn't want Pammy to keep talking. I didn't want to get to know her. I didn't want to care about what was going to happen to her now that she was in the realm of the father.

"Clydie, can I confess you something? I never been this far before. I mean away-far. And this is far. You better believe it. This is son-of-a-bitching far and it gives me the shivers thinking about it. I want to call Arden and tell him where I'm at but that Doris says there's no telephone. Now how can you run a motel without a telephone. Arden is not going to take this too good."

I thought of the sheriff hanging half out of his car, draining himself into the corrugated half pipe. After you are dead you don't really keep bleeding, there's nothing to keep your blood moving except for gravity. If you are hanging upside down then gravity is a factor. It's called bleeding out the carcass.

"Clydie, how is it that your daddy and that Doris are related?"

She studied the ring. The gleaming Eye of the Idol. "She from your daddy's side of the family?"

I shrugged. She stabbed out another Salem. She gandered at her ring some more, tilting it this way and that way. She said, "You think it makes my finger look fat?" She was rolling, following the glinty glimmer of the Eye of the Idol into the darkness. She was rolling into the blackness after the imaginary man.

She knocked the stone against her dead tooth. *Tap-tap-tap*. She said, "It's real. Can tell by the sound." *Tap-tap-tap*. "See there? It's genuine."

I said, "His name is Raymond. Raymond Rohbeson."

She said, "Who is? What is?"

I pointed toward the office door. "Raymond Rohbeson."

She said, "Which?"

I didn't say anything.

She said, "Your daddy?"

I nodded.

"You say he's Raymond?"

I nodded.

She lit another smoke. She said, "Raymond Ro-what?"

"Rohbeson. With an 'h.' And he's not really my father."

"He's not the what?"

"He told me he wasn't really my father."

"Earlis did?"

"No. Not Earlis. Raymond. Earlis is a dead guy."

Pammy slapped me. She slapped me very hard across the face. When I told the truth about the father this was her reaction.

And after I jumped away and after Cookie lunged at her snarling with fangs exposed and ready to puncture, and after they did puncture and grip through the lard and held on through Pammy's jumping panicky yanks and after Pammy hollered, "EARLIS, HELP ME! GODDAMN IT HELP ME!" and after Cookie let go and precious blood drops flew and scattered, there came such a flashing light, blue-white and blinding, sending a brief shock of skin-searing heat and a deafening blast, an explosion coming at us in echoing waves and the ground trembled and rocks came loose and there was a sudden flurry of scattering lizards and dusty snakes shooting out of hidden places and Pammy screamed again and Cookie faded fast up into the rock face and I followed her.

Pammy screamed, "IT'S THE END OF THE WORLD!" In the open doorway of the office stood Auntie Doris calmly lighting a Salem. She said, "Oh, honey, shit. That ain't nothing but Dreamland."

The father came out behind her, buttoning his shirt and smoothing his hair and hitching his pants as he walked to the picnic table. And in the bug light his skin looked oily. And from the cavern opening, from the Lair of the Sequined Genius came a rolling cloud and a thick, searing smell, like burning wires and rotting eggs. Pammy was backing away with her arms out and her eyes wriggling in terror.

The father poured two tall ones. He said, "You ain't getting cold feet about our wedding, honey, are you? Did you know Doris here is a certified beautician?"

Doris took one of the highballs. She said, "You could use a set and a comb-out, hon."

Dreamland is Air Force. Top Secret. Located somewhere on the base that stretches on and on for miles, filled with such craters from the violent tests of all the interesting bombs that came after the A and the H. All the silent letters of the alphabet that exploded after those.

There are many people who know about Dreamland but there are not many people who know this: Dreamland is never in the same place twice. Dreamland roves about beneath the landscape. Sometimes it's under a dry lake bed, sometimes it is in the mountains, sometimes it roves off the base completely through a system of chutes and tunnels and natural underground passages. Dreamland is nowhere and everywhere at once. The billowing fumes that rose from the Lair of the Sequined Genius had me sick and kneeling in my hidey-hole. Pammy was also brought down. The father coughed a little bit and wiped his eyes but kept on drinking. Doris wasn't affected at all. She said she hardly notices it anymore but it did used to bother her. One time it turned her eyeballs blood-red and egg-yellow for a couple of hours but now she can't even smell it.

The father glugged his highball whole and poured again. "Radioactive shit. Fallout particles, that what it is? Shit is supposed to be bad for you."

"Oh yes," said Auntie Doris. "Real bad."

"Earlis," Pammy was crying. "Help me, Daddy-baby. I can't breathe, that son of a bitching dog bit me to where I am bleeding to death and your boy has been telling lies on you."

"You're fine," said the father, sitting comfortable. "You're doing great. What lies has Clyde been telling you?"

His voice was casual but I heard a tautness.

And Pammy told him what I said. Pammy spoke his real name right to his face and he said she ought to know better than to listen to a turd like me. He said it wasn't exactly all lies because partly his name was Ray.

"Earlis-Ray is my name, honey, but true family just call me Ray. Clyde's just trying to welcome you into the family is all." The sound in the father's voice was chilling me. There is such a thing as Very Sensitive Vibration Feelers and the father had them when it came to me. The Navy sentence for treason is death.

"Come on, Pammy," said Auntie Doris. "Let's fix you up. What time is it? Gy-Rah ain't had nothing to eat tonight." Her big jaw lowered and her voice boomed, "GY-RAH!"

"I'm bleeding," said Pammy.

Doris said, "Come on inside. I'll clean you up. The dog did that? When I find her I'll break her neck for you, OK, hon?"

And the office door closed behind Pammy and Auntie Doris. And then it was silent. Just the father at the concrete table sipping a highball and saying my name. Speaking to me in a normal voice. "Clyde. I know you can hear me. I don't give a shit about that what you told Pammy. Come on out, Clyde, and have a drink with me."

chapter 49

T O MY house, to my house," said Vicky. "Turn here."

"New Orleans," said the Great Wesley. "South, good Hillbilly Woman."

"Alberta," said the Turtle. "Neil Young shall make our beds ready." And while he blabbed on a little about how Neil Young was excited about our visit, Vicky blabbed out things she wanted me to get from her room because I had to get these things because she was not going inside there was no way she was going inside, she did not want to see Susie. Her blabbing was interrupted occasionally by the Great Wesley leaning forward to say, "South, south. New Orleans! Naturally!" And I had my own opinion on a destination. You can say I had the way memorized. I was liking the sleek car very much. Liking the smooth quickness. It reminded me of Little Debbie.

It was because of the Stick I followed Vicky's directions. I wanted him to come with us. Vicky said, "Stop! Here! Don't park in front of my house," and I pretended to listen to her instructions while my heart pounded and I wondered if I could convince the Stick to come along.

I walked the warm sidewalk and Vicky shouted after me that if I forgot her HeavenScent perfume she would kill me.

There were no lights on in the house except the jumping light of the TV in the front room. I whisper-shouted for the Stick from the bushes beneath his open bedroom window. I backed up to see the attic oval window, to see if his face was peering down at me. There was no one. I cupped my hands around my mouth. "Stick! Stick! It's Roberta. It's me."

Click. The porch light came on. Green light shed itself onto my skin, onto my hands as I climbed the porch steps. I waited for the door to open but it didn't. There was no sound but the mumble of the TV. A man's voice, a lady's voice, and audience haw-hawing. I knocked. Tap-tap-tap.

"SHIT AND GODDAMN!"

I called through the door. "Is the Stick there? I'm looking for the Stick. Is he home?"

Nothing.

"Mr. Tallusoj?"

"SHIT AND FUCK TO YOU! THE INTERRUPTION! AND GODDAMN TO YOU!"

I waited but no one came. I knocked one more time but much harder and the door flew open and the green arm of Susie Home-maker shot out of the smelly darkness and dragged me inside.

And there was a great struggle and I was kicking and fighting but Susie Homemaker was very strong. He was grunting low terrible grunts and I could not reach Little Debbie and I could not find a biting place and my breath was leaving me, Susie was crushing me and there were the popping lights bright and blue swimming in front of my eyes and then there was a sick crack, some sick bashes and Susie's arms shriveled and I jumped away screaming, yanking on the door which would not open. The Stick grabbed on to me shouting, "Wait! Wait!"

He bashed Susie on the head so hard with a bottle of Whitley's that Susie was sent into panic-jerks and clawing at the chest and then a huge arch of the back like horrible electrocution and then stillness. And then blood. Blood looking very thick in the bouncing blue light of the television, blood coming from Susie's ear and Susie's mouth.

The Stick ran to the phone. He picked it up, started dialing

Emergency and slammed it back down. He picked it up again and did the exact same thing. He shouted, "I don't know what to DO! What should I fucking DO?!" And he was shaking and freaking severely.

I said, "Go get a blanket. He just needs a blanket." But I saw the extensions of the extremities, the toes and fingers stretching out and then nothing. Nothing. Empty eyeballs reflecting the TV light.

I stared at the body of the creature who attacked me, now covered to the chin with a torn and pilled blanket. Tucked in. Blood wiped away. Blank eyes staring as always at the nonstop box displaying so many unreachable worlds. I stared at the stillness of Susie Homemaker and felt a certain emotion wave pass over me. I have noticed while watching *Nightmare Theater* that there is a strange sort of feeling that comes when a monster finally dies. Sometimes it is sadness. Sometimes it is vomiting.

"Fuck, fuck, fuck." The Stick was rocking and smoking. He was sitting with his arms wrapped around his knees and he was crying. "I fucking killed him. I killed Susie. I can't fucking believe it. It's over. It's over. I'm free."

I came down the stairs in my original clothes and I carried a pile of random things from Vicky's room. I said, "You're coming with me, Stick. Come on, get up."

There is a certain spreading blankness that covers over the mind after you kill someone. A certain blank tide washing in, smoothing thinking into something of a horizon line. The Stick stopped talking. He did not look well. After some urging sentences he finally followed me out the front door.

Vicky hissed and swore at me because I brought her brother and forgot the HeavenScent.

chapter 50

T WAS morning in the desert and I was awakened by growling and barking and then a yipe. The father kicked Cookie away and yanked me up out of the hidey-hole. "Clyde. You stupid piece of shit." He snorted. His lips moved a cig from one side of his mouth to the other. He gripped my arm and shoved me down the hillside in front of him. "I put all my goddamn faith in you, Clyde." His eyeballs were red. All of his eyeball veins looked like they were leaking. His hair was sticking up and a bad smell drifted over him. He grabbed the back of my neck and dug in his fingers. "I got some bad news for you, Clyde."

We heard music. Both of us heard sudden music so loud that we started and the father released his grip and I tore down the hill.

The music came from the Lair of the Sequined Genius. It was the kind of music people call mood music. Music for the background. It kept playing even when the amplified voice began to speak. "Today on the Sequined Genuis Hour, poetry about irritation."

The voice of Gy-Rah welcomed listeners to his show. He said, "I will begin with a new poem called 'My Dark Itching.' "

The father headed toward the cave entrance.

"Ray!" Auntie Doris stepped out of the office with a pot of coffee and two cups. "Many a man has been lost in that snarl of caverns. And if it's Gy-Rah you're after, he's not there."

"I hear the bastard," said the father. "That's the Sequined Gonad, ain't it?"

They both paused to listen to the amplified words. Gy-Rah spoke them slowly and dramatically.

"*My dark itching protean*
results in terpsicorean
actions dissilient,
mother,
I need my liniment."

Auntie Doris poured herself some coffee and said, "Burma Shave."

She lit a cig and looked at the father's car sitting in the middle of her gloss-top asphalt. She called, "Ray, I think I'm going to kill you. Gy-Rah is going to have to melt it back down for me and he's not going to like that. Come get your coffee. Gy-Rah will be back after his show is over."

They drank coffee and Doris talked about her parking lot. She told the father it was her invention, it was a vision-maker. In heat waves created by the desert sun and the black shine of bitumen, entire worlds could be seen.

"I'll tell you this," said Doris. "It beats television."

The father said, "I don't see nothing."

"Shit on you, Ray," said Auntie Doris. "You broke it is why. Has to be smooth. Yesterday I saw a man standing there that had six peckers."

"Haw," said the father.

"Haw-haw shit," said Doris Horace. "Looked like the Powder Monkey."

Time ticktocked. Gy-Rah read more poems about his itching problem.

I heard the father ask about the suitcase. Auntie Doris said she didn't know where it was but it was around somewhere, she'd seen it, Gy-Rah had it, he didn't give a shit about it. She didn't think there was going to be any trouble except for Gy-Rah feeling so polluted by the father's visit that it might be a while before he showed himself.

Neither of them said anything about Pammy. I wondered where she was. I wondered how her midnight beauty treatment went.

Doris said, "Goddamn you look like Old Dad, Ray." Tears spilled from her eyes. "I miss him. I feel like shit whenever I think of what I did to that man."

"You made it up to him, Doris."

"I was dazzled by the Powder Monkey. You understand."

And they talked about the Powder Monkey. A high-wire man named Carl who left the circus in Baraboo to join so many other high-wire men that streamed into the Black Canyon looking for a job on the dam. During the first year of blasting the Powder Monkey was important. After the High Scalers drilled into the rock face the Powder Monkey scrambled across sheer clifs to set the fuses and the dynamite. Carl loved attention and did his work in his circus outfit. Glittering panties that flashed and caught the eye miles away. With the money he made he built the Lucky Chief on a site that he thought would bring him millions. The Lair of the Sequined Genius dwarfed Mammoth Cave. The splendor of its interior formations was unparalleled. He worked hard on the place, wiring the cavern with lights and speakers. Leveling walkways and putting in pipe handrails. Dreaming of the busloads of tourists who would come to see the cavern and stay at the Lucky Chief and lay such baskets of cash at his feet. And then Dreamland came along. The first horrible blasts sent bad smells rolling out of the cave. No tourist would put up with that. The Powder Monkey fell despondent and lost his will to live.

Doris said, "He drank three bottles of government iodine and went into the cave and just never came out."

"Shit," said the father.

"It's a shame," said Auntie Doris. "Because the government has been very good to us. They pay me and Gy-Rah to stay."

"What the hell for?"

"We're useful to them."

"How?"

"Classified, Ray."

"You are full of shit, Doris."

"Am I?"

And the conversation was mellow like this and they went on drinking heavily and talking like this and the sun arched from one side of the landscape to the other. Cookie and I came out of hiding. We took a walk. We turned around and came back. And then it was dark. And I kept on thinking about Fernst. I had been feeling bad about Fernst. I meant to kill Pammy but instead I killed Fernst. And now I found myself feeling bad about Pammy. Found myself feeling curious about her condition and location and why she had been absent all day.

The father and Auntie Doris had gotten very slurry in their words. I could not understand what they were saying and they could not understand each other but it did not stop them from talking. They kept on talking until a weak beam of light appeared in the darkness, bouncing and approaching. Auntie Doris said, "Thas Ghy-Rath naw."

Gy-Rah's prissy voice crackled from a loudspeaker. "I am out of ointment. For this and this only I return. Mother, make ready. Arrival is in progress. ETA thirty seconds—" A painted-over bread truck with a bad muffler and high wiggling antennas rolled straight at the father with one headlight shining. From the four-horned speaker on top of the cab the distorted voice said, "Pollutant, be GONE!"

The father suddenly tore toward the truck. The speakers blared, "INvader! INtruder! MOTHER!" In an attempted tight turn the engine died. The father yanked open the driver's door and Gy-Rah flew out of the passenger side. He was a tall person with a pear-shaped body and skinny arms and a face that looked like a horse and a rat and a nearsighted hog all crossed together. He wore short-shorts and his legs were bony. He was visible only for a moment before he shot into the office door and slammed it behind him.

Auntie Doris puffed calmly on her Salem. She said, "He doesn't like you, Ray."

The father threw open the back doors of the truck and began yanking out contents, all electrical, all bouncing onto the asphalt. The father shouted, "GodDAMN it. Where IS it?"

Doris rose. "I'll talk to him. Calm down. We're going to work this out. Quit throwing his equipment around. He'll get a rash."

The father jumped out of the truck. "*I'll* talk to him. I'll—" Auntie Doris went into the office and slammed the door.

The father stood there. He tapped some polite taps. "Doris, you going to let me in?" He stood a moment longer and then walked across the gloss asphalt to the car, popped the trunk, pulled out a crowbar, and carried it back to the office door. He tapped again.

"Avon calling," said the father.

He tried the door. Locked.

I laid low in the shadows. I knew what mood he was in.

He called to me. "Where you at, Clyde. I could use some help here."

And then he saw Cookie. I watched him squat down and call to her sweetly. Talk to her convincingly. There is a saying about dogs. That they can sense a person's intentions. That they have a special power of knowing if a person is good or bad. It isn't true. If the camouflage is good enough, the dog will believe.

"Come here, darling, come here, baby girl. Sweet girl, pretty girl, that's right, that's right."

My throat closed up when I saw Cookie wag her tail a little and step toward him. And then the yipe. "Got your damn dog! Clyde!" He jerked her by the leg and she yelped again. I came running.

chapter 51

HERE ARE we go-ing?" asked the Stick. He wanted to ride in the front seat and I wanted him to ride in the front seat but Vicky had the front seat and wouldn't give it up. She said, "I'm not riding with the psy-chos. They're psychos, Roberta. Real ones. Suppos-edly they are geniuses but they are the fucked-in-the-head kind."

I turned a tight curve and floored it onto the highway that passed through a tunnel and opened onto a bridge. "What direc-tion is this?" asked the Great Wesley.

"East," I said.

And there were some tangled protests. Beneath us the tires sung on the grated bridge. My stomach was churning. It is true that I am a person with black pockets of evil and hatred in my heart. There are underground places inside of me. Many under-ground Dreamlands that rove. A cold flavor was in my mouth and it made saliva flow over my lips. The second rush of Creeper was beginning. Vicky whapped the side of my head and shouted, "Roberta, you're not LISTENING!"

My jaws were very clenchy and my forehead was ice-cold and itching terribly. We were almost to the other end of the bridge and I was concentrating hard on the road, trying to see only the road and block out all other things so I missed what it was that the

Stick said to make Vicky go so insane and caused a fight to break out, legs and arms flying. I got kicked in the head really hard. I saw the swimming lights. We swerved all over the road. When the violent tangle ended the Stick's face was badly gouged and his nose was dripping ferociously.

"I hope you die," said Vicky, "I hope you fucking bleed to death. Hey, everybody, you want to know something about my brother? He still pisses the bed."

There was a second violent outbreak and in a weird way it helped me concentrate on my driving. It took the place of the hollow roaring in my head, like a jet flying low.

And then the fight was over and all was quiet for a while. All was peaceful and glidey-smooth in the sleek car.

"Seriously," said the Stick. "Where are we going?"

"Scene of the crime," I said.

"What crime?"

And during those first hours of our journey, as we climbed through the mountains on the familiar curving road, I told them. I told them everything I have told you. And Vicky slept through most of it. But the Turtle and the Great Wesley and the Stick hung on my every word.

"He put her in the trunk," I said, and a chill shot up my back when I remembered him slamming Cookie in. The father nudged a pack of cigs at me. I shook my head. Cookie cried a little at first and then stopped. The father explained how everything depended on me now. This was the final test. Was I Navy? If I was Navy I would go into the office and flush Gy-Rah out. I would get him to tell me where the last suitcase was. If I was Navy everything would be fine, but if I wasn't, my story was going to have a sad ending.

While he was talking, Gy-Rah shot out of the office door and disappeared into his lair. And the father hit me for that. Hard. Like it was me who gave Gy-Rah the signal.

"That's my half brother, Clyde. Supposed to have an IQ of a million and a half." And the father gave me some gnarly family tree explanations, about how Old Dad lost Doris to Carl Horace. Called Haywire Horace. Scared of nothing. Hung off ropes a thousand feet in the air. Just swung down and snatched Doris away from Old Dad. She was Navy. She was slaughterhouse. She was Old Dad's dream. Haywire was Air Force. He was circus. It never should have happened, but it did.

"You know why they called him Haywire, Clyde? It ain't what you guess. You ever hear of Bent Nail Syndrome? When you get a hard-on your dick kinks. He was famous in Baraboo."

"Hillbilly Woman," interrupted the Turtle. "Bent Nail Syndrome. I too am afflicted. Yes. It is a poignant condition. It is said that Bent Nail caused Hamlet's madness."

The Stick said, "Hamlet's not a real person."

The Turtle said, "Bent Nail knows no boundaries."

The Great Wesley again. "Please, Hillbilly Woman. Continue."

"Wait," said the Turtle. "Before you go on, there is something I must say."

We waited.

"What?" asked Vicky. "God! Just *say* it!"

"Yes. Absolutely." The Turtle cleared his throat. "I would like to say I also still piss the bed."

"The best people do," said the Great Wesley.

chapter 52

AVERNS ARE wonderful things. Sometimes the walls are made of alabaster and sometimes gypsum. Sometimes other things. The cavern that was Gy-Rah's lair was enormous. The Powder Monkey's work had made it an easy stroll down stepped walkways to a mysterious world that had once been an underground river. There were domed places, oval indentations where loose stones swirled in the ancient eddies, cutting the stone above and below in the most elegant way, shapes very Roman. Shapes you see on *Gladiator Theater*, Channel 11, Saturdays at two.

While the father explained my job to me, handed me the gun called the Luger, told me how to hold it and fire it, my mind was drifting to the movie called *The Time Machine* where monsters with glowing red eyes and bloody teeth freaked around in worlds underground. The main girl in the movie was named Weena and she didn't know the god she worshipped was created by the monsters. A god that opened its loving mouth and then sucked you into the meat-saw room. There were very obvious clues that made you shout at the TV, saying "No, Weena! No!" and as I half listened to the father explain the Navy way of flushing an enemy out of hiding, I wondered if someone somewhere was yelling warnings at me. Someone watching the movie of my life and shouting, "No! No! Turn back before they eat your legs!"

"What you have to do, Clyde, is simple. You got to go in there and flush him out. I don't care how you do it, but don't goddamn kill him. You can wing him but do not kill him, all right? Flush him into the clear and I'll take it from there. Go. No. Do it. Here." And so I had the gun. A loaded gun handed to me with trust and confidence.

But I didn't turn back. I entered the Lair of the Sequined Genius with a gun in my hand. Weak lights flickered in the descending blackness. I was surprised by the coolness of the air, surprised by the little sounds of dripping. A bit of water still passed through parts of the cave. Condensation made the pipe handrail slick to the touch.

As I walked, I wondered if I really could shoot the man in the short-shorts. There were so many other people I'd rather shoot at. And I was distracted by this thought when the lights went off.

Blackness.

"Psssst!"

An amplified whisper bounced and echoed around me.

"Pssst! You. Troglodyte. Abomination. I see you."

The sound came from everywhere at once. Whispers though a microphone can be so horrifying. Little whispered words and little evil insults.

"Pollution. Poison. Carrion."

A flame flickered behind a hoard of stalagmites.

The hissing voice of Gy-Rah said, "I see the gun. I see the gun clearly. Were you really planning on shooting me, you revolting pygmy?" The fire flicker went out. Gy-Rah laughed. From the blackness he whispered, "Take aim now."

It was quite a lucky shot. I didn't hit him but the blast made him holler, "Ooh, my balls! Ooh, my balls!" The lights came on and I saw him clutching his sequined privates. He'd clipped himself on a stalagmite.

"My ointment! You have activated my dark itching! I must have my ointment!" In the pale light I saw he was badly afflicted with a weepy scaly rash that thickened his eyelids and circled his elbows and from the way he was wriggling I could tell there were some other bothersome areas as well.

"You must run at once to Mother and get my ointment or I will go mad. The luminous green balls of genius which roll in my brain inform me I must surrender. Oh this itches! Tell me what you want! Speak!"

"The dog," I said.

"Dog?"

"The white dog."

"Peanut?"

"Give her to me."

"She is yours! My ointment! Go!"

"And I need the suitcase."

"The—"

"The blue suitcase full of money."

"Yes."

"I need it."

"My itching! I implore you."

"The suitcase."

"There is a complication."

I shot the gun again. I was really enjoying shooting off the gun. There was a ricochet sound. Some chunks fell off the cavern walls.

"I'll take you to it," said Gy-Rah. He put his hands up and waddled his behind as he walked ahead of me. This is how he came out of the cavern. The way I'd seen prisoners do it a million times.

The father popped up from behind the car and smiled very hugely at me. With his glowing cig clamped between his teeth he was clapping his hands. Clap, clap, clap, for a job well done. "Shit, Clyde! Damn, Clyde! Goddamn great, Clyde! Balls-out son of a bitching Navy all the way, Clyde!"

And then I shot him.

Gy-Rah ran. The father rolled on the asphalt clutching his leg. "Shit, sniper! Clyde! I been shot!"

He was twisting his head like an upside-down rooster to see where the shot had come from even though he was looking straight at me when I fired at him. His eyes saw me but his mind refused the knowledge.

I ran to him and said, "Car keys! Car keys!" He heard the urgency in my voice and tossed them to me without hesitation. Maybe he thought I was going to roll the car between him and his assassin. Maybe he thought I was wanting to shield him from harm. What I did was start the car and back over his foot.

Gy-Rah pounded on the office door. It flew open, he was yanked in, and Pammy was shoved out. The door slammed and locked.

Pammy looked sick. She wobble-walked toward the father. Her hair was deteriorated to the very scalp, looking like a couple of wispy feathers on a just-hatched bird. She closed one eye to get focus and her legs gave out.

I drove fast and talked loudly to Cookie, saying I would pull over in a minute, I'd pull over and get her out. I jumped out of the car, popped open the trunk, and of course it was empty.

For a while I lay on the hood of the car, staring up into the darkness. Staring up at the stars. The thousands and thousands and thousands of stars. Some fall and leave trails. Some go out without anyone even noticing.

chapter 53

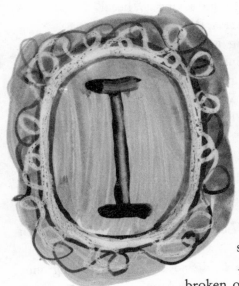

STOPPED THE car and Vicky woke up. She said, "Where the fuck are we? I'm fucking starving."

"The Top o' the Pass," said the Great Wesley. "It is real."

I stepped out into the cool night air. Vicky said, "There a bathroom?"

"Around back," I said. "That way."

All of the windows were broken out and the door hung half torn from its hinges, but the carefully placed stones in the wall were still there. And I walked to them and put my hands upon them and they were cold and they refreshed me. It was just an hour or two before sunrise. Vicky came back. "I can't pee back there. Too weird." She tramped into the bushes.

The Turtle got out and the Stick got out but the Great Wesley said he did not feel capable. The Turtle leaned into the car and gently urged him and the Great Wesley gently refused and I felt a sad tightness in my throat from their tenderness toward each other. Their soft voices twining.

The Stick walked over to me and put his hands near mine on the wall. He said, "This has been the weirdest night."

Vicky came back. "I'm so fucking hungry!" She poked her head inside the doorway of the dead gas station store. "Smells pukey. Let's go."

And we drove down the other side of the mountain and the car filled up with cigarette smoke and Vicky named the things she wanted to eat, Tiger Tails and Chick-o-stix and the list went on. And I freaked her by taking my hands off the steering wheel and lifting my feet from the pedals and saying "Wheee!"

"Fuck, Roberta! You're sick, Roberta!" said Vicky.

And the rays of morning light fell around us as we rolled out of the dark mountains and into the flat yellow cowboy world. Irrigating jets pulsed over the fields. Migrants in beat-apart hats bent and picked. The Great Wesley and the Turtle were sleeping. Vicky said, "Why the fuck are you crying? We need a gas station. We need a store."

In the rearview mirror I saw the Stick staring out the window. He looked so pale and worn out but his eyes were alive, taking in the openness, the pale colors, the immensity of the morning sky. He was taking the new world in.

"Fuck, Roberta!" said Vicky. "What are you slowing down for? Drive!"

I stopped alongside a field and called to two migrants. Women who stood up when they heard me ask about the grandma-ma.

One woman said, "*¿Que? ¿Que quieras?*"

The other, "*La abuela. La bruja.*"

"*¿La bruja? ¿La abuela mysteriosa, sí?*"

"The grandma-ma," I said. "Little. Very old."

"*Sí. Sí. Muerta.*"

I said, "What?"

The first woman put her hands together in a praying way and pointed up. Her friend slapped her hand and pointed down.

The smell of the stockyards was too much for Vicky. "Roll up the window!" But the smell was the reason I kept driving slow. The creature smell so powerful and alive and lonely and hopeless.

The Great Wesley sat up. "I was dozing, I'm afraid. What did I miss?"

"The grandma-ma is dead," said the Stick.

I turned down a road that got smaller and smaller, running along the railroad tracks, running along the canal. I was heading toward the Knocking Hammer, but it was the train I wanted to see. I heard it pounding behind me. I stopped the car and jumped out.

Vicky screamed just a moment before the whistle split the air. I jumped away from the engine onto the gravel between the tracks and the canal, wanting the exhilaration, needing the exhilaration. I kneeled be-side the roaring train and I felt nothing.

A hand grabbed my arm and I nearly lost my balance. The Stick had dodged with me. He dodged the train right behind me. I never even saw him. He was shouting something at me but I couldn't hear him over the train.

"What?"

He cupped his hands. "Do you think we have a chance?"

The train shot away. Going balls-out full speed on such a beautiful stretch of track, such a clean straightaway on such a clear day, the thunder and the roar faded and was gone.

"Do you?" asked the Stick.

I shook my head no.

He put his arm around me. I thought he wanted to comfort me but the Stick was falling over. He was in a lot of pain. Some-thing inside of him had gone very wrong.

The Turtle helped the Great Wesley up the embankment. I was shocked by how the Great Wesley looked in the daylight.

How washed-out and frail he was, how gingerly he moved his slippered feet. He looked around him blinking and he made me think of Cookie. The way her intelligent eyes blinked at the surrounding world, her ears up, the interested way she sniffed the air.

"Lovely," said the Great Wesley. "Perfect. Ideal."

His bathrobe fell open and in the sunlight his white skin and sudden dinger were exposed, and I saw the huge scar running up the center of his chest. It had been violently stitched. The procedure is called cracking. The procedure is last-ditch emergency and it is called cracking the chest.

"Wesley," I said.

"FUCK!" said Vicky when she caught up to us. She placed her hands on her own chest and stepped forward and back in horror. "Fuck! Fuck! What happened?"

The Great Wesley said, "My intentions were good but my aim was bad."

"What the fuck does *that* mean?"

"My dear girl," said the Great Wesley, "I missed."

And he sat down quite suddenly. And the Stick was down and then the Turtle and then me. The last one standing was Vicky.

She said, "What the fuck are you guys *doing*? We have to go, man!"

I said, "Where?"

The Great Wesley pulled out the very last of the ancient substance and a slender bone pipe with elaborately carved vines winding around it. He said, "I should like a good smoke with all of you, as all of you are dear, dear friends of mine, and I should like to hear the conclusion of the tale of the Hillbilly Woman, which I assume was a very happy one."

"No." I shook my head. "Not really."

"Of course it was," said Wesley. "You are here with us, aren't you?"

"Fuck this," said Vicky. "I vote no. I'm not staying here. Where *is* this? This isn't even anywhere!" But in the end she sat with us. In the end she stayed.

Chapter 54

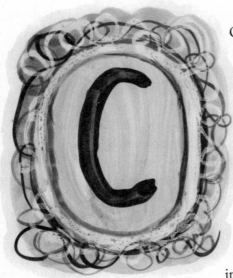

OOKIE. WHERE was she? Had he killed her? He was that kind of person. The father was very much that kind of person. But he was also the kind of person who would not kill her if she was still useful.

I didn't mean to fall asleep. I did not expect the crashing to come so hard. I closed my eyes and when I opened them again the morning had come.

My heart was pounding hard. I prayed she was still alive. I prayed I wasn't too late. When I got to the parking lot, Gy-Rah's truck was gone. The broadcasting equipment the father had hurled out the night before lay in glinting pieces and trailing wires. I scanned for the father. Was he waiting for me? Was he hiding behind a rock and taking aim?

Pammy was at the concrete picnic table with her head down on her arms. Around her were many empty booze bottles. Poor Pammy. Her head was so scalded. The shriveled fuzz of hair was so pathetic. There were broken bottles around her feet. I remembered her miserable wobbling the night before. I was feeling sadness for her, which made me wish some happiness for her. And then I saw the flies.

A great black cloud of flies buzzing and ringing her neck and turning the ground beneath her into a living carpet. They were on her legs and they covered the sheeting blood on her chest. Her throat had been cut.

The office door was open. I whispered, "Cookie? Cookie?" There was a blood trail through the door to the couch. A blood-soaked towel and scissors and part of a ripped sheet and full ash-trays and highball glasses laying on a sick green carpet. The walls and low ceiling were spackle-shot, very bumpy with little glitters glinting. The curtains were shut. I whispered, "Cookie? Auntie Doris?"

In the bedroom. In the bedroom. The blood on the ceiling and the blood on the walls, back-splatter, back-splatter in welts, smeared hand marks streaking downward. The lamp knocked over, the bed rolled cock-eyed. On the rug I saw Sheila. Sister to Little Debbie. I saw Sheila and beside her I saw a thumb.

And then I saw the hand it came from. Auntie Doris was on the other side of the bed. Her blank eyes were open and she was curled up like a child.

From the parking lot came the sound of the bad muffler, the engine rattle, and the speaker sound. The father's voice amplified, "Clyde, Clyde. You miss me, son? I sure miss you."

I froze. The gun was in the car. I picked up Sheila. The father said, "Where are you, son?" Cookie yelped. "I have your little doggie here." The engine stopped. "Come out, come out, wher-ever you are," There was a scuffle and the father said, "You stu-pid bitch. Hold still." He was talking to Gy-Rah.

I stepped out of the office to see the father standing behind him with a knife pressed to his throat. Gy-Rah's eyes were rolling like a cow's.

The father said, "Clyde. Clyde. Look at him. Old Dad sneaks off to Nevada, dinks Doris three times and *this* is what she poops out. Old Dad leaves me with nothing, and sends a third of his for-tune to this. There's no god, Clyde. Remember that."

Cookie ran. Cookie disappeared into one of a thousand hidey-holes and I was glad for her. I was hoping that she would not come out again until the father was gone. Truly gone for all time.

"You Navy, Clyde? Are you?"

I held Sheila behind me. I nodded.

"*Say* it, goddamn you."

"I'm Navy."

"You're Navy *what?*"

"I'm Navy, *sir.*"

"Then we don't need this pussy anymore."

Gy-Rah was able to walk quite a distance with his throat cut. The father had time to tap out a cig and light it before Gy-Rah went down like a dropped marionette.

The father gestured all around. His eyes were red-rimmed and dull. He gestured to Pammy and the office and to Gy-Rah's last writhings. He gestured to his split pant leg with white rag bandages wrapped beneath it. He said, "Can you believe this world of shit?"

He was stiff-leg walking to the car. He got in on the passenger side. "Here it is." He lifted the gun. "Here's what that son-of-a-bitching sniper used on me, Clyde, ain't it? Run up to the table and get a bottle of Whitley's. This morning has been a bitch and I could sure use a drink. Fish around in that pile of shit I yanked out of the truck, see if you can't find a couple of cables and harnesses. Do you know that little bastard had the goddamn gall to offer me a blow job? And do you know I had the goddamn gall to take him up on it? Speed it up, Clyde. It's getting hot and we got a long day ahead of us." He flipped down the visor and looked at himself in the mirror. "Got a goddamn pimple. Hurts like shit, too."

He gave the directions and I drove. Little Debbie and Sheila were snuggled together beneath my shirt. The father was humming and drinking and smoking and yawning. He said, "Stop the car, son." He held the gun against the side of my face. He said, "Give me your knife, son."

I reached for Little Debbie and he said, "Don't try it, son. Just hand her over." He took her from me and kissed the blade. "She's such a pretty little girl."

The road got steeper. The father kept the gun on me. "God-

DAMN I am tired." He kept yawning and popping his eyes. "When all this is over, I'm going to take a nice nap. That little faggot surprised me. Do you know he told me he had six peckers?" The father held up a splayed hand and the thumb on his gun hand. "Six! Told me he was some kind of wonder of nature. I said, 'Well let me have a look.' Only two of them were worth anything. Turn here. Turn here. Yes, I see the sign, if I don't give a shit about it, you don't either. You Navy, Clyde? Because right now I need a goddamned commando."

The road we followed was so rocky that I had to drive very slow. It wound up and up and up. The father made some melting-brain comments about keeping the car in motion, keeping the momentum going on the impossible road winding so steeply between boulders.

He drained the Whitley's fast. "Stop," he said. "Stop here. Here."

He asked me again if we were partners and I said we were. He told me to get the cables and he kept the gun on me. When I turned my back, BLAM! He shot the gun off very close to my head. I smelled the burning. "Goddamn snipers are everywhere, aren't they, Clyde?"

We climbed the rest of the way, going slow because of the father's bad leg. He was sweating hard in the face. We were up very high and it was getting to him. He sat down. "This is as far as I go, son." Beside him was a rusted iron U-bolt embedded into the rock. The father pinged the gun barrel against it. "History, Clyde. This here? The boys who built the great dam put these in. The Powder Monkey himself did this one. They didn't have no banks nearby during the construction, a lot of shifty little shits were crawling all over and waiting to rob you. Haywire blasted his safe-hole on the other side of this rock. Hung over the edge and made himself a Wells Fargo. Gy-Rah got me this far but the shit didn't bring no cables. You follow me, Clyde? These rings are going to hold your cable. Gy-Rah said the suitcase was there, just a twenty yards down from the edge. Wish I had a drink to offer you before you go."

He told me to thread the cable through the parallel U-bolts. Told me he'd anchor them good for me, that no one could beat a Navy man when it came to knots. All I had to do was fasten the harness around me and work the drop-pulley to lower myself down.

He said, "Go on now, son. That's right. You see Hoover Dam yet? She's supposed to be goddamn spectacular."

My legs were shaking. The cables were stiff and there were complications of leather straps looking ancient and crumbled. I will admit I was freaking badly, I will admit I looked back to see the tipping glint of the waving of the gun. The father looked bad. Greenish and thin and his hair stood up. He was laying on his stomach. The height had gotten to him.

I crawled to the top edge and looked over. I was surprised to see that the U-bolts continued over a descending platform. It was still a long way to the real edge. I dropped the cables over.

In the distance I saw the dam, her high white wall holding back the unnatural lake, unnaturally blue water glinting in such a dead world.

The father shouted, "Clyde? How's it going?" He pulled the cable and felt the resistance.

"Clyde? You got it? Tug if you got it."

Nothing happened. He yanked on the cable but it wouldn't budge. There was an echo that faded fast every time he shouted my name. I wondered how long it would be before he decided to climb up to the edge. I'd have one chance. There could be no hesitation. Sheila was ready. Sheila had no problem with the idea of turning against him.

He swore. He spat. He kept yanking on the cable. The sun burned down on him. He hollered and hollered. Finally he began his upward crawl, clinging to the cable that would not budge because I tangled them bad through the U-bolts. Jamming every hook and pulley and strap in an impossible snarl.

Fear is cumulative. It rises to a breaking point and then a person freezes. "Clyde! Goddamn it!"

I crouched just under the ledge with my back flattened against the rock wall. A few pebbles came tumbling over when he got to the edge. And then I saw his jug-eared shadow. By the time he realized what happened it was all over. He tried to say some gurgley last words but I couldn't really make them out. It's hard to enunciate with a slashed windpipe.

Chapter 55

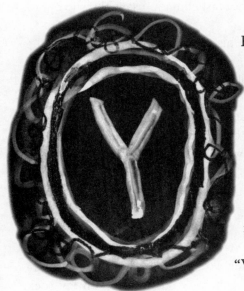

ES," SAID the Great Wesley. "The son shall bathe his hands in parent's blood, and in one act be both unjust and good." He nodded. "Burma Shave."

"Yes," said the Turtle.

"The money," said Vicky. "What about the money?"

"It's still there," I said.

"Where?"

The Stick rolled up onto his side and lay back down. He said, "Cop. Cop. There's a cop."

The white car was pulled over and I saw the yellow county star on the side. A big-bellied man was walking around the Jaguar. Vicky was backing away into the scrub. With a bored and irritated expression the man in tan and brown signaled for us to come down the embankment. He called us hippies. I started laughing.

I had so many thoughts right then. Ideas on what to do scattered in a thousand directions, what could I do to keep it rolling, keep the motion going. I thought of the Stick's question. "Do you think we have a chance?" And suddenly I thought, Yes! Yes! But the sound of the splash behind me changed everything. Wesley went over the canal edge, hit the rushing water, and was carried away so fast. I jumped up running alongside the canal and it seemed like he was waving to me, shouting some encouraging words to me but I couldn't hear what they were because the Turtle was screaming, "Wait for me! My dear, dear Wesley! Wait! Wait!" and he ran so fast, chasing after the shape of the disappearing Wesley, but he was not fast enough. I saw him slip out of his shoes and jump in.

The cop hopped back in his car and took off. I was sure he was going for help but no one ever came. In a certain way it didn't surprise me. I know things about cops. About fathers. About the world.

I ran to get the Turtle's shoes. It seems strange to me now when I think of how convinced I was that he would need them. How convinced I was that I would see them both again. But they were never found. Not by us. Not by anybody. There is a part of me hoping that maybe they made it. Made it to wherever people like us finally go.

We were at the Yakima bus station, Vicky was slurping down a strawberry milk shake that she would later be very sorry she ordered. I bought the tickets back to Cruddy City with my sock monkey money. We left the sleek car on a side street with an empty gas tank and the keys in the ignition. I was thinking about how close we were to the Knocking Hammer. How it would have been nothing to drive on a mile farther and lay my eyes on it again, something I had been wanting to do and planning to do for so long. Take the whole journey again, re-trace the trail of the father to the very cliff edge. But the urge had drained away.

The Stick was ill. He was having trouble moving, but he told me there was nothing wrong with him. And I believed him. I believed him completely. The father spoke the truth when he said that people lie and lie and lie. Even the best people do, sometimes.

I said, "You want me to get you some aspirin?"

Vicky said, "He can't have aspirin."

I said, "Why not?"

The Stick said, "Shut up, Vicky."

She shrugged. "Fine with me."

The Stick said, "So you cut his throat?"

I nodded.

"And you know for sure he's dead?"

"He's dead."

"Didn't you stay to make sure?"

"I got bored."

"Bullshit," said Vicky. "None of it ever happened. It's all bullshit. Nobody would leave that much money behind. How much did you say it was?"

"Thousands. Thousands and thousands."

"Such bullshit."

Our bus boarded. The doors whooshed open and we climbed on. I carried the shoes of the Turtle and the robe of the Great Wesley. "To the back," I said. "All the way back."

Vicky wanted to hold the Turtle's shoes and I was very surprised when she cried a little over them. I couldn't cry. The Stick got the window seat. He leaned back and said, "And then what?"

The flat landscape moved behind him, looking oddly fake. "And then what happened?" He closed his eyes.

And then what happened was I made my way back to the car and I started shaking very violently and it was a long time before I could drive and it was very hard to drive once I could and I made it back to the Lucky Chief and I threw up and hollered for Cookie and I kept hollering for Cookie and I popped the trunk and took a handful of money out of one of the suitcases and then I dragged both of the Samsonites into the cavern, deep, deep, deep into the cavern and I hollered and hollered for Cookie and I heard her barking and she came running and she was wagging her tail very hard and I picked her up and kissed her and we walked into the sunlight. The End.

"The END?" said Vicky.

"The End," I said.

"What a fucked-up bullshit waste-of-time story! God, Roberta! I could slap you right now."

"You could," I said. "But it would be a terrible idea."

She was picking at the Turtle's shoes. At the silver foil around the insole. She pulled it away and found a rectangle of origami paper. Inside were two perforated sheets. A miniature deck of cards printed on each. "It's blotter," she said. "It's actual blotter." There were two more sheets in the other shoe. There were 127 hits of blotter in all.

And after a moment there were only 121. She took three hits and gave me three hits. I snuck one to the Stick.

The bus bounced, Vicky got carsick, the strawberry milk shake found its way to the floor. She took three more hits. When we got to Cruddy City we were so blasted we could hardly maintain enough to get the 7 Dunbar bus home. The Stick said he was feeling better, that in fact he was feeling perfect. Vicky wanted to go home. None of us could think of a better idea. She walked very fast and we fell behind and the Stick put his arm around me. He said, "I'm a bleeder. Did Vicky tell you? I'm a bleeder." But I didn't know it was a situation. A condition. I just thought it was a thing you say when you are very high, like I'm an eater or I'm a breather. And we were so very high. All the streetlights shot rays at us and the cars left trails for us. All the ugly things around us looked beautiful. I missed the Turtle and the Great Wesley very much right then.

The Stick said, "My real name isn't the Stick. My real name is—" He said something unpronounceable. Something that sounded slightly like "the Stick," but had more letters in silent combinations. I tried to repeat it and he laughed.

He said, "I have a crush on you, Roberta."

I told him my name was no longer Roberta. I told him my name was Junior Bizarre and Vicky heard this and she fell on the grass laughing and having contortions and it took us a very long time to make our way to the hedges that surrounded the Tallusoj house.

He stopped at the broken front gate. I could tell that even in his blasted condition that he was thinking about Susie. He hadn't told Vicky. He said, "Vicky, Vicky. Um—um, Susie—"

Vicky said, "Fuck Susie. I'm sick of Susie."

She bounced up the porch ahead of us. The TV light was jumping in the window. The green porch light was on. He looked at me. Did we leave the TV on? Did we? I thought we turned it off.

Vicky shoved open the door.

"SHIT AND GODDAMN! THE INTERRUPTION! MY PROGRAM!"

The resurrected Susie lay back in his flowered bathrobe with his vulnerables spreading. He had a plastic tumbler of Whitley's in one hand and a Swisher Sweet in the other.

"Fuck off, Susie," said Vicky. "Cover yourself up."

"SHIT AND GODDAMN! I HAVE TO GET ORGA-NIZED!"

Later, in the attic, in the candlelight, the Stick and I lay together having some revelations.

He said, "I do still piss the bed."

I said, "I killed a lot of people."

He ran his finger over the inside of my arm and said the words spelled in scars.

I'm sorry.

He said, "Can I see your knife? Can I see Little Debbie? Is that what you used to do this?"

I handed her over.

He said, "What happened to Sheila?"

"She's with the father. If he fell, she is at the bottom. If he dried out like beef jerky, she is still his companion. Before I left I shoved her in pretty hard."

He ran his fingers over the raised letters again.

"You did this."

I nodded.

"*Are* you sorry?"

"No."

And we were quiet. And I crawled to the oval window. I was looking into the sky, I was wanting to find a satellite for him. I was thinking there had to be one tumbling somewhere above us. I didn't see him do it. Make the deep silent slices upwards from his wrists. "I'm a bleeder," he said, "I'm a bleeder, I'm a bleeder." But I didn't know what he meant until it was too late.

And I know I was screaming and I know I was scrambling after him out of the window and along the dormer ledge but I cannot say if he jumped or he fell. It seemed like he did neither. To me it seemed as if he took a calm step into thin air.

And so the ambulance came and so the cops came and I was very hysterical and Vicky was very hysterical and so we were all taken to Emergency and so the mother was contacted and came in screaming with her neck cords sticking out shouting she would kill me she would kill me she was absolutely going to kill me and so I shouted back that she should do it, I didn't care and so she was restrained and so I was restrained and so the cops asked me questions and so Vicky yelled from the next cubicle Don't Narc Me Out, Roberta! Don't! Don't! Don't!

And so we were kept overnight for observation and so the surgery man came in to say, "I'm afraid we struck out, I'm afraid he did not make it. He did not make it. I'm sorry. I'm sorry." And so the Stick was gone.

And so Susie was taken away and so Vicky was taken to a foster home, which she busted out of immediately. And so she called me said would I meet her, would I go with her because it turns out Neil Young is playing at the Hec Edmondson pavilion and it's festival seating and if we get there before the sun comes up we will be the first in line and then we will be in the front row when he sings "Cinnamon Girl."

And so that is what I am about to do right now. Sneak out and meet Vicky by the Diggy's Dumpster. And then tomorrow night, after the concert she promised she will come with me to the train tracks. And she promised she will give me the little push I need unless something happens and she gets together with Neil Young.

And so if you are reading this, if you are holding this book in your hands right now it means my plan worked completely, I am gone. I am gone. I got my happy ending.

And so whoever you are, if you want the money, you can have it. My description of the location is decent and followable. But watch out for Dreamland. Beware of the Air Force. Stay Navy all the way.

That is all.

This is the End.

I dedicate this book to my sister, Julie.

fuck you roberta !!!
I hate you roberta !!!
where are you ??

ABOUT THE TYPE

Cruddy is set in Monotype Fournier—discovered in the 1930 edition of *Moby Dick* designed and illustrated by Rockwell Kent. The typeface itself was recut for Monotype in 1924 under the direction of Stanley Morison. The original was created by Pierre Simon Fournier around 1742 and called "St. Augustin Ordinaire" in his *Manuel Typographique*. The earliest of the "transitional" typefaces, Fournier was a bridge to the more severe "modern" style made popular by Bodoni later in the century.